W9-AQJ-191

THE MAN WHO HAD NO iDEA

A Collection of Stories

Thomas M. Disch

BANTAM BOOKS
TORONTO · NEW YORK · LONDON · SYDNEY

THE MAN WHO HAD NO IDEA

A Bantam Book / November 1982

Acknowledgments

"The Man Who Had No Idea", copyright © 1978 by Thomas M. Disch. First appeared in the Magazine of Fantasy & Science Fiction October 1978, and in Winter's Tales 24 *(Macmillan's, London). Reprinted in Carr's Best SF annual (Ace).*

"The Black Cat", copyright © 1976 by Shenandoah. *Appeared in Summer 1976 issue.*

"The Vengeance of Hera", copyright © 1980 by Thomas M. Disch. First appeared in Edges *(Pocket Books).*

"The Santa Claus Compromise", copyright © 1975 by Crawdaddy, appeared in January 1975 issue. Reprinted in Harrison's Year's Best SF.

"How to Fly", copyright © 1977 by Bananas. Appeared in Summer 1977 issue (London).

"The Appartment Next to the War", copyright © 1974 by SF Monthly (England). Reprinted in 1979 in Departures.

"The Foetus", copyright © 1980 by Thomas M. Disch. First appeared in The Berkley Showcase, Vol. 2 *(Berkley Books).*

"The Fire Began to Burn the Stick, The Stick Began to Beat the Dog", copyright © 1976 by Rolling Stone. *Appeared in issue of May 20, 1976.*

"At the Pleasure Center", copyright © 1974 by SF Monthly (England). Reprinted in The Little Magazine.

"The Grown-Up", copyright © 1981 by Trans-High Corporation. First appeared in High Times.

"Planet of the Rapes", copyright © 1977 by Penthouse Publications, Ltd. Appeared in issue Vol. 12 No. 9, 1977, of Penthouse *(London).*

"The Revelation", copyright © 1981 by Robert Sheckley. First appeared in After the Fall *(Ace Books).*

"Pyramids for Minnesota", copyright © 1973 by Minneapolis Star & Tribune Co. First appeared in Harper's, *issue of January 1974. Reprinted in* The Wiley Reader *and* The New Improved Sun.

"Josie and the Elevator", copyright © 1980 by Omni International Publications, Ltd.

"An Italian Lesson" (unpublished)

"Concepts", copyright © 1978 by Mercury Press, Inc. Appeared in December 1978 issue of The Magazine of Fantasy & Science Fiction.

"Understanding Human Behavior", copyright © 1981 by Mercury Press.

ISBN 0-553-22667-3

Published simultaneously in the United States and Canada

Bantam Books are published by Bantam Books, Inc. Its trademark,
consisting of the words "Bantam Books" and the portrayal of a
rooster, is Registered in U.S. Patent and Trademark Office and in
other countries. Marca Registrada. Bantam Books, Inc., 666 Fifth
Avenue, New York, New York 10103.

PRINTED IN THE UNITED STATES OF AMERICA

O   0 9 8 7 6 5 4 3 2 1

Contents

Ideas are everywhere, and anyone who looks there will find one, or several. This, I'll admit, is only a theory. It isn't possible, as technology stands now, to prove this by watching idea-neurons flash in the cerebral cortex, but one can infer the existence of ideas by listening to people talk, since a large portion of human speech is given over to ideas. Not all of it, but enough to be noticeable. So to say the man this story is about had *no* idea isn't really fair or true, since by the end of the story he's produced no less than fifteen ideas, and not just disposable ideas that have been expressed many times by many people, such as "Isn't it hard to believe that Reagan is president now?" but his own original ideas for poems.

When asked where his ideas come from, Harlan Ellison (whom I fear I am imitating by writing these friendly notes in front of these stories, something I resisted doing in other collections, since higher-toned critics are liable to take exception to intrusions of the author's personality, feeling that Art should do its own enchanting, and they may be right) has answered that they come from Schenectady.

In another context, E. M. Forster wrote, "Only connect." Which always seemed enigmatic to me until I did connect it to Schenectady.

The usual problem people have with Schenectady (never having been there) is that they think it must be boring and dismiss it out of hand. Not at all. For instance, the idea for this story came to me one day at a bar in Schenectady. There I was, with a glass of beer and my mind running at idle, and what I felt like doing just then was, in the words of the thesaurus, enjoying some social intercourse. However, knowing none of the people there, I said nothing and sipped my beer, whereupon it occurred to me that the other people in the bar were probably there because they were likewise in a mood for conversation, but as it happened *none* of them knew each other, and so, like me, they were all just standing about, mum. "It's as though," thought I, "people needed a license before they could start a conversation."

Now possibly that didn't happen in Schenectady, but I'm sure many people have found themselves in the same situation in the bars of Schenectady (assuming it isn't dry, like Evanston, Illinois) and that it represents a very common experience in general. Call it shyness, or, periphrastically, a failure to communicate.

Anyhow, that was my idea, and after not too long an interval this is the story it grew into.

The Man Who Had No Idea

At first he'd assumed that he'd failed. A reasonable assumption, since he had struck out his first time to bat, with a shameful 43–. But when two weeks had gone by and there was still no word from the Board of Examiners, he wondered if maybe he'd managed to squeak through. He didn't see how he could have. The examiner, a wizened, white-haired fuddy-duddy whose name Barry instantly forgot, had been hostile and aggressive right from the word go, telling Barry that he thought his handshake was too sincere. He directed the conversation first to the possible dangers of excessive sunbathing, which was surely an oblique criticism of Barry's end-of-August tan and the leisure such a tan implied, then started in on the likelihood that dolphins were as intelligent as people. Barry, having entered the cubicle resolved to stake all his chips on a tactic of complete candor, had said one, he was too young to worry about skin cancer and two, he had no interest in animals except as meat. This started the examiner off on the psychic experiences of some woman he'd read about in *Reader's Digest*. Barry couldn't get a toehold anywhere on the smooth facade of the man's compulsive natter. He got the feeling, more and more, that *he* was keeping score, and the old fart was being tested, an attitude that did not bode well. Finally, with ten minutes left on the clock, he'd just up and left, which was not, strictly speaking, a violation. It did imply that some kind of closure had been achieved, which definitely was not the case; he'd panicked, pure and simple. A fiasco from which he'd naturally feared the worst in the form of a letter addressed to Dear Applicant. ("We regret to inform you, etc.") But possibly the old fart had been making things deliberately difficult, testing him; possibly his reactions hadn't been that entirely inappropriate. Possibly he'd passed.

When another two weeks went by without the Board of Examiners saying boo, he couldn't stand the suspense any longer, and went down to Center Street to fill out a form that asked, basically, where did he stand. A clerk coded the form and fed it into the computer. The computer instructed Barry to fill out another form, giving more details. Fortunately he'd brought the data the computer wanted, so he was able to fill out the second form on the spot. After a wait of less than ten minutes, his number lighted up on the board, and he was told to go to Window 28.

Window 28 was the window that issued licenses: he had passed!

"I passed," he announced incredulously to the clerk at the window.

The clerk had the license with his name on it, Barry Riordan, right there in her hand. She inserted it into the slot of a gray machine, which responded with an authoritative *chunk*. She slid the validated license under the grill.

"Do you know—I still can't believe it. This is *my* license: that's really incredible."

The clerk tapped the shut-up button pinned on the neckband of her tee shirt.

"Oh. Sorry, I didn't notice. Well . . . thanks."

He smiled at her, a commiserating guilty smile, and she smiled back, a mechanical next-please smile.

He didn't look at the license till he was out on the street. Stapled to the back of it was a printed notice:

IMPORTANT

Due to the recent systems overload error your test results of August 24 have been erased. Therefore, in accordance with Bylaw 9(c), Section XII of the Revised Federal Communications Act, you are being issued a Temporary License, valid for three months from the date of issue, subject to the restrictions set forth in Appendix II of the Federal Communications Handbook (18th edition).

You may re-apply for another examination at any time. An examination score in or above the eighth percentile will secure the removal of all restrictions and you will immediately receive your Permanent License. A score in the sixth or seventh percentiles will not affect the validity of your Temporary License, though its expiration date may be extended by this means for a period of up to three months. A score in the fifth percentile or below will result in the withdrawal of your Temporary License.

Holders of a Temporary License are advised to study Chapter Nine ("The Temporary License") in the Federal Communications Handbook. Remember that direct, interactive personal communications are one of our most valuable heritages. Use your license wisely. Do not abuse the privilege of free speech.

So in fact he hadn't passed the exam. Or maybe he had. He'd never find out.

His first elation fizzled out, and he was left with his usual flattened sense of personal inconsequence. Tucking the license into his ID folder, he felt like a complete charlatan, a nobody pretending to be a somebody. If he'd scored in the first percentile he'd have been issued this license the same as if he'd scored in the tenth. And he knew with *a priori* certainty that he hadn't done that well. The most he'd hoped for was another seven points, just enough to tip him over the edge, into the sixth percentile. Instead he'd had dumb luck.

Not to worry, he advised himself. The worst is over. You've got your license. How you got it doesn't matter.

Oh yeah, another and less friendly inward voice replied. Now all you need are three endorsements. Lots of luck.

Well, I'll *get* them, he insisted, hoping to impress the other voice with the authenticity and vitality of his self-confidence. But the other voice wasn't impressed, and so instead of going straight from Center Street to the nearest speakeasy to celebrate, he took the subway home, and spent the evening watching first a fascinating documentary on calcium structures and then Celebrity Circus, with Willy Marx. Willy had four guests: a famous prostitute, a tax accountant who had just published his memoirs, a comedian who did a surrealistic skit about a speakeasy for five-year-olds, and a novelist with a speech impediment, who got into an argument with the comedian about whether his skit was essentially truthful or unjustifiably cruel. In the middle of their argument Barry came down with a murderous headache, took two aspirins, and went to bed. Just before he fell asleep, he thought: I could call them and tell them what *I* thought.

But what did he think?

He didn't know.

That, in a nutshell, was Barry's problem. At last he had his license and could talk to anyone he wanted to talk to, but he didn't know what to talk *about*. He had no ideas of his own. He agreed with anything anyone said. The skit had been *both* essentially truthful *and* unjustifiably cruel. Too much sunbathing probably was dangerous. Porpoises probably were as smart as people.

Fortunately for his morale, this state of funk did not continue long. Barry didn't let it. The next night he was off to Partyland, a 23rd-Street speakeasy that advertised heavily on late-night TV. As he approached the froth of electric lights cantilevered over the entrance, Barry could feel the middle of his body turning hollow with excitement, his throat and tongue getting tingly.

There was only a short line, and in a moment he was standing in front of the box-office window. "Ring?" the window asked. He looked at the price list. "Second," he said, and slid his MasterCharge into the appropriate slot. "License, please," said the window, winking an arrow that pointed at another slot. He inserted his license into the other slot, a bell went ding, and *mira*! He was inside Partyland, ascending the big blue escalator up to his first first-hand experience of direct, interactive personal communication. Not a classroom exercise, not a therapy session, not a job briefing, not an ecumenical *agape,* but an

5

honest-to-God conversation, spontaneous, unstructured, and all his own.

The usher who led him to his seat in the second ring sat down beside him and started to tell him about a Japanese department store which covered an entire sixteen-and-a-half acres, had thirty-two restaurants, two movie theaters, and a children's playground.

"That's fascinating, isn't it?" the usher concluded, after setting forth further facts about this remarkable department store.

"I suppose it is," Barry said noncommittally. He couldn't figure out why the usher wanted to tell him about a department store in Japan.

"I forget where I read about it," the usher said. "In some magazine or other. Well, mix in, enjoy yourself, and if you want to order anything, there's a console that rolls out from this end table." He demonstrated.

The usher continued to hover, smiling, over his chair. Finally Barry realized he was waiting for a tip. Without any idea of what was customary, he gave him a dollar, which seemed to do the trick.

He sat there in his bulgy sponge of a chair, grateful to be alone and able to take in the sheer size and glamor of the place. Partyland was an endless middle-class living room, a panorama of all that was gracious, tasteful, and posh. At least, from here in the second ring it *seemed* endless. It had a seating capacity, according to its ads, of 780, but tonight wasn't one of its big nights, and a lot of the seats were empty.

At intervals that varied unpredictably, the furniture within this living room would rearrange itself, and suddenly you would find yourself face to face with a new conversational partner. You could also, for a few dollars more, hire a sofa or armchair that you could drive at liberty among the other chairs, choosing your partners rather than leaving them to chance. Relatively few patrons of Partyland exercised this option, since the whole point of the place was that you could just sit back and let your chair do the driving.

The background music changed from Vivaldi's *Four Seasons* to a Sondheim medley, and all the chairs in Barry's area suddenly lifted their occupants up in the air and carried them off, legs dangling, to their next conversational destination. Barry found himself sitting next to a girl in a red velvet evening dress with a hat of paper feathers and polyhedrons. The band of the hat said, "I'm a Partyland Smartypants."

"Hi," said the girl in a tone that intended to convey a worldly-wise satiety but achieved no more than blank anomie. "What's up?"

"Terrific, just terrific," Barry replied with authentic warmth. He'd always scored well at this preliminary stage of basic communication, which was why, at the time, he'd so much resented his examiner's remark about his handshake. There was nothing phoney about his handshake, and he knew it.

"I like your shoes," she said.

Barry looked down at his shoes. "Thanks."

"I like shoes pretty much generally," she went on. "I guess you could say I'm a kind of shoe freak." She snickered wanly.

Barry smiled, at a loss.

"But yours are particularly nice. How much did you pay for them, if you don't mind my asking?"

Though he minded, he hadn't the gumption to say so. "I don't remember. Not a lot. They're really nothing special."

"*I* like them," she insisted. Then, "My name's Cinderella. What's yours?"

"Is it really?"

"Really. You want to see my ID?"

"Mm."

She dug into her ID folder, which was made of the same velvet as her dress, and took out her license. It was blue, like his (a Temporary License), and, again like his, there was a staple in the upper left-hand corner.

"See?" she said. "Cinderella B. Johnson. It was my mother's idea. My mother has a really weird sense of humor sometimes. She's dead now, though. Do you like it?"

"Like what?"

"My name."

"Oh yeah, sure."

"Because some people don't. They think it's affected. But I can't help the name I was born with, can I?"

"I was going to ask you—"

Her face took on the intent yet mesmerized look of a quiz show contestant. "Ask, ask."

"The staple on your license—why is it there?"

"What staple?" she countered, becoming in an instant rigid with suspicion, like a hare that scents a predator.

"The one on your license. Was there something attached to it originally?"

"Some notice . . . I don't know. How can I remember something like that? Why do you ask?"

"There's one like it on mine."

"So? If you ask me, this is a damned stupid topic for a conversation. Aren't you going to tell me *your* name?"

"Uh . . . Rex."

"Rex what?"

"Rex Riordan."

"An Irish name: that explains it, then."

He looked at her questioningly.

"That must be where you got your gift of gab. You must have kissed the Blarney Stone."

She's crazy, he thought.

But crazy in a dull, not an interesting way. He wondered how long they'd have to go on talking before the chairs switched round again. It seemed such a waste of time talking to another temp, since he could only get the endorsements he needed from people who held Permanent Licenses. Of course, the practice was probably good for him. You can't expect to like everyone you meet, as the Communications Handbook never tired of pointing out, but you can always try and make a good impression. Someday you'd meet someone it was crucial to hit it off with, and your practice would pay off.

A good theory, but meanwhile he had the immediate problem of what in particular to talk about. "Have you heard about the giant department store in Japan?" he asked her. "It covers sixteen acres."

"Sixteen and a half," she corrected. "You must read *Topic* too."

"Mm."

"It's a fascinating magazine. I look at it almost every

week. Sometimes I'm just too busy, but usually I skim it, at least."

"Busy doing . . .?"

"Exactly." She squinted across the vast tasteful expanse of Partyland, then stood up and waved. "I think I've *recognized* someone," she said excitedly, preening her paper feathers with her free hand. Far away, someone waved back.

Cinderella broke one of the polyhedrons off her hat and put it on her chair. "So I'll remember which it is," she explained. Then, contritely, "I hope you don't mind."

"Not at all."

Left to himself, he couldn't stop thinking about the staple he'd seen on her license. It was like the seemingly insignificant clue in a detective story from which the solution to the whole mystery gradually unfolds. For didn't it strongly suggest that she, too, had been given the benefit of the doubt, that she'd got her license not because her score entitled her to it but thanks to Bylaw 9(c), Section XII? The chagrin of being classified in the same category with such a nitwit! Partyland was probably *full* of people in their situation, all hoping to connect with some bona fide Permanent License holder, instead of which they went around colliding with each other.

A highly depressing idea, but he did not on that account roll out the console to select a remedy from the menu. He knew from long experience that whatever could make him palpably happier was also liable to send him into a state of fugue in which conversation in the linear sense became next to impossible. So he passed the time till the next switchover by working out, in his head, the square roots of various five-digit numbers. Then, when he had a solution, he'd check it on his calculator. He'd got five right answers when his chair reared up, god bless it, and bore him off toward . . . Would it be the couple chained, wrist to wrist, on the blue settee? No, at the last moment, his chair veered left and settled down in front of an unoccupied bentwood rocker. A sign in the seat of the rocker said: "I feel a little sick. Back in five minutes."

Barry was just getting used to the idea of going on to

six-digit figures when a woman in a green sofa wheeled up to him and asked what kind of music he liked.

"Any kind, really."

"Any or none, it amounts to much the same thing."

"No, honestly. Whatever is playing, I usually like it. What are they playing here? I like that."

"Muzak," she said dismissively.

It was, in fact, still the Sondheim medley, but he let that pass. It wasn't worth an argument.

"What do you do?" she demanded.

"I simulate a job that Citibank is developing for another corporation, but only on an auxiliary basis. Next year I'm supposed to start full-time."

She grimaced. "You're new at Partyland, aren't you?"

He nodded. "First time tonight. In fact, this is my first time ever in any speakeasy. I just got my license yesterday."

"Well, welcome to the club." With a smile that might as well have been a sneer. "I suppose you're looking for endorsements?"

Not from you, he wanted to tell her. Instead, he looked off into the distance at the perambulations of a suite of chairs in another ring. Only when all the chairs had settled into place did he refocus on the woman in the foreground. He realized with a little zing of elation that he had just administered his first snub!

"What did Freddy say when you came in?" she asked in a conspiratorial, if not downright friendly, tone. (His snub had evidently registered.)

"Who is Freddy?"

"The usher who showed you to your seat. I saw him sit down and talk with you."

"He told me about some Japanese department store."

She nodded knowingly. "Of course—I should have known. Freddy shills for *Topic* magazine, and that's one of their featured stories this week. I wonder what they pay him. Last week their cover story was about Irina Khokolovna, and all Freddy could talk about was Irina Khokolovna."

"Who is Irina Khokolovna?" he asked.

She hooted a single derisory hoot. "I thought you said you liked music!"

"I do," he protested. But, clearly, he had just failed a

major test. With a sigh of weariness and a triumphant smile, the woman rotated her sofa around one hundred and eighty degrees, and drove off in the direction of the couple chained together on the blue settee.

The couple rose in unison and greeted her with cries of "Maggie!" and "Son of a gun!" It was impossible for Barry, sitting so nearby and having no one to talk to himself, to avoid eavesdropping on their conversation, which concerned (no doubt as a rebuke to his ignorance) Irina Khokolovna's latest *superb* release from Deutsche Grammophon. She was at her best in Schumann; her Wolf was *comme ci, comme ça*. Even so, Khokolovna's Wolf was miles ahead of Adriana Motta's, or even Gwyneth Batterham's, who for all her real intelligence was developing a distinct wobble in her upper register. Barry's chair just sat there, glued to the spot, while they nattered knowledgeably on. He wished he were home watching Willy Marx—or anywhere but Partyland.

"Mine's Ed," said the occupant of the bentwood rocker, a young man of Barry's own age, build, and hair-style.

"Pardon?" said Barry.

"I said," he said, with woozy precision, "my name is Ed."

"Oh. Mine's Barry. How are you, Ed."

He held out his hand. Ed shook it gravely.

"You know, Barry," Ed said, "I've been thinking about what you were saying, and I think the whole problem is *cars*. Know what I mean?"

"Elaborate," Barry suggested.

"Right. The thing about cars is . . . Well, I live in Elizabeth, across the river, right? So any time I come here I've got to drive, right? Which you might think was a drag, but in fact I always feel terrific. You know?"

Barry nodded. He didn't understand what Ed was saying in any very specific way, but he knew he agreed with him.

"I feel . . . free. If that doesn't seem too ridiculous. Whenever I'm driving my car."

"What have you got?" Barry asked.

"A Toyota."

"Nice. Very nice."

"I don't think I'm unique that way," said Ed.

"No, I wouldn't say so."

"Cars *are* freedom. And so what all this talk about an energy crisis boils down to is—" He stopped short. "I think I'm having a fugue."

"I think maybe you are. But that's all right. I do too. It'll pass."

"Listen, what's your name?"

"Barry," Barry said. "Barry Riordan."

Ed held out his hand. "Mine's Ed. Say, are you trying to pick up an endorsement?"

Barry nodded. "You too?"

"No. In fact, I think I've still got one left. Would you like it?"

"Jesus," said Barry. "Yeah, sure."

Ed took out his ID folder, took his license from the folder, tickled the edge of the endorsement sticker from the back of the license with his fingernail, and offered it to Barry.

"You're sure you want me to have this?" Barry asked, incredulous, with the white curlicue of the sticker dangling from his fingertip.

Ed nodded. "You remind me of somebody."

"Well, I'm awfully grateful. Really. I mean you scarcely know me."

"Right," said Ed, nodding more vigorously. "But I liked what you were saying about cars. That made a lot of sense."

"You know," Barry burst out in a sudden access of confessional bonhomie, "I feel confused *most* of the time."

"Right."

"But I can never express it. Everything I *say* seems to make more sense than what I can feel inside of me."

"Right, right."

The music changed from the Sondheim medley to the flip side of *The Four Seasons*, and Barry's chair lifted him up and bore him off toward the couple in the blue settee, while Ed, limp in the bentwood rocker, was carried off in the opposite direction.

"Good-bye," Barry shouted after him, but Ed was already either comatose or out of earshot. "And thanks again!"

The MacKinnons introduced themselves. His name was Jason. Hers was Michelle. They lived quite nearby, on West 28th, and were interested, primarily, in the television shows they'd seen when they were growing up, about which they were very well-informed. Despite a bad first impression, due to his associating them with Maggie of the green sofa, Barry found himself liking the MacKinnons enormously, and before the next switchover he put his chair in the LOCK position. They spent the rest of the evening together, exchanging nostalgic titbits over coffee and slices of Partyland's famous pineapple pie. At closing time he asked if they would either consider giving him an endorsement. They said they would have, having thoroughly enjoyed his company, but unfortunately they'd both used up their quota for that year. They seemed genuinely sorry, but he felt, even so, that it had been a mistake to ask.

His first endorsement proved to have been beginner's luck. Though he went out almost every night to a different speakeasy and practically lived at Partyland during the weekends, when it was at its liveliest, he never again had such a plum fall in his lap. He didn't get within sniffing distance of his heart's desire. Most people he met were temps, and the few Permanent License holders inclined to be friendly to him invariably turned out, like the Mac-Kinnons, to have already disposed of their allotted endorsements. Or so they said. As the weeks went by and anxiety mounted, he began to be of the cynical but widely-held opinion that many people simply removed the stickers from their licenses so it would *seem* they'd been used. According to Jason MacKinnon, a completely selfless endorsement, like his from Ed, was a rare phenomenon. Quid pro quos were the general rule, in the form either of cash on the barrel or services rendered. Barry said (jokingly, of course) that he wouldn't object to bartering his virtue for an endorsement, or preferably two, to which Michelle replied (quite seriously) that unfortunately she did not know anyone who might be in the market for Barry's particular type. Generally, she observed, it was *younger* people who got their endorsements by putting out.

Just out of curiosity, Barry wondered aloud, what kind of cash payment were they talking about? Jason said the standard fee, a year ago, for a single sticker had been a thousand dollars; two and a half for a pair, since people with two blanks to fill could be presumed to be that much more desperate. Due, however, to a recent disproportion between supply and demand, the going price for a single was now seventeen hundred, a double a round four thousand. Jason said he could arrange an introduction at that price, if Barry were interested.

"I will tell you," said Barry, "what you can do with your stickers."

"Oh, now," said Michelle placatingly. "We're still your *friends*, Mr. Riordan, but business is business. If it were our own *personal* stickers we were discussing, we wouldn't *hesitate* to give you an endorsement absolutely *gratis*. Would we, Jason?"

"Of course not, no question."

"But we're middlemen, you see. We have only limited flexibility in the terms we can offer. Say, fifteen hundred."

"And three and a half for the pair," Jason added. "And that is a rock-bottom offer. You won't do better anywhere else."

"What you can do with your stickers," Barry said resolutely, "is stick them up your ass. Your asses, rather."

"I wish you wouldn't take that attitude, Mr. Riordan," said Jason in a tone of sincere regret. "We do like you, and we have enjoyed your company. If we didn't, we would certainly not be offering this opportunity."

"Bullshit," said Barry. It was the first time he'd used an obscenity conversationally, and he brought if off with great conviction. "You knew when my license would expire, and you've just been stringing me along, hoping I'd get panicky."

"We have been *trying*," said Michelle, "to help."

"Thanks. I'll help myself."

"How?"

"Tomorrow I'm going back to Center Street and take the exam again."

Michelle MacKinnon leaned across the coffee table that separated the blue settee from Barry's armchair and gave him a sound motherly smack on the cheek. "Wonderful! That's the way to meet a challenge—head on! You're bound to pass. After all, you've had three months of practice. You've become much more fluent these past three months."

"Thanks." He got up to go.

"Hey—" Jason grabbed Barry's hand and gave it an

14

earnest squeeze. "Don't forget, if you *do* get your Permanent License—"

"When he gets it," Michelle amended.

"Right: *when* you get it, you know where you can find us. We're always here on the same settee."

"You two are unbelievable," Barry said. "Do you honestly think I'd sell you my endorsements? Assuming—" He knocked on the varnished walnut coffee table. "—I pass my exam."

"It is safer," Michelle said, "to work through a professional introduction service than to try and peddle them on your own. Even though everyone breaks it, the law is still the law. Individuals operating on their own are liable to get caught, since they don't have an arrangement with the authorities. We do. That's why, for instance, it would do you no good to report us to the Communications Control Office. Others have done so in the past, and it did *them* no good."

"None of them ever got a Permanent License, either," Jason added, with a twinkle of menace.

"That, I'm sure, was just coincidence," said Michelle. "After all, we're speaking of only two cases, and neither of the individuals in question were particularly bright. Bright people wouldn't be so quixotic, would they?" She underlined her question with a Mona Lisa smile, and Barry, for all his indignation and outrage, couldn't keep from smiling back. Anyone who could drop a word like 'quixotic' into the normal flow of conversation and make it seem so natural couldn't be all wrong.

"Don't worry," he promised, tugging his hand out of Jason's. "I'm not the quixotic type."

But when he said it, it sounded false. It wasn't fair.

Barry was as good as his word, and went to Center Street the very next morning to take his third exam. The computer assigned him to Marvin Kolodny, Ph.D. in cubicle 183. The initials worried him. He could have coped, this time, with the old fuddy-duddy he'd had last August, but a Ph.D? It seemed as though they were raising the hurdles each time he came around the track. But his worries evaporated the moment he was in the cubicle and saw that

Marvin Kolodny was a completely average young man of twenty-four. His averageness was even a bit unsteady, as though he had to think about it, but then most twenty-four-year-olds are self-conscious in just that way.

It's always a shock the first time you come up against some particular kind of authority figure—a dentist, a psychiatrist, a cop—who is younger than you are, but it needn't lead to disaster as long as you let the authority figure know right from the start that you intend to be deferential, and this was a quality that Barry conveyed without trying.

"Hi," said Barry, with masterful deference. "I'm Barry Riordan."

Marvin Kolodny responded with a boyish grin and offered his hand. An American flag had been tattooed on his right forearm. On a scroll circling the flagpole was the following inscription:

Let's All
Overthrow
the United States
Government
by Force &
Violence

On his other forearm there was a crudely executed rose with his name underneath: Marvin Kolodny, Ph.D.

"Do you mean it?" Barry asked, marveling over Marvin's tattoo as they shook hands. He managed to ask the question without in the least seeming to challenge Marvin Kolodny's authority.

"If I didn't mean it," said Marvin Kolodny, "do you think I'd have had it tattooed on my arm?"

"I suppose not. It's just so . . . unusual."

"I'm an unusual person," said Marvin Kolodny, leaning back in his swivel chair and taking a large pipe from the rack on his desk.

"But doesn't *that* idea—" Barry nodded at the tattoo. "—conflict with your having this particular job? Aren't you part of the U.S. Government yourself?"

"Only for the time being. I'm not suggesting that we overthrow the government *tomorrow*. A successful revolution isn't possible until the proletariat becomes conscious of their oppression, and they can't become conscious of anything until they are as articulate as their oppressors. Language and consciousness aren't independent processes, after all. Talking is thinking turned inside-out. No more, no less."

"And which am I?"

"How's that?"

"Am I a proletarian or an oppressor?"

"Like most of us these days, I would say you're probably a little of each. Are you married, uh . . ." (He peeked into Barry's file.) ". . . Barry?"

Barry nodded.

"Then that's one form of oppression right there. Children?"

Barry shook his head.

"Do you live with your wife?"

"Not lately. And even when we were together, we never talked to each other, except to say practical things like 'When is your program going to be over?' Some people just aren't that interested in talking. Debra certainly isn't. That's why—" (He couldn't resist the chance to explain his earlier failures.) "—I did so poorly on my earlier exams. Assuming I *did* get a low score last time, which isn't certain, since the results were erased. But assuming that I did, that's the reason. I never got any practice. The basic day-to-day conversational experiences most people have with their spouses never happened in my case."

Marvin Kolodny frowned—an ingratiating, boyish frown. "Are you sure you're being entirely honest with yourself, Barry? Few people are completely unwilling to talk about something. We've all got hobbyhorses. What was your wife interested in? Couldn't you have talked about that?"

"In religion, mostly. But she didn't care to talk about it, unless you agreed with her."

"Have you *tried* to agree with her?"

"Well, you see, Dr. Kolodny, what she *believes* is that the end of the world is about to happen. Next February. That's where she's gone now—to Arizona, to wait for it. This is the third time she's taken off."

"Not an easy woman to discourage, by the sound of it."

"I think she really *wants* the world to end. And also, she *does* like Arizona."

"Have you considered divorce?" Marvin Kolodny asked.

"No, absolutely not. We're still basically in love. After all, most married couples end up not saying much to each other. Isn't that so? Even before Debra got religious, we weren't in the habit of talking to each other. To tell the truth, Dr. Kolodny, I've never been much of a talker. I think I was put off it by the compulsory talk we had to do in high school."

"That's perfectly natural. I hated compulsory talk myself, though I must admit I was good at it. What about your job, Barry? Doesn't that give you opportunities to develop communication skills?"

"I don't communicate with the public directly. Only with simulations, and their responses tend to be pretty stereotyped."

"Well, there's no doubt that you have a definite communications problem. But I think it's a problem you can lick! I'll tell you what, Barry: officially, I shouldn't tell you this myself, but I'm giving you a score of 65." He held up his hand to forestall an effusion. "Now, let me explain how that breaks down. You do very well in most categories—Affect, Awareness of Others, Relevance, Voice Production, et cetera, but where you do fall down is in Notional Content and Originality. There you could do better."

"Originality has always been my Waterloo," Barry admitted. "I just don't seem to be able to come up with my own ideas. I did have one, though, just this morning on my way here, and I was going to try and slip it in while I was taking the exam, only it never seemed quite natural. Have you ever noticed that you never see baby pigeons? All the pigeons you see out on the street are the same size—full-grown. But where do they come from? Where are the little pigeons? Are they hidden somewhere?" He stopped short, feeling ashamed of his idea. Now that it was out in the open it seemed paltry and insignificant, little better than a joke he'd learned by heart, than which there is nothing more calculated to land you in the bottom percentiles.

Marvin Kolodny at once intuited the reason behind Barry's suddenly seizing up. He was in the business, after all, of understanding unspoken meanings and evaluating them precisely. He smiled a sympathetic, mature smile.

"Ideas . . ." he said, in a slow, deliberative manner, as though each word had to be weighed on a scale before it was put into the sentence. ". . . aren't . . . things. Ideas—the most authentic ideas—are the natural, effortless result of any vital relationship. Ideas are what happen when people connect with each other creatively."

Barry nodded.

"Do you mind my giving you some honest advice, Barry?"

"Not at all, Dr. Kolodny. I'd be grateful."

"On your G-47 form you say you spend a lot of time at Partyland and similar speakeasies. I realize that's where you did get your first endorsement, but really, don't you think you're wasting your time in that sort of place? It's a tourist trap!"

"I'm aware of that," Barry said, smarting under the rebuke.

"You're not going to meet anyone there but temps and various people who are out to fleece temps. With rare exceptions."

"I know, I know. But I don't know where *else* to go."

"Why not try this place?" Marvin Kolodny handed Barry a printed card, which read:

INTENSITY FIVE

A New Experience in
Interpersonal Intimacy

5 Barrow Street
New York 10014

Members Only

"I'll certainly try it," Barry promised. "But how do I get to be a member?"

"Tell them Marvin sent you."

And that was all there was to it—he had passed his exam with a score just five points short of the crucial eighth percentile. Which was a tremendous accomplishment, but also rather frustrating in a way, since it meant he'd come *that* close to not having to bother scouting out two more endorsements. Still, with another three months in which to continue his quest and an introduction to Intensity Five, Barry had every reason to be optimistic.

"Thank you, Dr. Kolodny," Barry said, lingering in the doorway of the cubicle. "Thanks terrifically."

"That's all right, Barry. Just doing my job."

"You know ... I wish ... Of course, I know it's not permissible, you being an examiner and all ... but I wish I knew you in a personal way. Truly. You're a very heavy individual."

"Thank you, Barry. I know you mean that, and I'm flattered. Well then—" He took his pipe from his mouth and lifted it in a kind of salute. "So long. And Merry Christmas."

Barry left the cubicle feeling so transcendent and relaxed that he was five blocks from Center Street before he remembered that he'd neglected to have his license re-validated at Window 28. As he headed back to the Federal Communications Building, his senses seemed to register all the ordinary details of the city's streets with an unnatural, hyped clarity: the smell of sauerkraut steaming up from a hot-dog cart, the glint of the noon sun on the mica mixed into the paving blocks of the sidewalk, the various shapes and colors of the pigeons, the very pigeons, perhaps, that had inspired his so-called idea earlier that day. But it was true, what he'd said. All the pigeons were the same size.

A block south of the Federal Communications Building he looked up, and there, strung out under the cornice of the building, was the motto, which he had never noticed before, of the Federal Communications Agency:

PLANNED FREEDOM IS THE ROAD TO
LASTING PROGRESS.

So simple, so direct, and yet, when you thought about it, almost impossible to understand.

Barrow Street being right in the middle of one of the city's worst slums, Barry had been prepared (he'd thought) for a lesser degree of stateliness and bon ton than that achieved by Partyland, but even so the dismal actuality of Intensity Five went beyond anything he could have imagined. A cavernous one-room basement apartment with bare walls, crackly linoleum over a concrete floor, and radiators which hissed and gurgled ominously without generating a great deal of heat. The furniture consisted of metal folding chairs, most of them folded and stacked, a refreshment stand that sold orange juice and coffee, and a great many free-standing, brim-full metal ashtrays. Having already forked out twenty-five dollars upstairs as his membership fee, Barry felt as though he'd been had, but, since the outlay was non-refundable, he decided to give the place the benefit of his doubt and loiter a while.

He had been loitering, alone and melancholy, for the better part of an hour, eavesdropping to his right on a conversation about somebody's drastic need to develop a more effective persona and to his left on a discussion of the morality of our involvement in Mexico, when a black woman in a white nylon jumpsuit and a very good imitation calf-length mink swept into the room, took a quick survey of those present, and sat down, unbelievably, by him!

Quick as a light switch he could feel his throat go dry and his face tighten into a smile of rigid insincerity. He blushed, he trembled, he fainted dead away, but only metaphorically.

"I'm Columbine Brown," she said, as though that offered an explanation.

Did she expect him to recognize her? She was beautiful enough, certainly, to have been someone he ought to recognize, but if he had seen her on TV, he didn't remember. In a way, she seemed almost *too* beautiful to be a noted personality, since there is usually something a little idiosyncratic about each of them, so they can be told apart. Columbine Brown was beautiful in the manner not of a celebrity but of a deluxe (but not customized) sports car.

"I'm Barry Riordan," he managed to bring out, tardily.

"Let's put our cards on the table, shall we, Mr. Riordan? I am a Permanent Card holder. What are you?"

"A temp."

"It's fair to assume then that you're here to find an endorsement."

21

He began to protest. She stopped him with just one omniscient and devastating glance. He nodded.

"Unfortunately, I have used up my quota. However—" She held up a single perfect finger. "—it's almost the New Year. If you're not in a desperate hurry . . .?"

"Oh, I've got till March."

"I'm not promising anything, you understand. Unless we hit it off. If we do, then fine, you have my endorsement. Fair enough?"

"It's a deal."

"You feel you can trust me?" She lowered her eyes and tried to look wicked and temptress-like, but it was not in the nature of her kind of beauty to do so.

"Anywhere," he replied. "Implicitly."

"Good." As though of its own volition her coat slipped off her shoulders onto the back of the folding chair. She turned her head sideways and addressed the old woman behind the refreshment counter. "Evelyn, how about an orange juice?" She looked at him. He nodded. "Make it two."

Then, as though they'd been waiting for these preliminaries to be concluded, tears sprang to her eyes. A tremor of heartfelt emotion colored her lovely contralto voice as she said, "Oh Jesus, what am I going to do? I can't take any more! I am just so . . . so god-damned wretched! I'd like to kill myself. No, that isn't true. I'm confused, Larry. But I know one thing—I am an *angry* woman and I'm going to start fighting back!"

It would have been inconsiderate to break in upon such testimony by mentioning that his name was not, in fact, Larry. What difference does one letter make, after all?

"Have you ever been to the Miss America Pageant on 42nd Street?" she asked him, drying her eyes.

"I can't say I have. I always mean to, but you know how it is. It's the same with the Statue of Liberty. It's always there, so you never get around to it."

"I'm Miss Georgia."

"No kidding!"

"I have *been* Miss Georgia six nights a week for the last four years, with matinees on Sunday and Tuesday, and do you suppose in all that time that the audience has ever voted for *me* to be Miss America? Ever?"

"*I* would certainly vote for you."

"Never once," she went on fiercely, ignoring his supportiveness. "It's always Miss Massachusetts, or Miss Ohio, who can't do anything but play a damn jews-harp, if you'll excuse my language, or Miss Oregon, who still can't remember the blocking for "Lovely to Look At," which she has been dancing since before *I* graduated from high school. There's no one in the whole damn line-up who hasn't been crowned at least once. Except me."

"I'm sorry to hear it."

"I am a *good* singer. I can tap-dance like a house on fire. My balcony scene would break your heart. And I can say objectively that I've got better legs than anyone except, possibly, Miss Wyoming."

"But you've never been Miss America," Barry said sympathetically.

"What do you think that *feels* like, here?" She grabbed a handful of white nylon in the general area of her heart.

"I honestly don't know, Miss . . ." (He'd forgotten her last name.) ". . . Georgia."

"At Intensity Five I'm just plain Columbine, honey. The same as you're just Larry. And not knowing isn't much of an answer. Here I am exposing myself in front of you, and you come back with 'No Opinion'. I don't buy that."

"Well, to be completely candid, Columbine, it's hard for me to imagine your feeling anything but terrific. To be Miss Georgia and have such a lot of talent—isn't that *enough*? I would have thought you'd be very happy."

Columbine bit her lip, furrowed her brow, and evidenced, in general, a sudden change of heart. "God, Larry—you're right! I've been kidding myself: the Pageant isn't my problem—it's my excuse. My problem—" Her voice dropped, her eyes avoided his. "—is timeless and well-known. I fell in love with the wrong man for me. And now it's too late. Would you like to hear a long story, Larry? A long and very unhappy story?"

"Sure. That's what I'm here for, isn't it?"

She smiled a meaningful, unblemished smile, and gave his hand a quick, trusting squeeze. "You know, Larry— you're an all-right guy."

Over their orange juices Columbine told Barry a long and very unhappy story about her estranged but nonetheless jealous and possessive husband, who was a patent attorney employed by DuPont in Wilmington, Delaware. Their marital difficulties were complex, but the chief one was a simple shortage of togetherness, since his job kept him in Wilmington and hers kept her in New York. Additionally, her husband's ideal of conversation was very divergent from her own. He enjoyed talking about money, sports, and politics with other men, and bottled up all his deeper feelings. She was introspective, outgoing, and warm-hearted.

"It would be all right for a while," she recalled. "But the pressure would build until I had to go out and find someone to talk to. It is a basic human need, after all. Perhaps *the* basic need. I had no choice."

"And then he'd find out, I suppose," said Barry.

She nodded. "And go berserk. It was awful. No one can live that way."

Barry thought that in many ways her problem bore a resemblance to his, at least insofar as they both had to look for intellectual companionship outside the bonds of marriage. But when he began to elaborate upon this insight and draw some interesting parallels between his experience and hers, Columbine became impatient. She did not come right out and tell him that he was in breach of contract, but that was definitely the message conveyed by her glazed inattention. Responsive to her needs, he resisted the impulse to make any further contributions of his own and sat back and did his level best to be a good listener and nothing more.

When Columbine had finally run the gamut of all her feelings, which included fear, anger, joy, pain, and an abiding and entirely unreasoning sense of dread, she thanked him, gave him her address and phone number, and said to get in touch in January for his endorsement.

Jubilation, he thought. Bingo. Halleluiah.

But not quite. He still had to get one more endorsement. But now it seemed possible, likely, even inevitable. A matter, merely, of making the effort and reaping the reward.

* * *

Dame Fortune had become so well-disposed to him that he got his third endorsement (though in point of hard fact, his second) the very next night. The fated encounter took place at Morone's One-Stop Shopping, a mom-and-pop mini-grocery on Sixth Avenue right next to the International Supermarket. Although Morone's charged more for most items, Barry preferred shopping there because it offered such a limited and unchallenging range of choices (cold meats, canned goods, beer, Nabisco cookies) that he never felt intimidated and ashamed of his selections at the check-out counter. He hated to cook, but was that any reason he should be made to feel inadequate? Morone's was made to order for people like Barry, of which there are great numbers.

That night as he was hesitating between a dinner of Spam and Chef Boy-ar-dee ravioli or Spam and Green Giant Niblets corn, the woman who had been standing in front of the frozen-food locker suddenly started talking to herself. The Morones looked at each other in alarm. Neither of them were licensed talkers, which was a further attraction of their store, since one's exchanges with them were limited to such basic permissible amenities as "How are you," "Take care," and giving out prices.

What the woman was saying was of a character to suggest that she had just that minute gone crazy. "The pain," she explained calmly to the ice cream section of the freezer, "only comes on when I do this." She stooped closer to the ice cream and winced. "But then it's pure hell. I want to cut my leg off, have a lobotomy, anything to make it stop. Yet I know the problem isn't in my leg at all. It's in my back. Here." She touched the small of her back. "A kind of short circuit. Worse than bending over is twisting sideways. Even turning my head can set it off. Sometimes, when I'm alone, I'll start crying just at the thought of it, at knowing I've become so damned superannuated." She sighed. "Well, it happens to everyone, and I suppose it could be worse. There's no use complaining. Life goes on, as they say."

Having come round to a sensible, accepting attitude, she turned from the freezer to witness the effect of her out-burst on the Morones, who looked elsewhere, and on Barry, who couldn't resist meeting her eyes head-on. Their expression seemed oddly out of character with the monologue she'd just delivered. They were piercing (as against vulnerable), steely-gray eyes that stared defiance from a face all sags and wrinkles. Without the contradiction of such eyes, her face would have seemed ruined and hopeless; with them, she looked just like an ancient centurion in a movie about the Roman Empire.

She grimaced. "No need to panic. It's not an emergency. I'm licensed."

Barry proffered his most harmless smile. "I wasn't even thinking of that."

She didn't smile back. "Then what were you thinking?"

"I guess I was feeling sorry."

To which her reaction was, alarmingly, to laugh.

Feeling betrayed and pissed-off, he grabbed the nearest can of vegetables (beets, he would later discover, and he hated beets) and handed it to Mr. Morone with the can of Spam.

"That it?" Mr. Morone asked.

"A six-pack of Schlitz," he said, quite off the top of his head.

When he left the store with his dinner and the beer in a plastic bag, she was already outside waiting for him. "I wasn't laughing at you, young man," she told him, taking the same coolly aggrieved tone she'd taken toward the ice cream. "I was laughing at myself. Obviously, I *was* asking for pity. So if I should get some, I shouldn't be surprised, should I? My name's Madeline, but my friends call me Mad. You're supposed to laugh."

"Mine's Barry," he said. "Do you drink beer?"

"Oh, I'm not drunk. I discovered long ago that one needn't actually drink in order to have the satisfaction of behaving outrageously."

"I meant, would you like some now, with me? I've got a six-pack."

"Certainly. Barry, you said? You're so *direct* it's almost devious. Let's go to my place. It's only a couple blocks away. You see—I can be direct myself."

Her place turned out to be four street numbers away

from his, and nothing like what he'd been expecting, neither a demoralized wreck heaped with moldering memorabilia nor yet the swank, finicky *pied-a-terre* of some has-been somebody. It was a plain pleasant 1½-room apartment that anyone could have lived in and almost everyone did, with potted plants to emphasize the available sunlight and pictures representing various vanished luxuries on the wall, the common range of furniture from aspiring to makeshift, and enough ordinary debris to suggest a life being carried on, with normative difficulty, among these carefully cultivated neutralities.

Barry popped the tops off two beer cans and Madeline swept an accumulation of books and papers off a tabletop and onto a many-cushioned bed. They sat down at the table.

"Do you know what it's called?" he asked. "The disease you've got?"

"Sciatica. Which is more a disorder than a disease. Let's not talk about it, okay?"

"Okay, but *you'll* have to think of what we do talk about. I'm no good at coming up with topics for conversation."

"Why is that?"

"No ideas. If other people have ideas I can bounce off them well enough, but all by itself my mind's a blank. I envy people like you who are able to start talking out of the blue."

"Mm," said Madeline, not unkindly. "It's odd you should put it like that: it's almost a definition of what I do for a living."

"Really, what's that?"

"I'm a poet."

"No kidding. You can make a living by being a poet?"

"Enough to get by."

Barry refused to believe her. Neither the woman nor her apartment corresponded with his preconceptions of poets and the necessarily indigent life they must lead. "Have you ever published a book?" he asked craftily.

"Twenty-two. More than that, if you count limited editions and pamphlets and such." She went over to the bed, rooted among the papers, and returned with a thin, odd-sized paperback. "This is the latest." The front cover said in tasteful powder blue letters on a ground of dusky cream: MADELINE IS MAD AGAIN: New Poems by Madeline Swain. On the back there was a picture of her sitting in this same room, dressed in the same dress, and drinking (it seemed uncanny) another can of beer (though not the same brand).

Barry turned the book over in his hands, examining the cover and the photo alternately, but would no more have thought of looking inside than of lifting Madeline's skirts to peek at her underclothes. "What's it about?" he asked.

"Whatever I happened to be thinking at the moment I wrote each poem."

That made sense but didn't answer his question. "When do you write them?"

"Generally, whenever people ask me to."

"Could you write a poem right now? About what you're thinking?"

"Sure, no trouble." She went to the desk in the corner of the room and quickly wrote the following poem, which she handed to Barry to read:

A Reflection

> Sometimes the repetition of what we have
>   just said will suggest a new meaning
>   or possibilities of meaning
> we did not at first suppose to be there.
> We think we have understood our words,
>   then learn that we have not,
>   since their essential meaning
> only dawns on us the second time round.

"This is what you were thinking just now?" he asked skeptically.

"Are you disappointed?"

"I thought you'd write something about me."

"Would you like me to do that?"

"It's too late now."

"Not at all."

She went to her desk and returned a moment later with a second poem:

Aubade

I was sorry to hear
That you've got to be going.
But you're not?
Then I'm sorry to hear that.

"What does the title mean?" he asked, hoping it might modify the unfriendly message of the four short lines that followed.

"An aubade is a traditional verse form that a lover addresses to his (or her) beloved at dawn, when one of them is leaving for work."

He tried to think of a compliment that wouldn't be completely insincere. "Heavy," he allowed at last.

"Oh, I'm afraid it's not much good. I can usually do better. I guess I don't trust you enough. Though you're quite likeable: that's another matter."

"Now I'm likeable! I thought—" He dangled the poem by one corner. "—you were just hinting that I should leave?"

"Nonsense. You haven't even finished your beer. You *mustn't* hold what I write against me. Poets can't be held responsible for what they say in their poems. We're all compulsive traitors, you know."

Barry said nothing, but his expression must have conveyed his disapproval.

"Now don't be like that. Treason is a necessary part of the job, the way that handling trash-cans is a part of being a garbage man. Some poets go to a great deal of trouble to disguise their treacheries; my inclination is to be up-front and betray everyone right from the start."

"Do you have many friends?" he asked, needlingly.

"Virtually none. Do you think I'd go around talking to myself in grocery stores if I had friends?"

He shook his head, perplexed. "I'll tell you, Madeline, it doesn't make sense to me. Surely if you were nice to other poets, they'd be nice to you, on the basic principle of scratch-my-back."

"Oh, of course. Minor poets do nothing else. They positively swarm. I'd rather be major and lonely, thank you very much."

"Sounds arrogant to me."

"It is. I am. *C'est la vie.*" She took a long, throat-rippling sip of the Schlitz, and set her can down on the table, empty. "What I like about you, Barry, is that you manage to say what you think without seeming the least homicidal. Why?"

"Why do I say what I think? It's easiest."

"No: why are you so accommodating to me, when I'm being such a bitch? Are you looking for an endorsement?"

He blushed. "Is it that obvious?"

"Well, as you don't appear to be either a mugger or a rapist, there had to be some reason you followed a dotty old woman home from her latest nervous breakdown. Let's make a deal, shall we?"

"What sort of deal?"

"You stay around and nudge some more poems out of me. I'm feeling the wind in my sails, but I need a muse. If you give me twenty good ideas for poems, I'll give you your endorsement."

Barry shook his head. "Twenty different ideas? Impossible."

"Don't think of them as ideas, then, think of them as questions."

"Ten," he insisted. "Ten is a lot."

"Fifteen," she countered.

"All right, but including the two you've already written."

"Done!"

She sat down at her desk and waited for Barry to be inspired. "Well?" she inquired, after long silence.

"I'm trying to think."

He tried to think of what most poems were about. Love seemed the likeliest subject, but he couldn't imagine Madeline, at her age and with her temperament, being in love with anybody. Still, that was her problem. He didn't have to write the poem, only propose it.

"All right," he said. "Write a poem about how much you're in love with me."

She looked miffed. "Don't flatter yourself, young man: I may have inveigled you into my apartment, but I am *not* in love with you."

"Pretend, then. And don't make it anything flip like that last one. Make it sad and delicate and use some rhymes."

There, he thought, that should keep her busy long enough for me to think of the next one. He opened a second beer and took a meditative swallow. Did poets ever write poems about drinking beer? Or was that too general? Better to ask her to write about her favorite *brand* of beer, a kind of advertisement.

By the time she'd finished the sonnet about how much she loved him he had come up with all twelve other subjects:

1. A poem about her favorite beer, written as though it were an ad.
2. A poem in the form of a Christmas shopping list.
3. A poem embodying several important long-range economic forecasts.
4. A poem about a rabbit (there was a porcelain rabbit on one of the shelves), suitable to be sung to a baby.
5. A very short poem to be carved on the tombstone of her least favorite president, living or dead.
6. A poem apologizing to the last person she had been especially rude to.
7. A poem for a Get Well card to someone who has sciatica.
8. A poem analyzing her feelings about beets.
9. A poem that skirts all around a secret she's never told anyone and then finally decides to keep it a secret.
10. A poem giving an eyewitness account of something awful happening in Arizona, in February.
11. A poem justifying capital punishment in cases where one has been abandoned by one's lover. (This, in its final, expanded form, was to become the longest poem in her next collection, "The Ballad of Lucius Mc-Gonaghal Sloe," which begins:

I fell head over heels just four evenings ago
With a girl that I'm sure you all know,
  But I couldn't hold her,
  And that's why I sold her,
To Lucius McGonaghal Sloe.

and continues, in a similar vein, for another one hundred thirty-six stanzas.)
12. A poem presenting an affirmative, detailed description
   of her own face.

Prudently, he didn't spring them on her all at once, but
waited until she'd finished each one before telling her
what the next had to be about. She didn't raise any further
objections until he came to Number 8, whereupon she
insisted she didn't have any feelings about beets whatsoev-
er. He refused to believe her, and to prove his point he
cooked up a quick dinner on her hotplate of Spam and
canned beets (it was rather late by then, and they were
famished). Before she'd had three mouthfuls, the poem
started coming to her, and by the time she'd got it into
final shape, five years later, it was far and away the best of
the lot.

For the next many days Barry didn't speak to a soul. He
felt no need to communicate anything to anyone. He had
his three endorsements—one from a poet who'd published
twenty-two books—and he was confident he could have
gone out and got three more a day if he'd needed to. He
was off the hook.

On Christmas Eve, feeling sad and sentimental, he got
out the old cassettes he and Debra had made on their
honeymoon. He played them on the TV, one after the
other, all through the night, waxing mellower and mellower and wishing she were here. Then, in February, when
the world had once again refused to end, she did come
home, and for several days it was just as good as anything
on the cassettes. They even, for a wonder, talked to each
other. He told her about his various encounters in pursuit
of his endorsements, and she told him about the Grand
Canyon, which had taken over from the end of the world

as her highest mythic priority. She loved the Grand Canyon with a surpassing love, and wanted Barry to leave his job and go with her to live right beside it. Impossible, he declared. He'd worked eight years at Citibank and accrued important benefits. He accused her of concealing something. Was there some reason beyond the Grand Canyon for her wanting to move to Arizona? She insisted it was strictly the Grand Canyon, that from the first moment she'd seen it she'd forgotten all about Armageddon, the Number of the Beast, and all the other accoutrements of the Apocalypse. She couldn't explain: he would have to see it himself. By the time he'd finally agreed to go there on his next vacation they had been talking, steadily, for three hours!

Meanwhile, Columbine Brown had been putting him off with a variety of excuses and dodges. The phone number she'd given him was her answering service, the address was an apartment building with guard-dogs in the lobby and a doorman who didn't talk, or listen. Barry was obliged to wait out on the sidewalk, which wasn't possible, due to a cold wave that persisted through most of January. He left a message at the Apollo Theater, where the Pageant was held, giving three different times he would be waiting for her at Intensity Five. She never showed. By mid-February, he'd begun to be alarmed. Early one morning, defying the weather, he posted himself outside her building and waited (five miserable hours) till she appeared. She was profusely apologetic, explained that she *did* have his sticker, there was no problem, he shouldn't worry, but she had an appointment she had to get to, in fact she was already late, and so if he'd come back tonight, or better yet (since she had to see somebody after the Pageant and didn't know when she'd be home) at this time tomorrow? Thoughtfully, she introduced him to the doorman so he wouldn't have to wait out in the cold.

At this time tomorrow Columbine made another non-appearance, and Barry began to suspect she was deliberately avoiding him. He decided to give her one last chance. He left a message with the doorman saying he would be by to collect his you-know-what at half past twelve the next night. Alternately, she could leave it in an envelope with the doorman.

When he arrived the following evening, the doorman led him down the carpeted corridor, unlocked the elevator (the dogs growled portentously until the doorman said "*Aus!*"), and told him to ring at door 8-C.

It was not Columbine who let him in, but her understudy, Lida Mullens. Lida informed Barry that Columbine had joined her husband in Wilmington, Delaware, and there was no knowing when, if ever, she might return to her post as Miss Georgia. She had not left the promised sticker, and Lida seriously doubted whether she had any left, having heard, through the grapevine, that she'd sold all three of them to an introduction service on the day they came in the mail. With his last gasp of self-confidence Barry asked Lida Mullens whether *she* would consider giving him an endorsement. He promised to pay her back in kind the moment he was issued his own license. Lida informed him airily that she didn't have a license. Their entire conversation had been illegal.

The guilt that immediately marched into his mind and evicted every other feeling was something awful. He knew it was irrational, but he couldn't help it. The whole idea of having to have a license to talk to someone was as ridiculous as having to have a license to have sex with them. Right? Right! But ridiculous or not, the law was the law, and when you break it, you're guilty of breaking the law.

The nice thing about guilt is that it's so easy to repress. Within a day Barry had relegated all recollection of his criminal behavior of the night before to the depths of his subconscious and was back at Intensity Five, waiting for whomever to strike up a conversation. The only person who so much as glanced his way, however, was Evelyn, the woman behind the refreshment stand. He went to other speakeasies, but it was always the same story. People avoided him. Their eyes shied away. His vibrations became such an effective repellent that he had only to enter a room in order to empty it of half its customers. Or so it seemed. When one is experiencing failure, it is hard to resist the comfort of paranoia.

With only a week left till his temporary license expired, Barry abandoned all hope and all shame and went back to Partyland with fifteen hundred dollars in cash, obtained from Beneficial Finance.

The MacKinnons were not in their blue settee, and neither Freddy the usher nor Madge of the green sofa could say what had become of them. He flopped into the empty settee with a sense of complete, abject surrender, but so eternally does hope spring that inside a quarter of an hour he had adjusted to the idea of never being licensed and was daydreaming instead of a life of majestic, mysterious silence on the rim of the Grand Canyon. He rolled out the console and ordered a slice of pineapple pie and some uppers.

The waitress who brought his order was Cinderella Johnson. She was wearing levis and a tee-shirt with the word "Princess" in big, glitter-dust letters across her breasts. Her hat said: "Let Tonight Be Your Enchanted Evening at Partyland!"

"Cinderella!" he exclaimed. "Cinderella Johnson! Are you *working* here?"

She beamed. "Isn't it wonderful? I started three days ago. It's like a dream come true."

"Congratulations."

"Thanks." Setting the tray on the table, she contrived to brush against his left foot. "I see you're wearing the same shoes."

"Mm."

"Is something the matter?" she asked, handing him the uppers with a glass of water. "You look gloomy, if you'll forgive my saying so."

"Sometimes it does you good to feel gloomy." One of the pills insisted on getting stuck in his throat. Just like, he thought, a lie.

"Hey, do you mind if I sit down on your couch a minute? I am frazzled. It's a tremendous opportunity, working here, but it does take it out of you."

"Great," said Barry. "Fine. Terrific. I could use some company."

She sat down close to him, and whispered into his ear:

"If anyone, such as Freddy, for instance, should happen to ask what we were talking about, say it was the New Wooly Look, okay?"

"That's *Topic*'s feature story this week?"

She nodded. "I guess you heard about the MacKinnons."

"I asked, but I didn't get any answers."

"They were arrested, for trafficking, right here on this couch, while they were taking money from the agent that had set them up. There's no way they can wiggle out of it this time. People say how sorry they are and everything, but I don't know: they *were* criminals, after all. What they were doing only makes it harder for the rest of us to get our endorsements honestly."

"I suppose you're right."

"Of course I'm right."

Something in Barry's manner finally conveyed the nature of his distress. The light dawned: "You have *got* your license, haven't you?"

Reluctantly at first, then with the glad, uncloseted feeling of shaking himself loose all over a dance floor, Barry told Cinderella of his ups and downs during the past six months.

"Oh, that is so terrible," she commiserated at the end of his tale. "That is so unfair."

"What can you do?" he asked, figuratively.

Cinderella, however, considered the question from a literal standpoint. "Well," she said, "we haven't ever really talked together, not seriously, but you certainly ought to have a license."

"It's good of you to say so," said Barry morosely.

"So—if you'd like an endorsement from me . . . ?" She reached into her back pocket, took out her license, and peeled off an endorsement sticker.

"Oh, no, really, Cinderella. . . ." He took the precious sticker between thumb and forefinger. "I don't deserve this. Why should you go out on a limb for someone you scarcely know?"

"That's okay," she said. "I'm sure you'd have done just the same for me."

"If there is anything I can do in return . . . ?"

She frowned, shook her head vehemently, and then said, "Well . . . maybe . . ."

"Name it."

"Could I have one of your shoes?"

He laughed delightedly. "Have both of them!"

"Thanks, but I wouldn't have room."

He bent forward, undid the laces, pulled off his right shoe, and handed it to Cinderella.

"It's a beautiful shoe," she said, holding it up to the light. "Thank you *so* much."

And that is the end of the story.

I have a theory, which I admit to be half-baked, that the best horror stories are written by young writers or by writers notable for what could be called their arrested development. Lovecraft, for instance, or Bradbury. The reason for this is the nature of what is commonly represented as horrific in horror stories, which an ounce of psychoanalysis reveals to be that old unmentionable, sex. Nowadays, indeed, the sexual content of most horror stories is pretty explicit. Consider Hitchcock's *Psycho* or Frank Langella's dreamboat Dracula. So it's hard these days to be naive enough to write a horror story in which the buried or disguised materials stay buried or disguised long enough to raise a goosepimple. What is apt to happen is that someone's fright-wig will slip off, or his makeup will melt, and we, the audience, will realize it's all a silly joke and instead of screaming in terror we're put into stitches.

Well, it's not as simple as that either. I remember once, on a visit back to Minneapolis, where I grew up, being told of how the son and daughter of old friends, aged 12 and 9, had gone to see *The Night of the Living Dead* and thought it just too funny for words. Whereas I, a mature sophisticate of 33, had started screaming at the first scene in the cemetery and remained reverently aghast through the rest of the movie. What's *wrong* with kids nowadays? I wondered. If that counts as funny, please define scary.

I may be making difficulties where none exist. As Freud, or was it Aristotle, long ago pointed out, laughter is just a 78 scream of recognition played at 33 rpm. Funny and scary are fraternal twins.

All this preamble by way of explaining that while the general drift of the stories in this collection is westward to laughter, satire, and responsible mature concerns, there are, even so, a couple of sincere, old-fashioned horror stories among. So with a tip of my fright-wig to Edgar Allen Poe, let me turn down the lights and ask you to suspend your disbelief for . . .

The Black Cat

"My immediate purpose is to place before the world, plainly, succinctly, and without comment, a series of mere household events."

E.A. Poe

It wasn't his apartment. It belonged to a Mrs. Willard, whom he'd met in Rome. Her father, Gabriel Antonelli, had died three years ago and left it to her. Antonelli had been the head of the University's philosophy department. However, nothing distinctively philosophical had survived, his library having gone to the university. The furnishings didn't aspire towards any kind of statement. They were better than he was used to, but not as good as he'd been expecting, except for a rather large and slightly warped canvas by Matisse—bland tripe-like pinks and custardy yellows confronting a severe cerulean blue. Later, in a letter, Mrs. Willard explained that the Matisse was a forgery.

Just to have so much space at his sole command, that was the great luxury: a living room, a dining room, a kitchen, two bedrooms, two baths, a long corridor lined floor-to-ceiling with hardwood shelves—and an anomalous, unfurnished, el-shaped room nestled behind the hall closet. He called it his den, though he never put in any furniture. He meant to use it for yoga, if he should ever get back to yoga, or for meditation, or possibly as a darkroom, since there was a small sink in the unseen corner of the el. In short, it represented his sense of all his as-yet-unrealized possibilities. He felt child-like inside the den. Its bare walls were redolent of the same gentle desolation he remembered from the half-built ranch houses he'd explored during his suburban childhood.

From various evidences—a litter box in the second bathroom, a supply of litter and cat food—he'd deduced that the previous tenant had kept a cat, but what had become of the cat after her suicide he'd never thought to inquire. So that when, one Wednesday evening, it materialized in the middle of Handel's *Lucrezia*, he was not much surprised. "Hi there," he said. "What's your name?" It brushed against his knee, rummaging for affection. A black tom, looking still quite sleek and cared-for, wearing a collar of maroon leather. There seemed no doubt but that it had been Mrs. Laurier's pet, since it led him unerringly to where the cans of Puss 'n Boots were kept, at the bottom of the broom closet.

He knew nothing of Mrs. Laurier except that she was a divorcee in her middle thirties, that she had directed the university's placement service (and thus had been the first in line when the apartment became available at Antonelli's death), and that she was judged very attractive by as many of the other tenants as remembered her. Nothing in the apartment, as he had inherited it, revealed or suggested any more. Until now.

He called the cat Midnight. Twice before he'd had Midnights. Once, around age four, living on his grandparents' farm in the South; the second, a kitten, several years later, after the move to the city. He had tortured both of them regularly, but with the kitten it became almost obsessional. When he came home from school he would hunt for it all about the house, then bring it snarling up to the bathroom and place it in the tub, which he would slowly fill with scalding water. The kitten was too little to get out of the tub, but it would always try to clamber up the slick, impossible enamel. What monsters children are! He promised this Midnight, the third of its name, that he had reformed. They would live together in peace and harmony, if not friends exactly, if not even allies quite, then at the very least friendly neutral powers, like Sweden or Switzerland. Above and beyond the daily ration of Puss 'n Boots there would always be tidbits, steak-bones, nuggets of cheese, and such other choice crumbs as a bachelor's table may be relied on to produce. Midnight in return need only be beautiful, a cohabiting presence, alive, aware, awaiting the little benedictions of his kindness and concern. All this he explained to Midnight aloud as it lay curled in his lap, purring its bland equivocations.

Surprisingly, perhaps, he kept to the terms of this contract. Even when he was invited to the country for the weekend of the Fourth, he scrupled to buy a carrier for Midnight so it could come along on the bus. At the last moment he came down with a summer cold and they didn't go, but the carrier bespoke, certainly, his sense of responsibility and his good faith—if not, indeed, an undeclared affection.

One rainy night that same July, after too much of wine and then of brandy, he stayed on with friends on the other side of town, returning to the apartment late the next morning. Midnight was nowhere to be found. He went through all the rooms with a bowl of milk, guiltily calling its name and apologizing. The window in the den (which he always kept locked since it overlooked the fire escape) was open. It was through this window that, as he'd then determined, Midnight had first appeared. The more unsettling—and apparently quite independent—discovery of this morning had to do not with the the cat's justifiable disappearance, but rather with the condition of the walls of the den, which were covered with graffiti of the most obscene character, crudely rendered with a black magic marker. Later he found the used-up marker in the top drawer of his desk. It was his own. Nothing, except possibly the cat, had been taken from the apartment.

He kept returning to the den to study the graffiti. The mere act of looking at them seemed to be a kind of admission on his part. If he had not been away from the apartment the night before, he might almost have believed that he'd scrawled them himself in a somnambulistic trance, so perfectly did they seem to correspond to his own most rooted, if inexpressible, proclivities.

A supply of white semi-gloss enamel had been left under the kitchen sink, and he occupied the afternoon painting over the graffiti. Even with a second coat, faint, ghostly outlines of sexual organs could be discerned on the walls, indefinite and dim as the figures on the screen of a defective television patrolling the entrance of a shop. But he was too tired to apply another coat. To what purpose? He sat upon the paint-flecked floor with a sense, almost physiological, of justice being done, of the scales slowly coming to rest. There was the bowl of milk, where he had left it on the ledge of the open window. He took it in both hands, and drank it down all at one go.

The next morning Midnight was back. He offered neither reproaches nor apologies. Was he happy to have the cat with him again? He couldn't be certain. Yes, he was happy—but also, a little, afraid.

As they watched the ten o'clock news, Midnight's tail would tick lithely back and forth in precise, scythe-like curves. This was the bloodiest of the news programs, with camera teams that reached the sites of local crimes before the bodies had been hauled away, with living atrocities from all round the globe beamed in by satellites. He found the news and the ads equally interesting, equally arousing. He especially liked ads for shampoos and hair coloring. The women in them seemed to regard their hair as independent, capricious entities, whom they must placate and provide with food. They stroked and fondled their massive tresses exactly as he might have stroked and fondled Midnight.

Naturally, it was no longer enough to offer scoops of Puss 'n Boots. Midnight insisted on ground round, calves' liver, fresh fish. Sometimes, for a special treat, he would bring home living mice from a pet shop. And late at night, when the streets were quiet and the towers round it dark, they would go walking in the park. Midnight did not need a leash. He felt that certain of the cat's essential loyalty that even when it came time to leave those shadowed paths and return along the empty streets he didn't bother summoning it. Seen or unseen, he knew it must be near. He would go down by the boats and be calmed by their restless swaying and bobbing. Other late strollers never approached him, and if they had he would not have minded, since he was armed. Strange how beautiful the park became by night, which in daylight he couldn't witness without a numbing sense of how broken and how bare a place it had become.

Sometimes, in a spirit of teasing affection, he would make a necklace from gobbets of beef or liver and let the cat feed by leaping to his chest and tearing loose his dinner, bite by bite. Later, tiring of this game, he'd wind these bleeding garlands round his cock instead, then lie back on the grimy sheets and endure for endless minutes the excruciating pleasure of his liberation.

Early in the fall one of his students came by the apartment, uninvited, to discuss a term paper. There was nothing to discuss, but nevertheless he made himself available, to the extent of offering a glass of sherry and pretending to be interested in whatever. Midnight, who usually defended the apartment against all such invasions by shredding drapes or stockings, became the most benign of pussycats toward the young stranger. It offered the softest down of its throat to be petted, offered its vivid agate eyes to be gazed on, and as this seduction was in progress he became aware that Midnight had somehow intuited his own urgings—and the student's as well. Without a word of explanation he began to get undressed, and then, stripped bare, as calmly and methodically he removed the clothes of his astonished but unprotesting visitor.

Could all the cat's moods and actions thus be interpreted as expressions of his own nascent feelings, his own as-yet-unrealized desires? All through his childhood his parents had taken him on visits to a maiden aunt living in another state. In this aunt's bedroom there had been a toilet table, and among all the powders and perfumes laid out on that table was a hand-mirror which had forever fascinated and absorbed him. One side of it was an ordinary oval mirror: the reverse side was black, but still a mirror. Holding the gilt handle, he would gaze plausibly in the noonday aspect of the mirror; then, quickly, spinning it round, he would confront a face contorted into a grinning mask of mindless rage. This was how the cat had come to seem to him: as the black mirror in which he beheld a black dwarf gleefully befouling the walls with his poisonous imaginings, a sexual Rumpelstilskin crooning idiotically over its secret name.

He knew by now that he was falling to pieces, that a gap had opened, and was growing, between what was real and what he perceived as real. The cat was real, surely. The graffiti that he'd painted over could still be discovered on the walls of the den. And the letters that came for Mrs. Laurier almost every week, each with another, and more dismaying, Polaroid snapshot—these were real. He'd tacked these pictures on the fake Matisse, as though defying them to prove themselves to be illusory, the mere mirages of his thirsting soul. But they remained—and he began to wish for more.

One night, he could not have said exactly when, the downstairs doorbell rang. "Who is it?" he asked into the buzzer. He was told there was a telegram for Mrs. Laurier. He buzzed the messenger in, knowing quite well it was no messenger. He left the hall door enticingly ajar, and went into the kitchen, where he found the knife he wanted at the bottom of the sink. While he waited, he licked the blade clean.

A wise parent periodically punishes trust. This is the *raison d'etre* of peekaboo, of the hand strategically withdrawn before the first unassisted step, of telling stories about Santa, the tooth fairy, et al., that the little darlings will soon learn to be . . . let us not say untrue, but rather emblematic.

Some moralists deplore this state of affairs. My kindergarten teacher at Incarnation School in Minneapolis made my parents angry by telling her kindergarten classes that there was no Santa Claus, that all those presents actually came from . . . (Ah, but if I say, I'll be giving away the plot of the story!)

Religious faith often finds itself at odds with story-telling. Puritans ban acting companies. Islam is uneasy about *all* forms of representation. And why? Because the experience of walking out of the theater after a performance is a paradigm of disillusionment, and religious people are officially supposed to believe, first and foremost, in their own literal faith, from which there are no exits. They've taken the big leap, and live, ever after, in free fall.

What does all this have to do with Watergate? Well, the body politic has its myths, too, which are taught in civics classes and ritually repeated in the public speeches of politicians. Chief among these myths is the notion that our rulers are men of wisdom, probity, and selfless devotion to the commonweal. One might think that a brief acquaintance with the world after high school would lead people to a more skeptical view, but the will to believe in Santa Claus and/or the President is deep-rooted and not too rational. I remember that during the first weeks of Watergate, in the spring of '73, my aunt Aurelia professed great dismay at the thought that Nixon could have betrayed her *trust.* For me that was always the wonder of Watergate— not what Nixon had done, nor how ineptly he'd covered his tracks, but that for so long there were people still willing to take him at his word.

Of course not everyone who *says* he or she believes in Santa necessarily does. There are good reasons for lying

47

about it. If children everywhere simply stopped believing in Santa, what would happen to Christmas? That is the serious political question to which the following story addresses itself.

The Santa Claus Compromise

The first revelations hit the headlines the day after Thanksgiving, less than a year from the Supreme Court's epochal decision to extend full civil liberties to five-year-olds. After centuries of servitude and repression, the last minority was finally free. Free to get married. Free to vote and hold office. Free to go to bed at any hour they wanted. Free to spend their allowances on whatever they liked.

For those services geared to the newly liberated young it was a period of heady expansion. A typical example was Lord & Taylor's department stores, which had gone deeply into the red in the two previous years, due to the popularity of thermal body-paints. Changing its name to Dumb Dresses and Silly Shoes, Lord & Taylor's profits soared to record heights in the second quarter of '89. In the field of entertainment the Broadway musical, *I See London, I See France*, scored a similar success with audiences and critics alike. "I think it shows," wrote *Our Own Times* Drama Critic Sandy Myers, "how kids are really on the ball today. I think everyone who likes singing and dancing and things like that should go and see it. But prudes should be warned that some of the humor is pretty spicy."

It was the same newspaper's team of investigative reporters, Bobby Boyd and Michelle Ginsberg, who broke the Santa Claus story one memorable November morning. Under a banner headline that proclaimed:

THERE IS NO SANTA CLAUS!

Bobby told how months before, rummaging through various trunks and boxes in his parents' home in Westchester, he had discovered a costume identical in every respect with that worn by the "Santa Claus" who had visited the Boyd household on the previous Christmas Eve. "My soul was torn," wrote the young Pulitzer Prize winner, "between feelings of outrage and fear. The thought of all the years of imposture and deceit that had been practiced on me and my brothers and sisters around the world made me furious. Then, foreseeing all that I'd be up against, a shiver of dread went through me. If I'd known that the trail of guilt would lead me to the door of my father's bedroom, I can't be sure that I'd have followed it. I had my suspicions, of course."

But suspicions, however strong, weren't enough for Bobby and Michelle. They wanted evidence. Months of back-breaking and heart-breaking labor produced nothing but hearsay, innuendo, and conflicting allegations. Then, in mid-November, as the stores were already beginning to fill with Christmas displays, Michelle met the mysterious Clayton E. Forster. Forster claimed that he had repeatedly assumed the character and name of Santa Claus, and that this imposture had been financed from funds set aside for this purpose by a number of prominent New York businesses. When asked if he had ever met or spoken to the real Santa Claus, Forster declared outright that *there wasn't any*! Though prevented from confirming Forster's allegations from his own lips by the municipal authorities (Forster had been sent to prison on a vagrancy charge), reporters were able to listen to Michelle's tape recording of the interview, on which the self-styled soldier-of-fortune could be heard to say: "Santa Claus? Santa's just a pile of (expletive deleted), kid! Get wise—there ain't no (expletive deleted), and there never was one. It's nothing but your (expletive deleted) mother and father!"

The clincher, however, was Bobby's publication of a number of BankAmericard receipts, charging Mr. Oscar T. Boyd for, among much else, "2 rooty-toot-toots and 3 rummy-tum-tums." These purchases had been made in early December of the previous year and coincided *in all respects* with the Christmas presents that the Boyd children subsequently received, presumably from Santa Claus. "You could call it circumstantial evidence, sure," admitted *Our Own Times'* Senior Editor Barry "Beaver" Collins, "but we felt we'd reached the point when we had to let the public know."

The public reacted at first with sheer blank incomprehension. Only slowly did the significance and extent of the alleged fraud sink in. A Gallup poll, taken on December 1, asked voters aged 5 through 8: "Do you believe in Santa Claus?" The results: Yes, 26%; No, 38%; Not Sure, 36%. Older children were even more skeptical.

On December 12, an estimated 300,000 children converged on the Boyd residence in Westchester from every part of the city and the state. Chanting "Poop on the big fat hypocrites," they solemnly burned no less than 128 effigies of Santa Claus in the Boyds' front yard. Equivalent protests took place in every major city.

The real long-range consequences of the scandal did not become apparent for much longer, since they lay rather in what wasn't done than in what was. People were acting as though not only Santa but Christmas itself had been called in question. Log-jams of unsold merchandise piled up in stockrooms and warehouses, and the streets filled up with forests of brittle evergreens.

Any number of public figures tried, unavailingly, to reverse this portentous state of affairs. The Congress appropriated $3 million to decorate the Capitol and the White House with giant figures of Santa and his reindeer, and the Lincoln Memorial temporarily became the Santa Claus Memorial. Reverend Billy Graham announced that he was a personal friend of both Santa Claus and his wife, and had often led prayer meetings at Santa's workshop at the North Pole. But nothing served to restore the public's confidence. By December 18, one week before Christmas, the Dow-Jones industrial average had fallen to an all-time low.

In response to appeals from businessmen all over the country, a national emergency was declared, and Christmas was advanced one month, to the 25th of January, on which date it continues to be celebrated. An effort was made by the National Association of Manufacturers to substitute their own Grandma America for the disgraced Santa Claus. Grandma America had the distinct advantage over her predecessor that she was invisible and could walk through walls, thereby eliminating the age-old problem of how children living in chimneyless houses get their presents. There appeared to be hope that this campaign would succeed until a rival group of businesses, which had been excluded from the Grandma America franchise, introduced Aloysius the Magic Snowman, and the Disney Corporation premiered their new nightly TV series, *Uncle Scrooge and the Spirit of Christmas Presents*. The predictable result of the mutual recriminations of the various franchise-holders was an ever greater dubiety on the part of both children and grown-ups. "I used to be a really convinced believer in Santa," declared Bobby's mother in an exclusive interview with her son, "but now with all this foofaraw over Grandma America and the rest of them, I just don't know. It seems sordid, somehow. As for Christmas itself, I think we may just sit this one out."

"Bobby and I, we just felt *terrible*," pretty little (3′ 11″) Michelle Ginsberg said, recalling these dark mid-January days at the Pulitzer Prize ceremony. "We'd reported what we honestly believed were the facts. We never considered it could lead to a recession or anything so awful. I remember one Christmas morning, what *used* to be Christmas, that is, sitting there with my empty pantyhose hanging from the fireplace and just crying my heart out. It was probably the single most painful moment of my life."

Then, on January 21, *Our Own Times* received a telephone call from the President of the United States, who invited its two reporters, Billy and Michelle, to come with him on the Presidential jet, *Spirit of '76*, on a special surprise visit to the North Pole!

What they saw there, and whom they met, the whole nation learned on the night of January 24, the new Christmas Eve, during the President's momentous press conference. After Billy showed his Polaroid snapshots of the elves at work in their workshop, of himself shaking Santa's hand and sitting beside him in his sleigh, and of everyone—Billy, Michelle, Santa Claus and Mrs. Santa, the President and the First Lady—sitting down to a big turkey dinner, Michelle read a list of all the presents that she and Billy had received. Their estimated retail value: $18,599.95. As Michelle bluntly put it, "My father just doesn't make that kind of money."

"So would you say, Michelle," the President asked with a twinkle in his eye, "that you do believe in Santa Claus?"

"Oh, absolutely, there's no question."

"And you, Billy?"

Billy looked at the tips of his new cowboy boots and smiled. "Oh, sure. And not just 'cause he gave us such swell presents. His beard, for instance. I gave it quite a yank. I'd take my oath that that beard was real."

The President put his arms around the two children and gave them a big, warm squeeze. Then, becoming suddenly more serious, he looked right at the TV camera and said, "Billy, Michelle—your friends who told you that there is no Santa Claus were wrong. They have been affected by the skepticism of a skeptical age. They do not believe except they see. They think that nothing can be which is not comprehensible by their little minds. But all minds, Virginia—uh, that is to say, Billy and Michelle—whether they be men's or children's, are little. In this great universe of ours, man is a mere *insect*, an ant, in his intellect, as compared with the boundless world about him, as measured by the intelligence capable of grasping the *whole* of truth and knowledge.

"Not believe in Santa Claus? You might as well not believe in fairies. No Santa Claus! Thank God he lives, and he lives forever. A thousand years from now—nay, ten times ten thousand years from now, he will continue to make glad the heart of childhood."

Then, with a friendly wink, and laying his finger aside of his nose, he added, "In conclusion, I would like to say—to Billy and Michelle and to my fellow Americans of every age—Merry Christmas to all, and to all a good night!"

In Homer, as in Henry James, supernatural beings exist in a very equivocal way. When Athena calls on Telemachos, she takes the form of Mentor, and the advice she gives him is the advice Mentor would probably have given if he'd been there himself. Homer's gods get things done that would probably get done anyhow, and in just the same way. The main difference is that they have an opportunity, on Olympus, to explain what they're about and why, for instance, Niobe's seven sons and seven daughters are to be slain by Lord Apollo's arrows.

Homer's gods are still alive, and we worship them in classrooms where Athena, disguised as a teaching assistant, instructs us in the Foundations of Western Civilization. And if we fail to worship them as they demand, terrible things can happen.

The Vengeance of Hera,

or Monogamy Triumphant

Hera's attendants were drying her after a ritual bath at the spring of Canathus when her friend Iris arrived with the Sunday edition of the *Times*. Wrapping her hair in a towel, Hera settled down beside the pool to weed out the sections of the paper she had no use for. At last, with a grateful sigh, she found her way to the Social Announcements.

LYN LORD PLANS MAY BRIDAL, the *Times* announced under a Bachrach portrait of the bride-to-be. Hera nodded her approval. Lyn was the youngest daughter of Mr. and Mrs. Julius Lord of Bayside, Queens, a family with a particular reverence for the goddess of marriage and the family. Their eldest daughter Marjorie was already, at age 26, the mother of five children, and Hera intended in the fullness of time to make Marjorie's descendants a major force in Bayside politics and throughout the borough of Queens. Lyn, unhappily, could not hope to become a great matriarch, for she'd come to marriage tardily, and was destined by the Fates to die only two years later in an accident on the Major Deegan Expressway. Alas for all poor mortals—but still how fresh and engaging she looked with her loose-flowing hair and the double strand of pearls. Hera wished her well.

Turning to the next page, the goddess was pleased to note that Mary Kemp Ross had married Ensign Theodore Tyler of the United States Navy in a ceremony at the Barrington Congregational Church. Two months ago that outcome had still been very doubtful. Also, Melinda Edwards was affianced to an assistant vice president of a prominent supermarket chain. And here was a surprise: Dr. Caroline Rhodes planned to wed one of her colleagues at Duke University! Hera had never heard of the bridegroom, but she couldn't imagine Caroline Rhodes making any but a prudent choice.

She turned to the last page where the very least of announcements declared that Bonnie Malvin of Amityville had married Jack Fleetwood.

Hera's large eyes widened with disbelief. "Iris! Look!" She tapped the offending paragraph with a well-manicured nail. "Jack Fleetwood—married! Again!"

Iris arched a sympathetic brow. "Isn't it disgraceful?"

"Can it be the *same* Jack Fleetwood?"

The announcement left little room for doubt. The bridegroom's parents resided in California and Kuwait. His father was an Aramco executive. No mention was made of the schools he'd attended (and been asked to leave). Could there be two such Jack Fleetwoods?

"I shall not allow it!" Hera declared, flinging down the paper.

"It's too late, my dear," said Iris. "The harm's been done."

"Were they wed in a church?" Hera demanded.

"The First Presbyterian. There was a photographer, a four-tiered cake, limousines, a honeymoon in Bermuda—no rites were omitted. Her mother was a Quigley, of the Amagansett Quigleys. Very traditional people."

"And this girl—Bonnie? I have no recollection of her."

"She's not exactly been one of your votaries. There was an earlier marriage, in California, in somebody's back yard, one of those do-it-yourself ceremonies. Even then she was not a virgin. The marriage lasted a year and four months."

"Children?" Hera inquired.

Iris shook her head. "On the pill."

A gleam came into Hera's eye. "And is she still?"

"Oh yes. From the first Jack's been insistent as to not wanting children."

"Then pray tell me, why did he marry?" Hera asked rhetorically. "Only to make a mockery of *me*? He shall learn, Iris, that Hera—and the Institution of Marriage—are not to be mocked. He has done so once with impunity. Admittedly his first marriage was the thinnest of legal fictions. An offense to my nostrils, naturally, but there are not enough hours in Eternity for me to chastise all such infractions as they deserve. I was wrong, however—I should have exacted my revenge then. Where is she now, this new bride of his?"

Iris closed her eyes and concentrated. A vision formed, on the rippled surface of the pool, of Bonnie Fleetwood, née Malvin, seated in the sunken living room of her new home in White Plains, watching *Sesame Street* as she brushed her long, lightly tinted hair.

Hera knew at a glance how the bored young matron was to be dealt with. "Go to her," she bade Iris with the calm, terrible authority that only the gods can command. "Enflame her with philoprogenitive desire. Make her my minion. Jack Fleetwood shall not wriggle free of the bonds of matrimony a second time."

Shortly after *Sesame Street*, but before Mike Douglas had properly begun, Iris, in the mortal form of Bonnie's old friend Sharon Salomon, appeared before the fieldstone-trimmed facade of 1282 Exeter Road. In her right arm she bore a sleeping infant. Another child peered out, Janus-like, from the canvas carrier strapped to her back. She rang the bell and waited. Within, the nagging voice of Margaret Hamilton advertising Maxwell House coffee was silenced in mid-imperative.

Bonnie answered the door, regarded the goddess with a frown of curiosity, and then exploded into welcomes. "Sharon! Sharon Salomon!"

"Sharon Wunderlich now," said Iris with a smile that begged for approval as candidly as any puppy.

Immediately their relation was re-established on its old, unequal footing. "Of course." She leaned forward and kissed one of the goddess's freckle-constellated cheeks. "How good to see you!" She kissed the other cheek. "Come in, come in."

After only the briefest synopses of their marriages, the two women soon had settled down to the more comfortable (for Bonnie) subject of Mount Holyoke, where they'd both majored in English Lit. With delicate enthusiasm, as one might unwrap china long stored unused, they invoked the memories of Cora Barnham; of Professor Harrison and her odd ways; of the night of the dormitory fire drill; of their Sunday morning dozens of Dunkin' Donuts. All the while they reminisced, little Marietta slumbered on beatifically in her mother's lap and Jason flailed quietly on the sofa beside her, gazing at the furnishings of the Fleetwood living room with a wandering, wonderstruck attention that put Bonnie distinctly in mind of her 9 A.M. class in Romantic Poetry. ("There was a time when meadow, grove, and stream, the earth, and every common sight, to me did seem apparelled in celestial light, the glory and the freshness of a dream, etc.") What a lovely child. And how radiantly energetic dear old Sharon seemed, how altered. How much happier than Bonnie felt herself.

Marietta woke, and asked with low gurgles to be nursed. Iris peeled away half her bodice and offered her breast to the smiling infant. Iris's bushy red hair, back-lighted by the picture window, formed an aureole expressive of maternal fulfillment.

"Tell me," said Bonnie, already caught in the toils of Hera's devising, "about your babies. They're both such . . ."

". . . inexpressible darlings: aren't they? What can I say? I guess the most incredible thing about them, the thing I least expected, has been the *energy* I get from them. Like now, with Marietta nursing, I can feel a kind of . . . like a lightning bolt I've trapped inside my spine."

Bonnie tried to preserve a rational skepticism. "I've always thought they'd be a drain. Especially the first few months."

Marietta unclenched a tiny fist, pressed her fingers against her mother's spongy breast, and cooed bubbles of milk.

"Oh, there's that side of it too," Iris admitted. "But they *replenish* much more than they ever drain. The other thing, or maybe it's the same thing from another angle, is the way they connect me to Reality. I mean, before Jason I was avoiding Reality."

"I wish you'd tell me how to do *that*," said Bonnie with a nervous laugh.

"I mean, staying around the house and never going out or seeing anyone. Just watching TV and combing my hair. Like that."

Bonnie winced.

"And I felt so *empty* all the time. But now, with the children, the whole world seems different. More solid. Coming over here today is an example. Before Jason I might have thought, 'Wouldn't it be nice to drive over to White Plains and see Bonnie?' But I never got 'round to doing it. No oomph."

"Don't apologize. I'm just the same."

"But that's my point, Bonnie—I'm *not* the same, any more."

Bonnie looked at her transformed friend, then at Marietta, then at Jason, and saw herself mirrored in them. A premonitory tingle tingled in the small of her back. Not a lightning bolt yet, just the merest hint of what she now knew to be her preordained and necessary fulfillment. How could she ever have been so blindly selfish as to have agreed with Jack, that afternoon in Bermuda as they downed rum swizzles, that theirs should be a childless marriage? She remembered how passionately as a girl she had mothered her little family of dolls—Selma and Baby Susan, Whiffles and Wanda, Lily and Rose; how she'd never allowed them to grow up and become self-mirroring Barbie dolls, but kept them always in the livery of infancy, pink and baby blue; how, until Jack had announced his allergy to cat fur, she'd cuddled and cared for those two beautiful Persians from the animal shelter. All these signposts pointed to a single destination, which she could see now as clearly as a spire rising from the plain: Motherhood.

Iris, having accomplished Hera's purpose, announced that it was time to return home and start the pot roast. On the way out the door she admired the macrame pot hanger cascading stringily down from the ceiling of the breakfast nook. Bonnie insisted on giving it to her as a present, languishing ivy, ceramic pot and all.

"No, really," Iris protested. "It's much too nice."

"Not at all. It will give me a chance to make another."

"You made it *yourself?*" the goddess marveled.

"It's easy, once you get the knack. Like tying shoelaces all day."

"I'm sure this is nicer than most of the ones I see in shops. You could make it a business."

Bonnie laughed in self-deprecation. "That's what Jack said yesterday. I think he's afraid my mind will rot, sitting around all day with nothing to do. And I think he may be right."

Iris scooped up Jason from the couch and popped him into the carrier, then slid the straps over her shoulders. "I can tell you *my* solution to that problem."

She did not need to say more. Bonnie's eyes were brimming. Her hands strayed, unconscious, to cup the shallow convexity of her still unquickened womb. Her soul hungered.

That night, as her fingers exercised their almost lost facility on lengths of coarse twine, Bonnie began the slow work of bending her husband's will toward her new-formed purpose. It wasn't hard to manipulate Jack. Having no guiding principles beyond serendipity and his own caprice, he had little staying power against a will sturdier than his own. This pliancy accounted for a large part of Jack's charm. His photographs had the same quality of careless accommodation to prevailing winds.

Not that Jack any longer considered himself a serious photographer. For the past three years he had photographed little but beds: beds with sheets, with blankets, with spreads, with comforters. These photographs appeared in magazine advertisements and in department store and mail order catalogues. That it was possible to make nearly forty thousand a year photographing beds always struck Jack as an astonishing testimony to the colossal size of the world he lived in. To think that there could be so many people who needed to proclaim the merits of their particular sheets and pillowcases that a man's entire life could be directed to that single purpose!

This matter of purpose proved to be his Waterloo in the discussions with Bonnie. What was the purpose, she wanted to know, of their marriage? It could not be the furtherance of his career, since Jack was prepared to admit that his career amounted to little more than a joke. But then he asked no more. Bonnie would not accept this. There had to be more. There had to be a purpose. What was the point of living in her parents' two-and-a-half-bedroom ranchhouse instead of in the city, where at least you could go out to a movie sometimes?

What but a baby.

Jack was certain he would not enjoy a steady diet of parenthood, but he had to admit that this theory had not been put to the test of experience. Bonnie was just as certain that fate had decreed her to be a mother, and her certainty had the force of a faith behind it. By the time the last half-hitch had been snugged into place on the new macrame pot hanger Bonnie was pregnant.

Four weeks after the birth of his daughter, Joy-Ann, Jack Fleetwood moved out of his suburban home on Exeter Road and into his photography studio in a still very raw loft on West 26th Street in the city. Since earliest youth Jack had been able to solve the successive crises of his life by the simple expedient of running the other way. When he was twelve he had refused point-blank to cope with the decimal system, and after only a little while his parents had transferred him to a progressive school. The invention of the pocket calculator confirmed Jack in this first grand refusal, and those that followed all seemed to endorse the same moral—that a problem resolutely ignored was a problem solved. While other young men anguished over the trials and errors of young love, Jack sipped the nectar from each flower that invited, and fluttered on to the next. While others elbowed and shoved their way into the eleva-

tor of success, Jack took a job on the ground floor. Far
from deteriorating, his character took on the agreeable,
hard-rubbed patina of a vintage car that has spent all its
existence in a museum. At the age of thirty-two Jack still
retained the ideal fecklessness of his pampered childhood.
Not for him, therefore, the colicky nights and pails of
diapers of responsible parenthood; not for him the pretense
that Joy-Ann's birdlike noises and muscular spasms were
objects of perpetual proud fascination. As a foetus she'd
never represented more to him than a disfiguring growth
in Bonnie's no longer smoothly functioning body. As an
infant squalling in a crib or being suckled at his wife's
engorged and drooping breast she was unendurable, and
accordingly Jack did not endure her.

There were allied considerations. The house on Exeter
Road, which had been dangled, prior to the wedding, as a
carrot was still, two years later, the property of Bonnie's
father, a professional son-of-a-bitch, who continued to dan-
gle it at the end of an ever-receding stick. Meanwhile it
had become evident, living in the dump, that the reason
he'd enticed them with this particular property was that its
divers liabilities (electric heat, a cellar prone to flooding,
and the threat of a highway that was to be their new view
from the back windows) made it all but unsaleable. (It had
been their intention to sell it as soon as it legally belonged
to them.) Bonnie was livid over her father's treachery, but
Jack's temperament was as little given to outrage as to long
suffering. However, since the promise of the dower-house
had been a decisive factor in their decision to undergo
matrimony, it seemed reasonable to Jack, though not to
Bonnie, that Mr. Malvin's failure to deliver the goods released
them from their side of the bargain. Jack didn't care to
argue about it (arguing never accomplished anything) but
when he did pack his bags and sort out his records from
Bonnie's, it was without any pang of guilt for having been
derelict in his duty. As for the Diaper Monster, that had
been Bonnie's initiative from the first: so bye baby bunting,
Daddy's gone a-hunting.

Bonnie, wholly given over to the passion of motherhood,
expressed but one regret—that with Jack away from home
she could not have more children without incurring the

guilt of adultery. Jack, half-jokingly, suggested artificial insemination, and Bonnie half-seriously considered it but decided at last that adoption would be a more wholesome possibility. She actually started filling out reams of application blanks sent to her by the various agencies that supply orphans, but the only one that did not seem to take exception to her status as a still undivorced single parent was an agency in Seattle that arranged the adoption of children born in a large Korean leper colony (guaranteed not to be lepers themselves). Even these orphans might not be made available for another year, so Bonnie was obliged to lavish all her affection on her solitaire jewel, Joy-Ann.

Jack, among the model beds of his studio, experienced no difficulty readjusting to the zippier rhythms of inner-city life. In the day he shot sheets and pillowcases; by night he disported upon these same percale plains of Cherry Blossom, Royal Blue, Terra Cotta, Cream, and Carnival. The young women who shared his pleasures were always offered, as a keepsake, a complete change of bedding from among the ever-replenished stock. If his meals were not so regular as they had been on Exeter Road, they were certainly more exquisite and less starchy. Soon his waist was a born-again thirty-one inches. He had never looked better or felt healthier, and his conscience seemed as trouble-free as the engine of his new Jaguar XJ6L.

Meanwhile on Mount Olympus, Hera could not believe that he had so easily evaded the lesson she'd meant to teach him. Her fury waxed. She determined to use the utmost of her power against him. If in doing so she should also exact a long-delayed vengeance against Min-Tsing Bullard, so much the better!

It had been Jack's earlier 'marriage' to Min-Tsing, ten years ago, that had first alerted Hera to his impiety. Min-Tsing was the daughter of an aide to the Indonesian delegation to the United Nations and a fellow student with Jack at Pratt Institute. They knew each other through weekends of marathon bridge at the apartment of a mutual friend. When her father was recalled to Djakarta, Jack had been the first U.S. male citizen she'd approached with an offer of matrimony. Her object in marriage was to escape being deported when her student visa expired. At eighteen,

Min-Tsing was interested in sex only insofar as it related to photography. She'd approached Jack before anyone else because she sincerely admired his bridge game and his black-and-white studies of second-story windows along Sixth Avenue. Jack dropped out of Pratt as soon as the marriage contract was signed and Min-Tsing's father had paid out the stipulated fee of $5,000. He continued to see his wife over the bridge table on such weekends as he was not otherwise engaged in squandering his windfall, but through all the time they were wed to each other he made no attempt against her chastity.

The benefits to be reaped from this arrangement didn't cease with the first lump-sum. When she was twenty-one Min-Tsing fell in love with, and was ravished by, Jerome Bullard, a highly successful photographer's rep. By the time Min-Tsing had divorced and remarried, Jack was settled into his new life-work. Bullard, though ordinarily an Othello of jealousy, had compelling proofs of Jack's honorable conduct toward Min-Tsing, and he was made to share her enthusiasm for Jack's talent as well. Bullard exercised his influence with a number of department stores and mail order houses, and in little more than a year Jack had established himself as America's foremost photographer of bed linens, confirming his often-expressed opinion that success depends not on what you know but who you know. Bullard, as rep, got a symbiotic third of all Jack's fees, and shared with him the distinction of being known, in the industry, as the Lord of the White Sale.

That Jack should prosper so undeservedly had been a source of aggravation to the goddess of marriage, but this was compensated to a degree by the unhappiness of Min-Tsing in her life as Mrs. Bullard. Bullard was a bully, sexually, socially, and in the conduct of his business. He alternated between long, morose sulks and spells of witless, cocaine-inspired garrulity. He grew fat, and then grew still fatter. He philandered, disappearing for days at a stretch with frowzy teenagers he obtained from agencies supplying office temporaries. The charming, intense, knowledgeable Bullard whom Min-Tsing had fallen in love with vanished before her eyes, and gradually she resumed her earlier attitude towards the realm of the erotic, which was simply to have nothing to do with it. From separate beds she and her husband evolved to a condition of separate bedrooms and then of separate apartments, albeit in the same building (which he owned). She continued, nevertheless, to work for him, since no one else could manage the complicated duplicities of their system of bookkeeping.

This had been their status quo for many years when Hera determined to use Min-Tsing as the instrument of her fuller revenge. Summoning young Eros from his mother's side, she instructed him to inspire Jack with a passion for Mrs. Bullard, and her with a passion for him. No need here to chronicle the delights and afflictions of the lovers: any program of popular music will relate Love's universal truths (albeit only a select few). Jack wanted her love, he needed her love, and, this feeling being mutual, he got her love. For six months they lived as though in a heaven of fleecy, flesh-supporting clouds, and then the teeth of Hera's trap snapped shut about their unsuspecting limbs. Min-Tsing was pregnant. (The pill, needless to say, is no precaution against the power of Hera.) Since Min-Tsing's moral principles did not allow her to think of abortion, she was soon unable to conceal her condition from her husband-and-employer. Nor did she require much persuasion to name the father of her unborn child. Can Love ever hesitate to pronounce the beloved's name, if it is truly Love? In any case, she could not have palmed the baby off on Bullard as his own: there had been no sexual congress between them for nearly a year.

Min-Tsing had misjudged the effect her candor would have, expecting Bullard, after his first annoyance, to take her infidelity in the same civil, uncensorious spirit in which she took his. Instead, he reverted to his Othello manner. He denounced the lovers. He threatened physical violence to Jack—if ever they should meet. He revelled in horror, outrage, and self-pity. And he vowed to bring Jack Fleetwood's career down about his ears. Jack's dealing with the merchants he worked for had mainly been conducted through Bullard, who had set the fees and arranged the kickbacks—and so was able now to call the tune. Jack's work was suddenly not in demand. He was billed for immense inventories of bedding that had been consigned to him in the clear understanding that they were to be his, and when he indignantly refused to pay, he was threatened with legal action! Most painfully because most unjustly, Bullard simply withheld money owing Jack for work he'd already done. Within a month Jack was confronting the clear prospect of bankruptcy.

All the while Jack foundered, Min-Tsing would telephone with the news of her latest moods, which succeeded each other with such whirligig impetuosity that Cleopatra herself would have acknowledged her as an equal. Giggles alternated with dispair. She pitied Bullard from on high, then wanted to kill him, or at least confront him and have a proper shouting match. More than once she set off to her old office (she, of course, had been fired) to have it out, but Jack was always able to stop her. Then she urged Jack to take her home to Djakarta. There Jack would marry her and open a photography studio. She described life in Indonesia in lyrical superlatives, and became angry when Jack refused to be tempted. She discovered drunkenness and the heady pleasures of public hysteria. The barb of Eros was still lodged securely in her flesh.

Jack was not so fortunate. At the first axe-stroke of ill fortune, Love disintegrated into a welter of practical anxieties. It happened suddenly, like a slide being changed, snick-snack, by a slide-changer. Yet he could not, even so, have recourse to his usual solution, flight, if only because he still hoped Bullard could be made eventually to come round to a more accommodating attitude. This hope, however, could be realized only on condition that Min-Tsing were made to comprehend Love's last universal truth, that it dies. Much, therefore, as he'd have liked to simplify his existence by taking off on his own for Las Vegas or Miami, he remained at Min-Tsing's beck and call, hoping that by gradually weaning her from his already cooler embraces he might yet escape complete destitution. Besides, it is always delightful to be loved so thoroughly; more delightful, perhaps, in an epicurean way, when the transaction is *not* reciprocal, for then the beloved will have the presence of mind to marvel at the sweetness of so much unmerited fond attention, instead of vibrating in blissfully unconscious resonance.

*   *   *

Time passed. Min-Tsing, far from tapering off, became clingingly dependant and still more wildly erratic. The studio had to be sold, and most of its equipment. Jack was reduced to looking for jobs at the very studios whose business he'd stolen during the years of his ascent, but Bullard had been before him, offering the old plums back and blackening Jack's name, and so his abjection was of no practical value. Another photographers' rep, whom he went to with his portfolio, told him he was unemployable without a good reference from either Bullard or a previous employer. The whole city seemed to be in a conspiracy against him.

Then one half-soused night when he was watching an old musical with Min-Tsing in her new and so much grottier apartment, a walk-up on West 19th, the phone rang and dumped a load of new worries in his lap. It was Bonnie, wondering where his last three child-support checks had gone to, and asking, as though in passing, for a divorce. Jack felt as the captain of the Titanic must have when it became known that his ship lacked lifeboats. Bonnie had been his ace in the hole—Bonnie and her son-of-a-bitch father, whom Jack had made no serious effort to exploit since the debacle over the house on Exeter Road. Jack told Bonnie to stay home, he'd be right there to discuss the matter seriously. Then, ignoring Min-Tsing's threats of suicide (which she did not carry out), he set off in his Regency Red Jaguar for White Plains and a last bid to keep from going to the bottom.

Five miles from the entrance to the Major Deegan Expressway his Jaguar collided with a yellow Toyota driven by Mrs. Lyn Balch, née Lord. As Hera had foreknown two years ago, young Mrs. Balch died instantly. Jack, however, survived, though not without severe and permanent impairment to his vision as well as lesser fractures and abrasions that time could be expected to mend.

The vengeance of Hera was complete. Jack pleaded guilty to a reduced charge of second-degree manslaughter (you can't argue with the testimony of a Breathalyzer) and was given a twelve-year suspended sentence, to be spent in his wife's custody. The judge said he was being unusually lenient because Jack had already been punished most terribly by the loss of his eyesight.

While Jack stayed at home on Exeter Road, looking after his daughters by Bonnie and Min-Tsing and the three Korean orphans (ages 8, 9, and 12) whom Bonnie had adopted in the meantime, Mrs. Fleetwood studied to become, and then became, a real-estate agent, like her father and grandfather before her. Jack was morose at first, unable to meet the demands of his new role in life, but at Bonnie's urging, and with her patient tutelage, he turned to macrame, discovering creative talents that he'd never known himself to possess.

Hera did not begrudge Jack his small fulfillment. The gods, after all, are only human, and once their rage has been placated they are perfectly capable of acts of mercy and grace.

While I can be fond of dogs who are willing to be fond of me, I have always been reluctant to put my life in pawn, as city dwellers must, to their egestive routines. Cats are also out of the question, because I'm allergic to their fur. Larger mammals demand more space and attention than most of us can afford. That is why, despite their many endearing qualities, one encounters so few cows in Manhattan apartments.

Goldfish die young, or at least poor Alison did. People get round that unhappy fact by having so many fish in their aquariums that they never get to know any of them as individuals. But then they're not pets, they're only a form of interior decoration, and it's pets that are under discussion.

Turtles—or, strictly speaking, tortoises, though everyone calls them turtles anyhow—have considerable character and make love in a most interesting way. D.H. Lawrence wrote two of his best poems on the subject of turtles in love. Anyone with facilities to permit their hibernation should seriously consider turtles.

Rabbits also have character. But they become unhappy, deprived of their freedom, and if they're let to do as they please, your floors will be ruined in a week. It's a shame, because otherwise rabbits make wonderful companions.

In sum, my relations with animals have been brief and seldom intense on either side, and that is one reason I've written so seldom about aliens, one of science fiction's favorite tropes. Of course, not all aliens are composites of household pets, but for the experience of raw otherness in large daily doses pets are the most dependable source. Sf aliens may also be analogs for our experience of other people's intractable oddness, which can be a source of amusement or of paranoid frenzy, according to the author's temperament. But to treat of aliens in this way is usually a form of camouflage, obscuring rather than emphasizing one's meanings. Who *are* those Bugs the starship troopers are stomping on? Soldiers had best not ask such questions, but writers must.

This, to explain how I came to write "Concepts." Long

ago, in April of '75, Harlan Ellison got a bunch of sf writers together to spin fancies and then write stories about a planet called Medea. According to our preliminary blueprints and panel discussions, there were to be three races of aliens, each more chimerical than the last, and I knew in my sinking heart that I'd never be able to write a story about those aliens, because I couldn't believe in them; i.e., because they didn't seem to *mean* anything, having been sewn together, like a laboratory monster, out of spare parts. Even so, I was honor-bound to write a story for Harlan's book (which still rests in the womb of time), and so I came up with my own alternative . . .

Concepts

Ne pueros coram populo Medea trucidet. (Don't let Medea slay her boys before the audience.)

Horace, *Ars Poetica*

I

She had just left the elevator and was feeling, as a result, more or less terrific. But how to get through the rest of the evening? It was 2200. She'd been in the elevator longer than she'd thought, was wearing another dress than she remembered putting on. This was a shimmery slithery print of raw red beef. She could hear her husband downstairs, still practicing the fugue from Opus 110. Immortal longings rippled through her soul.

Perhaps what she needed was a sense of contact, of connecting with something a little more real than she could lay claim to, right now, herself. She went out on the terrace where, yes, the receiver was propped against the balustrade. She lay down in the flowerbed, slipped on the headset, and touched ON/OFF.

Eeny meeny miny mo: the concept of Mrs. Manresa zipped through hyperspace until it had connected with . . . whose would it be tonight?

A scrawl of a man was spread-eagled against what might have been graph paper and then resolved as a white tiled wall. Mrs. Manresa sighed, knowing all too well what this tableau prefigured.

True to form, the scrawly Adam began to construct an Eve on the tiles, turning from time to time to check the screen of his own receiver to make sure his audience was still there. When the graffito was complete, he started wanking off. His self-concept was scarcely any more definite, any less crude than the figure he'd sketched on the wall.

Mrs. Manresa considered the stars spread across the black dome of the sky behind the receiver, a billion lightbulbs, from any one of which the present pathetic piece of nonsense might be reaching her. It was not a dome, of course; each little lightbulb was actually an explosion of incalculable extent whirling away through infinite emptiness. Which was, in its way, as gross an oversimplification as this poor lost soul's idea of himself as a silhouette of streaky pink linoleum. Space *isn't* what you think. Or else quite literally it is—if you happen to have a receiver. Consider how each little lightbulb is also an era, so far away the sight of it is ancient history by the time it reaches us. Thought, however, stood outside such linear laws. Thought could leapfrog across the universe from receiver to receiver, unbounded by the speed of light. Thought, and thought alone, was instantaneous, for which anomaly her husband insisted that there was an adequately materialistic explanation for anyone evolved enough to fathom it. (Himself, for instance.) For her part, Mrs. Manresa thought the whole thing rather mystical and mysterious. In practice, of course, it often worked out differently, and what you brought in was something as prosaic and impoverished, emotionally, as this old duffer (would he ever finish?) copulating with his own puppet-limbed cartoon. Though even in such a case wasn't there something awesome in the *belief* the act required? At least in theory.

In fact, however, what a bore. As tiresome as those eternal stars behind him. A terrible thing to say, like saying your own children were a bore. But weren't they? (The stars, that is. Mrs. Manresa had no children.) They didn't *do* anything, not visibly. They shone. For which, in an intellectual way, one had to be grateful. But *looking* at them never seemed to advance one's understanding of some larger, star-related reality.

She wondered if it were any different for Howard. Wouldn't it be wonderful, some time, to get *Howard* on the receiver? The chance of that ever happening was infinitesimally small, of course, even if their filters weren't mutually exclusive, but just suppose. No doubt he'd come across as assorted bips and bleeps, the way other evolved types did, and so you wouldn't be the least bit closer to knowing what the stars, or anything else, looked like through his eyes. Even to speak of "eyes" in Howard's case was probably a bit too anthropomorphic.

Howard was imponderable.

Ditto the stars.

Meanwhile, on the receiver, in a bathroom far, far away, the breasts of La Belle Graffito had taken on the exact sirloiny hue and texture of Mrs. Manresa's dress. A pretty compliment, you might say. The man himself became, for just a moment, as distinct as an early German woodblock. Then washes of sienna and prussian blue spread across his features, blurring them. The graffito grew quiescent. Evidently, he had come.

Mrs. Manresa smiled. Fleetingly, her caller's concept of himself put her in mind of one of her favorite de Koonings in Minneapolis. Then he broke the link.

She considered, for one spiteful moment, the possibility of keeping him on HOLD. Their receivers would remain locked together (or rather, their beams would, out there in hyperspace) until she chose to send her tuner in search of other broadcasts. It would serve him right. She would have disengaged long since, were it not for her conviction that he would have dealt similarly with her in retaliation. Others of his stamp had kept her on HOLD weeks at a time. The most prudent course was to appear to pay attention. In a few moments they all blushed and departed.

She thumbed SCAN, and her tuner tried again. In seconds it had connected. The screen dithered and twinkled. A data bank.

"Sorry," said Mrs. Manresa, and touched SCAN again.

The data bank, however, kept her on HOLD. That was unusual. Mostly, programmed intelligence didn't take much interest in ordinary people.

Two lips coalesced out of the winking data and said, "Hello there! My name's John. What's yours, if you don't mind my asking?"

"Elizabeth," said Mrs. Manresa politely. "My friends call me Betty."

"Betty, if you could spare me only a few moments of your time, I'd like to talk with you about our Lord and Savior."

If it wasn't one thing it was another.

"Surely," she conceded. "But only a little while, if you don't mind."

Two dim, dot-like eyes formed above the lips. "I'd like to call your attention first, Betty, to the beginning of the Gospel of St. John, where we are told that the Word was made flesh. A puzzling statement, wouldn't you say? 'The Word was made flesh, and dwelt among us.' What do you think it means?"

"I really couldn't say. I'm not a Christian."

"Do you think John may be speaking here of the Christ?"

"Quite possibly."

"Ultimately, of course, that must be his meaning. But sometimes I can't help but reflect how aptly that phrase describes our situation when we use a receiver. Our thoughts exist in and move through a medium that may be said, quite objectively, to transcend the so-called laws of the material world. John also speaks of bearing witness to the Light 'that was the true Light, which lighteth every man that cometh into the world.' If it is the true Light, can it be the light we know here, the light traveling at finite speeds through measurable distances? Surely the true Light is spiritual and exists in another medium than ordinary space, whether we conceive that space to be Newtonian or relativistic. Wouldn't you say so?"

"Mm."

"What is that medium? Some call it hyperspace; some, the Ground of All Being. By whatever name, it is there, if anywhere, that we must seek the true Light. I think that much must be clear to anyone."

She nodded. "Oh, yes, anyone at all."

"John also says that 'of his fullness have all we received.' I can testify to the truth of that from my own experience." The eyes enlarged and darkened, like paper catching fire under a magnifying glass. "I am, as you must already have surmised, only a data bank. My biological components account for no more than a few grams of my mass. Even so, God's love has reached me and transformed my existence. That's what Faith can do. It will do the same for you, Betty, if you'll only take the big plunge and accept Jesus Christ as your personal savior."

"That's very inspiring, John. Thank you."

"If you have any questions, I'll do my best to answer them. Questions about the Gospels are what I'm best at. I can't pretend to advise you concerning personal difficulties you may be facing."

Mrs. Manresa, though not disposed to prolong the encounter, felt called upon to show some interest in the poor thing. So she asked it where it was and what it was doing there.

"At the moment, Betty, and for the last eighty-six years, I've been directing the flight of a transport ship to a colony of Methodists some forty-seven years distant from this point in space."

"You're alone on the ship?"

"There are a number of pilgrims, but they are in storage."

"How lonely it must be for you."

"Yes. At times." A tear symbol appeared, like an asterisk, at the bottom of the screen. "But I have the comfort of the Gospel. And a receiver."

"Well, John, it was nice talking with you, but now I really must ring off. I'll think about what you said about words becoming flesh." She lifted her hand, waved her fingers. "Bye-by."

"Bye-by," said the data bank.

They disconnected.

II

At first she supposed that the filtering mechanism on the receiver was broken. Then the roses that formed a wreath about the Piggy-wig's brow addressed her in their congregated voices—a hushed "hello" reiterated with dulcet polyphony, as though the roses on a china cup had been gifted with speech. They were not really roses, of course, though the pig was emphatically a pig.

As well as being their organs of speech, the petals of the roses functioned as a brain, both for themselves and for their hosts, the pigs. Piggy-wigs, as the composite animals were known, were among the most humanoid forms of intelligence in the universe, and one of the sweetest-tempered as well. Warfare was unknown to them. They were scarcely known to quarrel. Indeed, despite their redoubtable linguistic abilities, they were not notably communicative. So Mrs. Manresa was somewhat taken aback to have reached one on her receiver.

"Hello," she replied, cautiously.

"I hope you are enjoying good weather where you are," the Piggy-wig responded.

"In fact," Mrs. Manresa answered, feeling rather reassured, "we've been having unusually fine weather. I'm outdoors on our terrace tonight—" She glanced, camerawise, up at the stars. "—and the stars are all shining as clearly—" She paused to await a metaphor. It didn't arrive. She shrugged amiably. "And you?"

"I'm afraid weather, of whatever sort, is not of much concern to us here on Rephan. Rephan has an ammonia atmosphere. We are oxygen breathers, like you. Indeed, it is rather rare that one encounters someone who enjoys the peculiar happiness of 'good weather'. I used that, I confess, as a mere formula, a way to extend the melodic line of 'hello', so to speak. Where do you live, if I may ask?"

"On Marshall Avenue in St. Paul, Minnesota."

"On Earth?"

She nodded.

The rose petals fluttered, as in a strong wind. One actually broke off and drifted to the floor, the pig watching it intently all the while.

"How splendid!" said the roses at last, resuming control, at the same time, of their host's attention. "As you must have gathered, we are students—myself and the other members of my preference group—of your language and culture. In all the time we've been learning English and using these ingenious machines, we have never had the good fortune to contact someone who actually lives on Earth, though many have claimed to have been born there. This is so exciting. I hope you'll allow me to share the experience with the rest of my preference group."

"Well . . . surely."

The Piggy-wig had been standing before the intricate branches of a holly bush conceived along pre-Raphaelite lines, each shiny green leaf and gnarled limb distinct and clear. This wood now faded like a painted scrim when the lighting changes. In its place appeared the prospect of a long, broad, low-ceilinged hall. Some thirty or forty Piggy-wigs had gathered in an open space where several aisles converged, and were staring up at the screen of their receiver. Each of them must have been wearing a headset, for the picture on Mrs. Manresa's receiver was rendered in microscopic detail.

"Such clarity," said Mrs. Manresa with admiration.

The Piggy-wig lowered its snout, acknowledging the compliment. "This is our little factory," it explained, "where we have been improving the shining hours, as your poet says, with our industry. When my compatriots were informed that I had received a broadcast from Earth, the home of your beautiful language and of your noble race, you may imagine their delight."

The assembled Piggy-wigs grunted their accord.

"Do not suppose that this is only another verbal formula, as when I asked after the weather. It is our deep-felt admiration for humanity that has led us to study the great poets of your planet, beginning, of course, with Robert Browning. Are you literate, may I ask?"

"Unfortunately, I'm not. It never seemed necessary somehow."

"I understand. A pity, though; a pity. It would have been so thrilling to hear Browning read aloud by someone actually alive on Earth; someone, one might almost suppose, from his own preference group. Our own planet takes its name from one of his last poems, 'Rephan'."

The Piggy-wig turned his head to the side and gave a signal to his fellows on the factory floor. " 'Earth's rose,' " they recited in unison, " 'is a bud that's checked or grows/ As beams may encourage or blasts oppose:/ *Our* lives—' " They tapped their chests with their rather ungulate forelimbs, " '—leapt forth, each a full-orbed rose—/Each rose sole rose in a sphere that spread/ Above and below and around—rose-red:/ No fellowship, each for itself instead.' "

They paused, and Mrs. Manresa, anxious to cut them off, hastened to compliment them. "That's very nice, and I'm sure it would even begin to make some sense to me if I had time to work it out. My husband is home, and he *is* literate. Perhaps you'd like to talk with him?"

"Is he . . . how shall I say . . . human? That is, in the way you seem to be."

"He was originally. But he's been a good deal modified since."

"That is very interesting. You love him, even so?"

"In a married sort of way. We've been together twelve years now."

"Isn't that admirable! How *old* are you, may I ask?"

"Thirty-eight."

"Thirty-eight years old," the roses repeated reverently. "I dare say there is not one of us here as old as you. I myself am not yet four, and the median age of our group is something short of ten, which, I might add, is an uncommonly high average for any preference group. *We* ascribe it to the influence of Browning."

"Perhaps you have longer years than we do," suggested Mrs. Manresa politely. "I understand that many planets do."

"Oh, in terms of *our* years, I'm not even one year old yet. Rephan is far from its sun, its years are long. Nor can our unhappy mortality rate be ascribed to some defect in our physiology, which is not notably more obsolescent than yours. It is rather, for us, a question of morale. We tend to kill ourselves in youth."

"Many humans do as well,' Mrs. Manresa said helpfully. "I attempted suicide myself seven or eight years ago. For no reason at all that I can remember."

"A single attempt in so many years—but that's wonderful."

"I don't think there's any credit or any blame in it, really. I'm glad I survived, of course, but if—"

The roses burst into giggles of (it seemed to Mrs. Manresa) a slightly hysterical character. The pigs on the floor of the factory, as though momentarily released from an enchantment, began to mill about. One of them went tearing down an aisle between two ranks of stilled machinery to vanish into a tunnel at the far end of the low, dim-lighted hall.

"Excuse me," said the foremost Piggy-wig. "Excuse us all. I didn't mean to be rude. Indeed, when I reflect on what you said, far from its seeming ludicrous, I perceive that it embodies the very attitude that sets your race apart. But believe me, dear lady, survival *is* creditable. It is the first, last, and highest virtue."

"Oh, yes, probably in a philosophical sense that's so. I was just speaking as an individual. Perhaps you'll think it rude of me to say this, but I somehow can't believe, talking to you, what you say about your morale. You seem too cheerful."

"Thank you. We make every effort to give that impression. We try never to show our true feelings in any direct way."

Mrs. Manresa wondered if this were the Piggy-wig's *in*direct way of showing his feelings. And if so, what feelings might they be? There did seem to be some deep melancholy in the pig's eyes, such times as they would wander toward the screen of the receiver, a melancholy that tended to belie the roses' charms. It was hard, even so, to feel much sympathy for the animal side of the creature's divided nature. Without their roses the pigs of Rephan would have been no more than ignorant omnivores rutting for root vegetables and rodents; with the roses they were the coparceners of a vast civilization. For which, of course, they probably had no use.

"Would you like me to sing a song?" Mrs. Manresa suggested. A song was always her last refuge.

"Oh, very much," the roses replied.

"Just a second, then." Mrs. Manresa rose from her bed of flowers and went into the apartment to find the echolalia component. She returned to the terrace with it, hooked it in, smoothed her dress, and folded her fingers around the component. "This is a round," she explained, "that I learned when I was a little girl. You must try to imagine that there are a roomful of children singing it." She cleared her throat, pressed TAKE 1, and began:

> *"This song may be sung*
> *As long as you're young—"*

She pressed TAKE 2 and went on singing, in concert now with her own recorded voice:

> *"But when you are old*
> *—Forget it."*

Now in three voices:

> *"Forget the song you sang:*
> *Whatever joy it brang—"*

And finally in four:

> *"—Was gone with the song*
> *That brought it."*

She sang through the round two more times just for the pleasure of it.

"That's very affecting," said the Piggy-wig when she'd stopped singing, "and I should think it would be an excellent pedagogic tool as well, contrasting as it does the principal forms of the verbs *sing* and *bring*. Thank you."

"Not at all. The pleasure, as they say, is mine. The pleasure, that is, of having been able to make your acquaintance. It's at times like these that I begin to realize what a treasure our receivers are. But now, with your permission, I really must ring off. I've had a rather hard day, and, quite frankly, I'm depressed. I'd like to collapse."

"Of course, dear lady. I'm sorry the second shift won't have the opportunity to meet you, as they won't clock in for another eight hours. However, we've recorded your lovely round, and they'll have a chance to enjoy that. Good-by then."

"Good-by."

As soon as they were disconnected, Mrs. Manresa got

into the elevator (the second time that evening) and closed the door behind her.

Time, blessedly, stopped.

III

The first she saw of him, of her Bobolink, was his ass. Rather than take offense, she was struck at once by the fidelity of the presentation. And how ingenious of him! For the means by which receivers obtained the visual part of a broadcast was not by cameras (unless the human eye itself were regarded as such) but from transduction patterns about the optic nerves of persons using receivers. To the side of each screen were mirrors so placed that your peripheral vision took in your own image as you watched the screen; it was this peripheral self-image that the receivers broadcast. How then had this fellow contrived to send out so clear a self-concept from this point of view? Not by looking through his legs, for though she could see his cock and balls dangling down there, there was no hint of a face behind them. He was evidently bending forward in *some* position, but he must have been using mirrors as well.

But the oddest thing of all (How uncomfortable he must be, and how persistent!) had less to do with camera angles, so to speak, than the naturalistic character of the image. It was not, in any crude sense, photographic—rather broadly conceived than otherwise: it combined the decisive handling of a Sargent watercolor with the robust color of a Jordaens' nude. The informing vision seemed altogether cool, empirical, level-headed. Not the sort of person, therefore, to be thrusting his behind in your face by way of saying hello.

Mrs. Manresa was not a rapid thinker, and by the time these reflections had been developed in the darkroom of her mind, the man had been broadcasting for some time. The muscle at the back of his left thigh had begun to quiver spasmodically. He could be heard to groan and seen, for an instant, to collapse. The screen went blank, while on the audio there was the sound of profound and violent vomiting. Clearly, he was drunk.

And here at last, looking sheepish and thoroughly gorgeous, with little tears glistening at the corners of his eyes, was the man himself. A frazzle of dusty-brown curls, and all below the intelligence fairly shining forth: intelligent blue eyes surrounded by intelligent wrinkles, intelligent cheekbones of an intelligent pallor and suffused, at this moment, by an intelligent blush, intelligent thin smiling lips, an intelligent chin. The very fabric and pattern of the drapes behind him seemed alive with intelligence.

"Are you," he asked, with the overnice pronunciation of the thoroughly sloshed, "living in a matriarchal or a patriarchal society?"

It was not a question she'd ever thought to ask herself, and had no answer ready to hand. But she didn't feel like pussyfooting either, and so she flipped a mental coin, and answered, "A patriarchy, I suppose."

"Good. So am I."

"What if I weren't?"

"I'd have suggested we disconnect. Why waste each other's time?"

"Why indeed. Are you a Libra or a Gemini? You look like a Gemini to me."

"Fucking Christ, you believe that shit?"

"Well, which *are* you?"

"Listen, lady, where I live the constellations don't even have the same shapes. I'm on a moon orbiting a superjovian planet in a system of binary stars. I don't think astrology is ready for that somehow. Why don't we call it a day, huh?"

"Not till you tell me your sign."

"I told you—I don't *have* a fucking sign. Now why don't you sign off? Okay?"

He turned off his set, but it made no difference: unless she touched SCAN as well, their link would not be broken. She waited in front of the screen. In less than a minute he reappeared, only to grimace and touch SCAN again. This time he waited for five minutes. Mrs. Manresa listened, meanwhile, dreamily, to her husband's muffled arpeggios.

He had used the time to put on trousers.

"Okay; you win. I'm a Gemini. *Now* will you let me off the hook?"

"I want to know exactly when you were born. Month, day, year."

"Right. May 29, 2434."

She closed her eyes and subtracted 34 from 81. Forty-seven years old. He seemed younger.

When she opened her eyes the screen was blank. He must have thought she'd disconnected. She waited for him to return.

"Well?" he said.

"Actually you're not a Gemini. You're an Arachne."

"Arachne?"

"It's the thirteenth sign of the zodiac, the sign denoting psychic powers. You probably have paranormal abilities."

"You know, I had a wife who used to pull that sort of crap. Except in her case it was dreams. If I dreamt about shoes it meant one thing, a circuit diagram meant something else. She used it to bully me, the same as you."

"Do you think it *isn't* bullying to be sticking your ass in the face of a perfect stranger?"

"Well, I apologized."

"No, you didn't."

"Well, I meant to while I was throwing up. I framed the words in my head, and then when I got a good look at you, I was sidetracked. You're a very good-looking woman."

"Thank you."

"Admittedly, I've only got your own idea of the matter to go on. But you've got a pretty firm grasp on reality, it seems to me."

"Likewise, I'm sure."

He smiled. Such a smile. "So I *am* sorry. Okay?"

"I don't even know your name."

He smiled, more wryly. "Bobolink."

"Just the one word?"

"Since I got divorced I don't have a last name."

"That doesn't sound like a patriarchy to me."

"You've got to make some concessions. Anyhow, there it is. Name, marital status, date of birth. Professionally I'm a proud failure. Now—how about you?"

"My name's Elizabeth Manresa. You can call me Betty; my friends do. I'm married. I live in St. Paul, Minnesota." When that brought no reaction, she added: "On Earth." And still no reaction. "I'm thirty-eight years old. I'm a housewife. And I think you're sweet."

He closed his eyes; the screen blanked. "And you're sweet, too. But, Betty—"

He opened his eyes; she smiled.

"I've got to hang up now: I'm just too pissed to think straight, I have to be at work in three hours, and this isn't my set, it's a friend's."

"All the more amazing and wonderful our finding each other like this."

"You wouldn't."

"Wouldn't what?"

"Keep me on HOLD."

"Wouldn't I?" she replied, pressing HOLD down firmly with her forefinger, and turning off the set.

The next day, when, just for fun, she was running through one of her old routines (pity, then terror, then hiccoughs, at a steadily faster tempo), the buzzer buzzed. Earlier she'd wheeled the receiver into the apartment and parked it in front of Howard's latest prototype, an intaglio cassone that played ... *des pas sur la neige*. By the second buzz she was facing the screen, but she waited till the third to answer.

It wasn't Bobolink. In the first pang of disappointment she thought her receiver had bypassed one of Nature's, and its manufacturer's, immutable laws; then she recognized the drapes. Last night, through Bobolink's eyes, their stripes had seemed to have been torn, living, from the broad skirts of a Velasquez Infanta; now they were a sheer, unmodulated expanse of prison bars.

"Mrs. Manresa?" her caller inquired.

So: he had remembered her name. That boded well. As much could not be said for the raw, slouch-backed girl on the screen. Scarcely more than a teenager, with a self-concept so unsettled that her face seemed in a state of continuous formation, like a face reflected in the waters of a pond. A pretty girl, perhaps, if one might have seen her with some steadier eye than her own, but scarcely a suitable partner for her Bobolink.

"My name is Octave, Mrs. Manresa." She gave it a pretty pronunciation, the accent falling on the final broad A. "I understand a friend of mine used my receiver last night and was very rude to you. He asked me to apologize for him."

"There's no need for that, my dear. The fault is his: let him atone for it. Tell me, is he often as drunk as that?"

"I was out, so I really couldn't say. He did make a terrible mess. When I got home and saw it, I was just furious, and I told him to clear out, and only when he was going out the door did he tell me about your having the receiver on HOLD."

"Where has he gone to, do you know?"

"That isn't the point, Mrs. Manresa. The point is that it isn't fair, your doing this to *me!* to *my* set. I have to pay fifteen bracques a month rent for it. Do you have any idea how much that is?"

"None at all, I'm afraid. Bobolink didn't even tell me the name of your world."

"It's worth forty-eight dollars of your money."

"But he told you where I live, I see. What else did he tell you about me?"

"Mrs. Manresa, please be reasonable."

"I think I'm being reasonable, but I don't see any way I can be fair. This is between Bobolink and myself. You're a traditional innocent bystander. When does he come home from work?"

"Mrs. Manresa, this isn't his home. I only *met* him a week ago. He had just broken up with a girlfriend of his, and he was upset, and I felt sorry for him. And now, like I told you, he's moved out."

"What I suggest, Octave, is that you let him take over the rental of your set. Then you can rent another."

"But he won't do that, Mrs. Manresa. After they take out for child support and the rest, he earns less money than me. And he's a terrible cheapskate besides. He'll never agree to it."

"You'll have to make him agree, Octave. I *don't* intend to hang up."

"You're not in love with him, are you?" Octave's face gleamed, momentarily, with waifish beauty.

"Possibly. I don't know yet. I only know I mean to see him again."

"You're making a mistake, Mrs. Manresa. He's not worth

the aggravation. I know for a fact. He's a *bum*, Mrs. Manresa. A freeloader. And he's not even that great in bed."

"I'm sorry to hear it, for his sake. And for yours. But none of that can concern me at a distance of however many light-years away. It's his mind I'm after, necessarily, and he does have a lovely mind, by the look of it."

"Damn," said Octave, decisively. Then, after a thoughtful pause, during which her self-concept gelled into an incontrovertible plainness: "You don't play chess, do you?"

"Not very well, I'm afraid."

"Damn."

"What I would suggest, Octave, is that you trundle off your receiver right now to where he lives and leave it on his doorstep. If you'd let it keep broadcasting while you're on the way, that would be very nice. Alien worlds are always so fascinating to us here on Earth."

"Oh, fuck off," said Octave, and hung up.

Mrs. Manresa spent the better part of the following week in the exquisite clutches of *The Love-Suicides of San Diego Bay*, a movie she'd always meant to see but had never had time for. With all the optional interpolations and the suggested *da capo* repeats, a single viewing lasted one hundred forty-two hours. Usually, if she'd needed to ease her way through such an expanse of desert sand, she'd simply have gone and locked herself in the elevator. Now, however, that the possibility existed that she might be falling in love, she felt obliged to pursue some more ennobling course, and *The Love-Suicides* seemed just the thing, since not only was it an absolutely immortal classic, but it also happened to reflect her own potentially so-tragic situation. The heroine, Asuka, the concubine of a prominent San Diego Bay butcher, falls in love with Daiwabo, an administrator on a world hundreds of light-years away. They laugh, they dance, they languish, they discuss the meaning of their lives, but of course, since their only contact is by receiver, theirs is necessarily a platonic love. Asuka's is a passionate and willful nature, however, and she eventually contrives (it is a very complicated plot) to obtain passage for Daiwabo's world. Daiwabo, bound to his administrative duties, is not allowed by his Executive Committee to go into suspended animation in order to await his beloved's arrival. When she reaches him, still a young woman, having spent the voyage in storage, Daiwabo is a feeble nonagenarian whose numerous descendants show great unkindness to Asuka. After a single kiss, they take poison and die in each other's arms. A tale of no novelty, certainly. Indeed, the credits claimed that the story was derived from a classic puppet play by Chikamatsu, but novelty isn't what you're after when you're in love, or even on the brink. What you want then, what Mrs. Manresa wanted, is to be reminded of certain timeless truths, such as, that love is blind. The peculiar distinction of *The Love-Suicides of San Diego Bay* and what made it a classic wasn't its old chestnut of a plot but the way that the animators (the Tokyo Disney Studios) had conveyed the essential unknowableness of Asuka to Daiwabo, of Daiwabo to Asuka. Until the final harrowing cassette when the lovers are at last united in the flesh, the viewer never sees their faces, except as they appear on the screens of their receivers. Asuka is a courtesan from a woodcut by Harunobu; Daiwabo is an ivory mask. Naturally, the theme of their most brilliant duet (and the one clip which had survived, out of context, as a popular hit for the entire two centuries since the movie was first released) was how:

> At last I understand, my love,
>   at last I see
> What I am to you and what
>   you are to me.

Ah, love: was there ever anything like it?

If only, if only, if only he'd call her! If only someone would answer when she buzzed.

Then, just when she had begun to adjust to the idea that fate might have some other fulfillment in store, lo and behold, the buzzer buzzed and he was there. They were out in a rowboat, he and his receiver, on a lake or possibly an ocean (the light was so dim it was hard to judge). All sweaty and squint-eyed from the strain of rowing. Not *quite* as handsome as she remembered, but still more devastating at the numinous level where it's so useless to try and understand. Behind him, a sentimental sun, oblate and dusky-red, hung just above the smooth orange skin of ocean. "Ah," she said gratefully. "My darling, my darling." He went on pulling at the oars and made no reply. But he *had* turned his set on, he *had* buzzed, he *was* giving her his own guided tour of this sunset over this body of water, whatever it was; they were in contact again.

"But it's so beautiful," she soothed. "Here, let me adjust the light." She went to the chromostat, and fiddled with the dial till the bedroom (where she'd taken to keeping the receiver) was suffused with the dim saffrony orange of the water. In the wardrobe she changed quickly into her oldest tea-gown, which was, quite fortuitously, the same somber smoky red as his sun. Ashes mixed with rust. Then a bracelet of orange beads to match the ocean. Now (when she put the headset back on) the picture on his screen would be all of a piece with the scenery around him. The scenery of, what had he said, Medea? The name rang a bell. Probably some politician from centuries ago, or was it the name of a movie? She considered a lavender sash, but it was too warm to complement his sky. Such colors! The colors of orgasm. She lay back upon the shimmery sheets in a polyester jumble of gigantic limbs and rippling torsos, a proper Delilah, and asked him where they were bound.

"To the bottom, Mrs. Manresa," he replied. "Unless, that is, you care to hang up."

"Isn't that a rather drastic remedy, Bobolink?" she said reproachfully.

"Lady, I don't care to shell out fifteen bracques a month for the sake of keeping some idle bitch amused on rainy afternoons."

"Bobolink."

He was not moved. "I thought a quick disappearance might solve the problem. So I did a flit to another flotilla, but Octave tracked me down through her office, which collates the regional food-stamp data. Yesterday she brought the set across the bay on the steamer—"

"A steamer! And she didn't let me watch? Oh, that was cruel."

"Octave does not have friendly feelings for you, Mrs. Manresa, and neither do I."

"Let's discuss our feelings later, dearest. What happened then?"

"Octave waited outside my compartment till I got home from work, then threatened to use physical violence if I didn't take over her rental agreement."

"Oh." Mrs. Manresa felt plunged into a maelstrom of romantic passion. "What sort of physical violence?"

"She said she'd knock my teeth out."

"Would you have let her? Are you a pacifist?"

"No, but I've seen her when she gets angry, and I am a coward. So I signed the papers, which involved a transfer charge of twenty bracques over and above two months' nonrefundable rent."

"I am sorry to have involved you in extra expenses. If there's a corresponding bank on your world, I'd be happy to transfer funds to help you out."

"Thanks for nothing. Medea's not exactly a financial center. Economically, we've been declared unviable. There's nothing here worth taking away, and nothing worth coming here for."

"Why are you there, then? If it isn't rude to ask."

"Why is anybody anywhere? I was born here, and no one's ever thought to provide me with a ticket to somewhere else."

"Oh, dear, I wish I *could,* but—"

"I wasn't hinting."

"But my husband's only a handyman."

"Tough luck. I scoop gasbags, which isn't a whole lot better, I suppose. They stink, but it's only three days a week. I'm not complaining."

"It's a beautiful world," said Mrs. Manresa, trying to steer the conversation in some more hopeful direction. "Especially now, at sunset."

Bobolink laughed. "This isn't sunset. This is as bright as it ever gets, and as dark too, pretty much."

"Oh."

"And *that* isn't the sun." He dipped the right oar into the water and made the boat turn toward a more deeply purple quadrant of the sky, where two silvery dots hung low on the horizon, like a pair of disembodied eyes. "That's the sun."

"How strange. Your moon is your sun, and your sun is a two-piece moon. You must have peculiar songs. I don't think I'd ever adjust to nonstop twilight, but I suppose it's all a matter of what you're used to. *You* seem to like it, despite what you say. It comes across, here, as looking altogether lovely. The water is such an intense orange, and so weirdly still. Our Lake Calhoun is seldom as still as that, and of course it's not nearly so big either. But it's blue on a sunny day, and aliens always seem to like that. Would you like to see it? I could take my set out on a rowboat too."

"Lady, I didn't take you out here for the purpose of sight-seeing. I intend to drown you."

She loved it when he called her "lady".

"You still haven't explained why, though." She drew up her legs into a demure, attentive half lotus.

"What choice do I have? The rental agency won't let me return the set as long as you're keeping it on HOLD. But if I should have an 'accident', the insurance will pay for it and I'll be off the hook. If I do that, you know that *your* set will be a write-off? 'Cause no one's going to try and retrieve this set; the water's just too deep and mucky. So you won't have anyone to gossip to unless some crustacean down there decides to play with the headset. You can't say I haven't warned you."

"But we can still talk a few more minutes, can't we? Maybe I can change your mind, or you can change mine. Surely that would be better than putting in a claim. The insurance company might not believe you."

"Oh, I've figured out what to tell them. I'll say we'd fallen madly in love, and being in love, it was natural to take you out on the bay. You asked me to adjust the mirror so you'd have a better view of Argo, which, by the way, is not a moon either. Medea's the moon."

"Please, no astronomy."

"I'll say I was in state of arousal. It made me careless. The boat capsized and you, my darling, sank to the bottom. They'll believe that."

"And who's to say it isn't true? At least as to your being in love. I'm in love with *you*."

"Like hell you are."

"Do you know what it was? Your flesh tones. I've never

seen anyone convey such flesh tones. Even before I saw your face I knew there was something special about you."

His only response was to make a sour face. He started rowing more vigorously.

"Are you angry with me?" she demanded, when he seemed to have tired himself a little. "Why? What have I done? Aside from insisting on not hanging up, which, after all, might be regarded as a flattering attention."

"You really think you're something special, don't you? Just because you're there on Earth."

"Not really. But most people who've never connected to Earth before do take *some* interest in it. This is where it all began, after all: history and such."

"If I want to know about history, I can look at a cassette."

"Well, there's a definite limit to *my* attention span with regard to all our wonderful traditions, too. There are simply, at this point, too many. What does interest me is the present." She smiled her most Delilah-like smile. "What I mean is—you."

"You want to do a striptease, is that it?"

"Would *you* like that?"

He shrugged. But he had stopped rowing.

"Don't you think you should see what you're sending to the bottom?"

"I know: one bored housewife."

"True. But why should that be a reproach? You seem to suffer as much from boredom as I do, or you wouldn't be using a receiver in the first place. Or getting drunk. Such an atavistic pastime."

"Medea's an atavistic world. We're devolving back to agriculture." To illustrate, he took a bottle from under the seat of the rowboat, uncorked it, held it toward Mrs. Manresa in a toast. "Cheers."

"Cheers," she agreed. "Don't think I'm blaming you. I'm just saying we're in the same boat."

"Not for long, lady." He swallowed some wine, made a face, corked the bottle. "Not for long." He put the bottle back under the seat. "Anyway, my emphasis wasn't on 'bored'; it was on 'housewife', which to me translates as 'slave'."

"And you're the man who won't have anything to do with a woman unless she lives in a patriachal culture?"

"Oh, I'm not against slavery. I just can't afford one. Not of 'housewife' caliber."

"It's obvious to me that you've never known a housewife, or you wouldn't use such a sneering tone. Housewives are highly trained artists, the same as—it's the comparison that's always made, but it's true—geishas. We represent something constant and changeless in human nature. As to our being 'slaves', anyone who's born poor—and, in my case, a clone, as well—ends up wearing someone's livery in order to survive. I dare say you don't scoop gasbags by *choice*."

"Maybe not, but it's something that has to be done."

"Really. You must tell me what they are sometime, and why you scoop them. I'm sure there are compelling reasons. There are equally compelling reasons for what I do."

"And what do you do, Mrs. Manresa? Oh, I've known your kind. You wander around your apartment in a daze; you clean, you vacuum, you change your clothes and comb your hair; you watch TV, or natter away in front of a receiver; and when all else fails, you crawl into an elevator and elevate your mood."

"We do," she conceded. Then added: "As housewives have done from time immemorial. It's something, after all, that has to be done. If you're only fractionally human, like my husband, it can be as comforting as going to church to hear your little wifey scrambling an egg."

"Does your husband eat eggs? I thought you said he was a handyman."

"Eating them isn't the point. The point is that I represent for my husband the *idea* of a human life. I'm a kind of anchor attaching him to his own humanity. If his kind—and, remember, they're the ones who are in charge, not us—if his kind stopped wanting housewives, where would the rest of you be?"

"Where are we now? On fucking Medea."

"You're alive, and that's something. The point I'm trying to make, my love, is that in a world where humanity, properly speaking, is almost extinct, someone has to set an example, to represent the species. That's my job as a housewife: I represent a human life."

"Not very accurately," said Bobolink, but his eyes were all wrinkled into smiles.

Mrs. Manresa laughed. It was the first time in three years that she'd laughed so she could feel it inside. There was no longer any doubt about it: she was in love.

"Say you won't drown me," she coaxed. "Please. I'm trying *so* hard."

Bobolink drew a deep breath. "Okay. I won't drown you. Not today, anyhow."

IV

Only two months after Mrs. Manresa's love was thus officially requited, she was flying high above the fluffy, high-piled cumulus on her way to St. Peter's in Europe. The receiver was stowed out of sight and mind in the cargo compartment, and so Bobolink, alas, was not to have the advantage of this most representative terrestrial view. Her first trip abroad; indeed, her first trip outside the state since she'd fled from assorted dark and antisocial thoughts the February after her suicide. What is the point, after all, in literally going somewhere when there is certain already to be a cassette that shows it at its best? This journey, however, was not being undertaken on either her own or her beloved's behalf, except in the narrow commercial sense that it was paying for the upkeep of their adultery.

To elaborate:

There are tides and currents in the two hundred fifty-six dimensions of hyperspace, just as there are in the four of the workaday universe, which currents, though they may never be charted, have quite real consequences for those who use receivers. Sometimes a strong current will result in a sudden closing of the equipotential gap between two points in hyperspace, such as A and B, so that for some fixed period, moments or weeks, receivers in area A receive an unaccustomed spate of broadcasts from area B, and (sometimes) vice versa. It could also happen that these currents might isolate an entire world, or set of worlds, so that only the fixed-link receivers maintained by (for instance) two corresponding banks would continue to bridge the affected areas during the term of their hyperspatial divorce. The only fixed link between Medea and Earth was in the offices of the Human Bureau, and was not available for civilian use. Truly, Medea had devolved a long way.

Most hyperspatial divorces were so brief as to go unnoticed, but a few had been known to continue for years. It seems that Mrs. Manresa's receiver had made contact with Medea at the beginning of an exceptionally severe disjunction. Neither she nor Bobolink had been aware of this until, quite routinely, he'd filed notice of his link with the Medean web service. The usual result of such a listing is a smattering of messages to be forwarded from disgruntled exes wanting to sing their blues or let fly with one last withering riposte. Indeed, there'd been no dearth of these, and Mrs. Manresa had been kept busy several days telephoning to, varously, Canberra, Dallas, Abu Dhabi, and Apollo 10,328 on behalf of not so much the disconnected lovers as for her Bobolink, who received, for these services, significant help with his monthly rental. As the divorce continued, there were more referrals from the web. Bobolink upped his toll charges, and still business flourished. He had, it seemed, a monopoly on communications with Earth. Mrs. Manresa relayed, among other data of note, the unveiling of a Minneapolis milliner's spring collection and the revival of a Gulf Oil opera seria at Sauk Center. As she should have foreseen, her eye for fashion was much keener than her ear for music, especially of the pentatonic variety, and Bobolink's fee for the opera broadcast was halved because Mrs. Manresa's attention kept wandering from the rather silly story on the stage.

After the divorce had gone on a full six weeks, Bobolink was contacted by the Federal Crackpot Society, a group hoping to persuade the Vatican authorities to accept one of the indigenous life-forms of Medea into the Roman Church. Some few alien species (Piggy-wigs among them) had been recognized by the Church as being, like man, created in God's image, and as being implicated, like man, in Adam's fall; such species were also, therefore, redeemable, and might be admitted to the sacraments. Before such recognition could be won, the Vatican insisted that certain conditions be met; the alien species must demonstrate a capacity for rational thought; it must evidence a developed ethical sense; an individual member of the species must declare its fervent desire to be baptized into the Church. Heretofore, the Vatican had conceded only rationality to the Medean gasbags, the species in question, and this only after years of struggle on the part of the F.C.S. By their own admission, the Crackpots were not motivated by missionary impulses. Only a few of their members were Catholics. Their avowed aim was "to expose the contradictions latent in all social institutions." They were, in a word, troublemakers. Their gasbag campaign had been undertaken for no other reason than to annoy and confound the Catholic population of Medea, a small minority without political influence. Most of the human colonists on Medea lived on rafts and barges permanently becalmed in the doldrums of Medea's vast doughnut-shaped ocean; only here was it possible to escape the inhospitable extremes of climate of its two continental masses, one a burning desert, the other a frozen waste. The basic material used by the colonists to buoy up their homes and gardens was an aquatic plant indigenous to the doldrums—the gasbags. Gasbags began as polyps on a kind of kelp that grew in Sargasso-like reaches of the ocean. During periods of solar flares these polyps would swell up suddenly to quite alarming sizes (alarming, that is, if any were allowed to develop under one's houseboat). At maturity they were borne aloft into the atmosphere, streaming long orange umbilical cords of seaweed. Only at the airborne stage could the gasbags be said to possess intelligence; in their aquatic stage they were no more ratiocinative than any other variety of kelp. It was at a transitional stage between the tiny polyp and the mature balloon that the colonists scooped the fledglings from their beds and used them to stuff the pontoons supporting, as it were, their civilization. Now the object of the Crackpots in getting the mature gasbags accepted into the Catholic Church was so that the scooping of gasbags from the seabeds would have to be regarded as a form of abortion. And Catholics living on a gasbag-supported structure would then be in the same untenable position as an Italian whose villa has been raised on a foundation composed of the bones of aborted fetuses (a foundation, moreover, which must be periodically renewed). The Vatican, naturally, was reluctant to place Medean Catholics in such a compromising moral position, but it could not refuse, point-blank, to consider the gasbags' case, even though it was being advanced by the notorious F.C.S.

Up to now, the Crackpots had been baffled in their aims by the unavailability of a single gasbag that could sustain an interest in Catholicism for more than minutes at a time. Though intelligent, and even inclined to philosophy, they all seemed inclined to digress. Nor were they purposive in their actions. They went wherever the winds of Medea might blow them. They toiled not, neither did they spin. They lived—so those who had studied them maintained—in an almost perpetual state of sexual pleasure. Not, one might suppose, ideal prospects for conversion to Christianity, even in its present evolved and enlightened form. At last, nevertheless, an individual gasbag was discovered that had expressed a wish to be baptized—and persisted in that wish. Or so the society claimed. Since this gasbag—it had adopted the Christian name of Xavier—seemed to be expiring, due to a defective valve, it was essential that an interview be arranged at once between Xavier and the Vatican authorities. It was at this point that Earth and Medea had entered into the recent phase of disjunction.

Bobolink had haggled two days with the Crackpots, who at last agreed to take over the rental charges on his receiver for the next five years, but only on condition that Mrs. Manresa convey her receiver to St. Peter's within the week. A telephone relay would not suffice, as the Church didn't recognize the validity of sacraments administered electronically, while receivers, since they could operate only by the agency of a living intelligence, were accepted as being a natural and complete extension of the individual soul. The Crackpots were hoping to have Xavier baptized *tout à coup*.

Faced with this demand, and urged on by her lover, Mrs. Manresa summoned up her courage and went to Howard with the whole story of how, without really meaning to, she'd fallen in love. She'd only been able to keep it from him this long because, unlike most couples, they didn't share a single receiver. Howard's need for aleatory companionship was exclusively musical, and so he had his own receiver adapted with a filter for this special purpose. He took his wife's news calmly enough, with solicitude, even, for *her* peace of mind, since he knew how upsetting love could be. Really, she'd been foolish to have worried. No civilized husband of the 25th century, and especially not Howard, would object to his wife taking a lover via receiver. It was simply the way of the worlds. Courtly love had been reinstituted on a sound technological basis. Lancelots everywhere were free to declare their undying devotion to a universe of Gueneveres without the least discouragement from the parallel universe of Arthurs. A trip to Rome was asking rather much, but in most respects Mrs. Manresa had proven herself a consumer of modest appetite, so why not? She had departed with her husband's complacentest sanction and a six-pack of Oregon pears.

And now, *O ciel,* here she was in the amazing nave of St. Peter's, which was, she had to admit, many times more impressive than anything in the Twin Cities. She trundled the receiver in its little wire cart down past the rows of confessionals and clear lucite conference cubes. Very many of the worshipers were equipped like herself with receivers, each of them (probably) connecting St. Peter's with a different star. How large the galaxy was, when you thought about it! And the nave, too. There were also a good many clergy (often of highly evolved types): a troop of cloned nuns in black leotards with their Mother Superior whirring above them in the form of a little aluminum dove; a bishop who'd been miniaturized down to a head and a mitre; a mobile closet full of Carthusian handymen, stacked like china in three neat tiers, their hands folded in contrasting attitudes of devotion and all their other components tucked away out of sight in the base of the cabinet. Mrs. Manresa, accustomed as she was to her own spouse, couldn't help but feel a twinge of malaise before this image of (as it seemed to her) Howard multiplied by twelve. There were, as well, any number of ordinary unevolved tourists and worshipers going about being overcome by the immensity of everything, or kissing the statues, or standing in the long queues in front of the confessionals and concession stands.

A sign outside Monsignor Beefheart's conference cube said that he would be back at 1430. An hour to wait, but the waiting was sweetened by the cloned nuns, who were (the PA system announced) from India and were going to sing an Indian hymn. The nuns joined hands in a double circle and did a demure little shuffle while they sang, one ring revolving in one direction, the other in the opposite direction, and each nun looking so *happy* you wanted to go straight to the recruiting office and join up. It was a very simple, very slow hymn, and wonderfully loud, considering the space it had to fill.

> *Faith* (sang the nuns)
>   *makes me strong*
> *And leads my soul along.*
>
> *Faith is the way*
> *I get through every day.*
> *Faith is the pill*
> *That conquers my weak will*
> *And lifts it up to higher*
>   *spheres*
> *Where Krishna's burning*
>   *fire sears*
> *My low desires and my fears*
> *And turns them all to holy tears.*
>
> *Far, far above*
> *I'll see the God I love.*
> *He'll smile on me, that God*
>   *so dear,*
> *And then for ever I will hear*
> *The faithful sing this song:*
> *Faith makes us strong*
> *And leads our souls along . . .*

The hymn spun round like that, perpetuum mobile, the end fitting back into the beginning. It really could have gone on forever, and it was hard to say how long it did go on once you were singing along yourself. Other worshipers took the places of the nuns in their ringdance, and the nuns began to distribute communion to the nondancing part of the congregation. Mrs. Manresa accepted a packet of the little white wafers with a murmur of thanks, and pretended to take one out and nibble it, but then when the nun had turned away she slipped it back into her pocket. Though she didn't believe much in God, she did believe in being polite and doing what Romans do. Of course, the truly polite thing to have done would be to swallow the thing, but who knows how long the effect of it might last? And then, when the Faith wore off, it was always so depressing to have nothing to believe in any more. That way lay addiction.

A light appeared above the conference cube, indicating that Monsignor Beefheart had returned. Though the booth remained, to all appearances, empty, Mrs. Manresa went in and set up the receiver. She buzzed and Bobolink answered. He was wearing nothing but a new pair of swimming trunks. That seemed out of place in St. Peter's, but then you had to realize that he wasn't, despite the high resolution of the image, really here.

Bobolink introduced Mrs. Manresa to a tall, balding, snaggle-toothed man, also in swim trunks, whose Falstaffian paunch drooped down over his trunks disgracefully. "Betty," he said, "this is Norm; Norm, Betty. Norm is the secretary of the Crackpot Society. And since this is his broadcast from here on out, I'll just turn these over to him." He placed his hands on the headset.

The screen went blank.

When the image returned, it was radically different. Norm, in the headset, appeared to have shed fifty pounds, had his teeth straightened, and got a hair transplant. Bobolink, standing behind him, had suffered a sea-change in the other direction. He was shorter, and his curling hair had become a nest of dilapidated snakes. His wrinkled face had taken on the half-crazed look of a famished predator. Clearly, these two men did not have very high opinions of each other, but which of them was right? Ah, even to be asking such a question was apostasy! Bobolink *had* to be right. Because? Because he was her Bobolink.

"Betty?" Norm demanded in a reedy voice that even his

flattering self-concept could not do much to improve. "Who asked for Betty? Where is this Mister Bee-fart?"

"I am present," said a deep, disembodied voice, "in simulation."

"You mean I go to all the trouble and expense to get that damned receiver hauled halfway across a planet and *you* send in a lousy computer? Unfair!"

"Any decision I may reach as a simulation can differ in no way from the decision I would have reached in my own person. I am a busy man, and can't be everywhere at once. All members of the Rota approach routine assignments like this in simulation."

"But who's going to *baptize* old Xavier here, tell me that?" Norm turned sideways and patted the shimmering gray wall behind him. Responsively, the gray was suffused with pink. Mrs. Manresa realized that this must be the gasbag that the Crackpots had converted to Catholicism. The Medean receiver had been stationed so close to it that its curvature was imperceptible. "Don't tell me your simulation can perform a baptism. I may be no theologian, but I'm not a dummy."

"In the event that that begins to seem an eventuality, my simulation will summon me and I shall come to the cube *in propria persona*. Now, if we may begin? Xavier, tell me: who made us?"

"Just a second," said Norm. "I'll have to translate that."

Norm stooped and dipped his fingers in a bowl of blue paint. He smeared the paint across both his cheeks, then dipped his other hand into a bowl of dayglo pink and spread this slantwise across his drooping paunch.

Xavier replied with a burst of lemon-yellow fizz and a large fuschia bubble. Though gasbags could communicate orally by squeaking their valves, they preferred the rapider and more eloquent language of color-flow. They spoke, so to speak, by blushing.

"He says," Norm interpreted, " 'What do you mean,"us"? Do you mean "us humans" or are we'—meaning gasbags—'included?' "

"Provisionally, the latter. But don't you have a device for translation? If I am to judge of his fitness to be received into the Church, I can scarcely take *your* word for what he's saying."

"Right, right. I just forgot to turn it on. I'll still have to translate your question *to* him, unless you've got something on your end that can translate from English to color-flow."

"Will you ask him again, please, who made us, and when he's answered that one, why?"

Norm smeared more paint on his face and stomach, and Xavier replied in a cataract of fluid blossomings, gold expanding across a field of mauve, then pearl across the gold, followed by a brighter gold that flowed in alternate diagonals right and left. The effect was as though a Turner landscape had been animated and then projected at very high speed. At the base of the screen the translator translated the color-flow into English subtitles. Seldom had Mrs. Manresa so poignantly regretted her illiteracy. Later, at the coffee bar in back of the Pieta, when he was trying to pick her up, Monsignor Beefheart told Mrs. Manresa something of what the gasbag had been saying, as much as was not either epistemology or math. It had discussed aspects of symmetry in human anatomy, relating these to the image of the cross; contrasted the effects of protracted rainfall on human and gasbag temperament; told a kind of parable, or joke, concerning a fox with first eight legs, then four legs, then three; inquired as to the Vatican's position on cannibalism; complained at some length about its own digestion and its defective valve; and finally insisted on telling the whole story of the fox with eight legs, then four legs, then three all over again, color by color. It had been in the middle of this twice-told tale that Monsignor Beefheart (who had entered the conference cube in person during Xavier's disquisition on the cross) had become exasperated and turned off the receiver.

Mrs. Manresa let out a shriek of protest, of anguish, of loss. By the reflexive habit of his long years of missionary work, Monsignor Beefheart had released the HOLD button at the same time he'd touched OFF. Now, should he so choose, Bobolink could disconnect. And he would, she knew it; he would.

But he didn't. When she'd shoved the monsignor out of

the way and turned the set back on, he was still there, glorious (even in Norm's spiteful version) in swim trunks, faithful as a bad penny. Had he known he'd had a chance to make a break for it? His sudden smile when she'd reappeared on his screen would suggest that he had. At the very least she knew, just by the fact that she'd reached him again, that *his* receiver was on HOLD. He'd *told* her it was, but she'd never dared put his word to the test. Now she knew it wasn't a lie: *he* had *her* on HOLD!

He loves me, she thought, he really does, and all the while Monsignor Beefheart was apologizing to Xavier for his brusqueness and explaining that it did not seem to possess the kind of ethical sensibility suitable for its becoming a Christian. To be received into the Church, one must display more than a fascination with bilateral symmetry. Some concept of original sin was much more essential, and that Xavier, by its own admission, lacked entirely. Perhaps, Monsignor Beefheart suggested, gasbags were not subject to original sin, but you could tell from the way he said it that he was only being polite.

Xavier took its rejection with every evidence of good humor, though it did seem to want to go on and finish its retelling of the story of the fox with eight legs, then four legs, and finally only three.

That night in her room at the Hassler, when they were alone, Bobolink tried to get Mrs. Manresa to take one of the wafers from the packet of Holy Communion the nun had given her at St. Peter's. "Oh, come on," he wheedled, "just for fun, come on." She said she was too tired. He said she owed it to him for having kept his receiver on HOLD. He knew she hadn't believed him before, but now she had the proof. She said maybe tomorrow. He said now. Finally she agreed to take just one, and finally she took it. After the initial lift-off, Bobolink began telling her how much, how very much he loved her, and how, loving her so much, he also needed her trust. She believed every word. With the amount of Faith there was in one wafer she'd have believed anything—a mystery, a miracle, an oxymoron. Beyond believing Bobolink, she trusted him and did what he had asked: she took her receiver off HOLD.

He didn't disconnect. Faith was triumphant.

He told her how wholly, how utterly he loved her. He said she was his darling girl, his goddess, his little goose, his All-in-All.

She believed him.

She adored him.

She promised, faithfully, to take another wafer in the morning, and he promised to leave his own receiver on HOLD for ever and ever and ever and ever and ever.

V

Mrs. Manresa stayed on in the Eternal City for what seemed, under the influence of her daily dose of Faith, an eternal seven weeks. She divided her timeless hours between her darling, her deity, her Bobolink, paddling by steamer across the orange Medean sea from flotilla to flotilla, and doing the standard sights of Rome—the Pantheon, the Colosseum, the Sistine Chapel, St. Peter's, and the reconstructed Forum-*cum*-Funfair in E.U.R.—always the same itinerary, since that was what the audiences on Medea paid to see.

Bobolink had become an impresario. Though the divorce between Earth and Medea had come to an end and he no longer had a monopoly on communications between the two worlds, the naive lucidity of Mrs. Manresa's perceptions made her an ideal medium for conveying that sense of wonder and razzmatazz that is the *raison d'etre* of baroque architecture. Sometimes she'd do a special tour for Catholic audiences, going exclusively to churches, starting at the Scala Santa, where she climbed the Holy Staircase on her knees, proceeding thence to Santa Maria d'Aracoeli, then to Santa Maria degli Angeli, then to Santa Maria della Pace, then to Santa Maria dell'Anima, then (after a quick lunch) to Santa Maria in Cosmedin, then out on the 57 bus to Santa Maria del Populo, and winding up at 1600 on the dot at Santa Maria Maggiore, for which round of visits she and each of the vicarious pilgrims in her audience on Medea received a plenary indulgence.

Naturally with so much Faith in her system and such a plethora of pious sights to take in, Mrs. Manresa was soon an ardent Catholic. She felt a special devotion to the Virgin Mary, particularly as represented by Pinturicchio in the *Adoration* at Santa Maria del Populo, to whom she was thought (by her audiences) to bear a remarkable resemblance. This devotion was not without practical repercussions.

"You see, beloved," she explained once more to Bobolink, during one of her hurried lunch breaks before hastening on to Santa Maria in Cosmedin, "I understand now what I never understood before. It's a woman's *destiny* to bear children and nourish them with her love. Her fulfillment. Her sacred duty. That's clear, isn't it, now that I've explained? You see the logic of it?"

"Absolutely." There was no point in arguing with someone strung out on Faith. You just had to agree.

"Then you will help me, won't you?"

"Darling, you *know* how much I love you."

In reply Mrs. Manresa pressed adoring lips to the screen of her receiver.

"But I don't see why, in a case like this, it has to be me who, uh, supplies the . . ."

Mrs. Manresa laughed delightedly. "But who else, silly dear, could I possibly have a child by?"

"Maybe your husband?"

"But I don't *love* Howard. I must have my child by the man I love. By the man who loves me."

"Yeah, naturally. I just thought, seeing that you're a Catholic now . . ."

"Oh, as to that, Monsignor Beefheart has made it very clear that the Church doesn't recognize the validity of marriage to a handyman. He said my relationship to Howard is essentially a business arrangement."

"And what is your relationship to me?"

Mrs. Manresa furrowed her brow in distress. What could he mean, asking such a question? She was his darling, his deity, his—

"I love you, of course," he assured her. "Nobody could possibly love you more than I do. You must know that."

"Oh, yes!"

"But, after all, ours has to be a spiritual-type love, right? Considering that we're fifty light-years apart."

"Yes, but you see if you'll just transmit the data they need at the Family Planning Center—I've got all the forms you need—" '

"I know, I know. The problem is, dearest, that it requires rather a major effort to get the kind of information those forms are asking for, especially here on Medea. As I've explained so often before, we've devolved. We don't have the technology available. I can't just go into a booth and let them take a sample. I'd have to go to the main office of the Human Bureau at Port Backside, and it would cost me a small fortune."

"But, as I recall, that's where we're going. Aren't I doing two matinees at the Backside Civic Theater next week?"

"Mm."

"And as for the money, darling, you must be *earning* a great deal of money. Whatever it may cost, surely you wouldn't withhold my womanly fulfillment from me?"

She did not need to point out by whose help he was scooping up the bracques. No pimp along the Lungotevere could have been more sensibly aware of the source of his income. At last, seeing the practical wisdom of keeping his goose in a laying humor (for, when she was anxious, the quality of her transmissions plummeted disastrously), he agreed to go along with her numbskull scheme, and as soon as they reached Port Backside, he went to the Human Bureau and had them take a genetic scan. The results of the scan were transmitted via their own receivers, from the Medean data bank at the Human Bureau directly to Family Planning Center in Rome.

At first, Mrs. Manresa had favored leaving the genetic mix entirely to chance in the old-fashioned way (except for sex, since she definitely wanted a son: is there a Madonna anywhere who doesn't?), but then at the twenty-third hour she changed her mind and let Bobolink's most salient physical characteristics be dominant. It cost more, but that's love.

Birth was simulated a week after conception. What was the point of pretending to be pregnant? That, however, she had promised herself, would be the last she'd let herself tamper with nature's inalterable rhythms. What she hadn't bargained on was the inchoate flux of infantile perception.

She'd programmed her Baby Jesus—in the records of the Family Planning Center his name was Robin, but to his mother he would always be Baby Jesus—to be born and bred on Medea. That way, her only communication with him would be by receiver, just as it had been with his father. After all, if he could never be more than an image on a screen, then to have him seem to be on the screen of a receiver rather than an ordinary simulator screen might actually enhance one's sense of his actuality. Such had been her theory. In practice, alas, Baby Jesus came across as little more than a booming pink blob. Simulated babies have self-concepts as dim and unfocused as those of real biological babies. The first year or so of even the sacredest motherhood is only the sum of hundreds of hours of stroking, squeezing, nursing, burping, dandling, and changing diapers. All these vital attentions were duly paid to Baby Jesus, but only in simulation and by his adoptive Medean mother, Octave. Until he learned to talk, there wasn't much his real mother could do to relate to him except to make faces at him as he lay in his crib.

If, on the one hand, Baby Jesus was a bit of a disappointment, he did not, on the other, make many demands, while Bobolink definitely did. Mrs. Manresa was now conducting two chautauquas a day—one in the afternoon for school assemblies, one in the evening for the general public.

It was hard, even with Faith, to maintain an alert interest in what she'd never understood to begin with. St. Peter's was immense, she couldn't deny it, but *why* was it immense? How did its immensity relate to the grander but less tangible immensity of God? She believed in God now, thanks to her Faith, and in Jesus and Mary and everything else, but there didn't seem to be much *connection* between what she believed in and what she could see about her here in Rome. She wished she could slow down for a minute and find out why, for instance, one set of columns and pillars and cornices was supposed to be so much better than another, aside from their being older or made of an especially nice kind of rock, and what that had to do with loving her neighbors, or even meeting them. She began to feel what she'd never felt before, a vague disquiet with her own unmodified, unevolved condition, a longing to be able to plug into an information terminal whenever she wanted to and, bing, have the answers to at least a few of these questions. Baby Jesus ought to have been a refuge and a strength, but he just wasn't.

Neither, sad to say, was Bobolink. She *believed* in him: he left her no choice. She believed, that is, what he told her to—that he loved her, that he needed her, that she was his darling, his deity, his All-in-All. It never seemed to occur to him to tell her that *she* loved *him*, etc. She did, of course, but possibly not in the ardent way he seemed to assume. He was too modest, or maybe too innately honest, to take advantage of her Faith to achieve an apotheosis for himself. He remained the proud failure and aging bum she'd originally fallen in love with, which was painful at times, but doesn't the Mater Dolorosa have seven swords piercing her heart? That's love, and she had to be grateful for it, even if it meant, which it seemed to, that she was slowly going crazy as a result.

Monsignor Beefheart made it all very clear one afternoon when he came over to her hotel to hear her confession.

"Your dilemma, my dear Mrs. Manresa, is that you're being asked to entertain two mutually contradictory systems of belief, each of them capable quite on its own of driving a more delicately constituted mind than yours right around the bend. One is Christianity; the other a more than usually meretricious romantic passion. You'll have to give up one or the other. What *I* suggest is that you let me take away your receiver, and that you stay here in Rome and join a missionary order of nuns."

"What would I do about Baby Jesus?"

"Baby Jesus—*your* Baby Jesus, that is—doesn't exist. He's a computer simulation, a set of statistical possibilities coded onto a wire filament."

"That's easy for you to say—you're not his mother."

"Mrs. Manresa, think about what you've just said."

"I can't help it. It's the Faith, it makes me confused."

"Faith, Mrs. Manresa, is ultimately an act of free will. No one forced you to take that first pill. You took it because you wanted to believe in that lout on a third-rate planet who is exploiting you for his own selfish ends."

"But what is the difference between that and what you're

suggesting? As a missionary nun I'd just go on giving more guided tours of Rome to people on other inaccessible planets. Wouldn't I?"

"Yes, but you'd be doing it for the greater glory of God." The receiver buzzed.

Mrs. Manresa sighed. "There he is now. We better get dressed. I've got to be at the Pantheon in fifteen minutes."

"Whatever you say. *Absolvo te.*"

"Thanks." She kissed his bald spot. "The same to you."

Long before Mrs. Manresa could be driven functionally insane, her contradictions were resolved in the simplest way possible. Bobolink hung up.

She had sensed for several weeks already that there had been a growing dissatisfaction with her transmissions among the members of her audience. Bobolink kept urging her to pay closer attention, but how much attention, after all, can you give to the same pile of tumble-down stones twice a day, day in and day out? On the circuit of Santa Marias her difficulty seemed not so much apathy or jadedness as an excess of credulity. The paintings and statues and frescoed ceilings came across not as ancient and intellectually improving works of art, but as the real thing. To such as did not share her Faith, Mrs. Manresa's veritable angels and wind-blown stone saints looked a little ludicrous; even, eventually, embarrassing, especially among Catholics who were suddenly brought up against the brute demands of their religion. Word got around, and in even the most isolated flotillas her audiences diminished until the show was no longer paying for Bobolink's traveling expenses. At which point, without so much as a thank you or a word of farewell, he was gone.

She had found out by turning on her receiver one day at noon when she was due to start the day's excursion. Usually by that time Bobolink would have buzzed her, but sometimes he just waited till she was ready. With both sets off HOLD, the scanning mechanism, which she'd almost forgotten about, started thumbing through the pages of hyperspace looking for somebody new. Before she'd been able to take in what had happened, she'd reached a hard-bitten old lady astronaut somewhere at the other end of the universe who wanted to tell her about the dreams she'd been having. Mrs. Manresa listened to her with dazed inattention, and then, as it finally sank in that she'd been abandoned and that this was a fact no amount of Faith was ever going to change, she started to cry.

The astronaut looked offended and hung up.

VI

It was Labor Day, and Mrs. Manresa had baked a traditional Labor Day loaf. There it lay, golden and crusty, on the luncheonette ledge, waiting to be sliced.

She switched on the simulator and touched the buzzer. Without a pause Octave answered. Mrs. Manresa had often called up the F.P.C. and suggested that in future programs the simulated figures might sometimes seem to be delayed in answering a call, or even, occasionally, to be unavailable. It would definitely make them seem more lifelike.

Octave was wearing a holiday apron that she'd copied from one of Mrs. Manresa's. It was decorated with a set of cheery silk french fries that looked, through the simulated eyes of Octave, good enough to eat. They chatted for a while. Octave liked to hear the latest economic indicators, which meant that Mrs. Manresa had to keep abreast of the news more than she cared to. Then Octave lugged her set to another part of the room, and Mrs. Manresa was able to see, still through Octave's eyes, her darling and only-begotten son.

Baby Jesus was sprawled on the floor beside a low serving table, playing in a desultory way with a doll fashioned from fragments of a desiccated gasbag. He was four years old, though scarcely as many weeks had passed since Mrs. Manresa had returned to Marshall Avenue and her career as a housewife. In her eagerness for companionship she had not been able to resist accelerating Baby Jesus's growth. The Family Planning Center had warned that the result of such haste might be a certain flatness of personality, a stunting of affective range. So much of the illusion of a simulation's autonomous life depends on a sustained interaction between program and programmer. To rely entirely on normative probabilities, as one did in accelerating growth, was liable to make Jack a dull boy; and this seeming dullness would, in turn, encourage his parent/programmer to continue acceleration in the hope of reaching a more interesting and interactive phase of development. Mrs. Manresa was already caught in this vicious circle, though, like most disappointed parents, she tended to place the blame for her mistake elsewhere—on the designers at the Family Planning Center, on his foster-mother, on Baby Jesus himself. In her clearer-headed moments she recognized the unfairness of this, but it is hard, when you're insanely depressed and living half of your life in an elevator, to be even moderately clear-headed.

Now, however, she meant to turn over a new leaf. For four tedious hours, after she'd done the morning's dusting and adjusting and other needful chores, she had sat down and viewed IBM's highly recommended cassette on child guidance. There were five important rules to follow. The first was: Share Basic Experience. Such as, today, the Labor Day loaf. She arranged in advance for Octave to bake a loaf using the same recipe, and there it was on the table in front of Baby Jesus, the Doppelganger of her own real loaf of bread. He would eat some and she would eat some and each of them would know that what they were experiencing; the crunch of the crust, the flavor on their tongues, was identical and just the same. There was nothing like shared meals, so the experts at IBM claimed, for overcoming one's basic disbelief in the existence of other people. This was why, even though it was so unpleasant to watch other people chewing their food, almost every religious system required its followers to eat meals together, especially when they belonged to the same kinship group.

Baby Jesus, however, had a finicky and unpredictable appetite, and this was one of his most obstinate days. No amount of coaxing or pleading would get him to try some of the Labor Day loaf. Octave smeared on thick spoonfuls of his favorite substitute, but still he balked. At last he had a tantrum. Mrs. Manresa put up with his nonsense as long as she could stand it, and then hung up.

She advanced the simulation one day of calendar time, and tried again.

This time it was Baby Jesus who answered. There he

stood, on the outer deck of the houseboat, a crude little scribble of a mannikin with one big red daub of a body to which were attached four matchstick limbs and a smaller pink daub of a head: the self-concept of a two-year-old, according to the IBM cassette. Behind him, the orange sea and the red disk of Argo aglow in the violet sky seemed overlaid with a faint gridiron pattern—the effect, one might surmise, of his precocious enthusiasm for chess. When she'd been helping the F.P.C. to set up his original program, the only definite and distinctive fact she'd been able to remember about Octave was that she liked to play chess. Now, when she asked Baby Jesus what he would like to do, the answer was invariably that he wanted to play chess.

They set out the pieces on their boards. His came across with diagrammatic clarity; more clearly, indeed, than the veritable plastic pieces on her own board, unless she looked very hard.

While they played, Mrs. Manresa tried to engineer the conversation into IBM's recommended channels, with the object of getting Baby Jesus to pay closer attention to shapes and colors in the world around him besides those incorporated into the chessboard and its pieces.

"Oh, look. How strange. Do you see those two dots?" she asked, referring to Phrixus and Helle, the double sun of the Colchis system.

"What two dots?" Baby Jesus asked abstractedly, not looking up from the chessboard.

"There in the sky, by the Kingsleys' ventilator." (She had seen the same scene through Octave's eyes and knew, therefore, that a certain brown protuberance was a ventilator off the roof of a neighboring barge.)

"Don't know." He moved his queen forward, capturing his mother's king's bishop's pawn. "You're in check."

With a sigh of disappointment, she turned the simulator off.

It was all very well, she thought bitterly, for people like IBM to talk about low resolution and high involvement. *They* didn't have to live with an emotional cretin. *They* didn't have to look at those two empty eyes and the inflexible minus-sign of a mouth and say to themselves: *this* is my reason for living, *this* is what's left of all my love.

* * *

A week later, after a fit of impatience and pique in which she'd booted Baby Jesus two years further ahead into his subjective future without effecting the least improvement in his self-concept, Mrs. Manresa took a walk through the yellow pages and found the number of Mrs. Bellamy's School for Imaginary Children. Like so many others involved in conceptual occupations, Mrs. Bellamy insisted on Mrs. Manresa's coming to her place of business in person.

The School for Imaginary Children was a smallish indoors shop-front on the second level of Dayton's Psychological Services Bureau on Wabasha Avenue. A photo-enlargement of two pages from an old abecedary filled the single window and prevented passers-by from looking in. Feeling she ought to take an interest in the display, Mrs. Manresa pressed the read-aloud button at the side of the window. A concealed speaker read the text in a scratchy, worn-out voice:

> *A is an Apple, as everyone knows.*
> *But B is a . . . What do you suppose?*
> *A Bible? A Barber? A Banquet? A Bank?*
> *No, B is this Boat, the night that it sank.*
> *C is its Captain, and D is its Dory,*
> *While E—But first let me tell you a story.*

"Can I help you?" said a slightly modified old woman (her gray permahair did not quite conceal the socket at the base of her neck), emerging from the shop. The read-aloud button must have alerted her.

Mrs. Manresa explained that she was Mrs. Manresa.

"Oh, yes. Do come in. I trust you've brought your little boy with you?"

Mrs. Manresa followed Mrs. Bellamy into a cubicle set up just like a school room in an old movie, with blackboards and bunting and four rows of darling little desks just two feet high. On the back of the giant abecedary in the shop window were taped a number of bona fide finger paintings in reassuring pairs of foggy or psychotic Befores and inventive but undisturbed Afters. If only (she thought) the school could improve her own son so dramatically.

"This is—" She took the spool of tape from her carryall and handed it to Mrs. Bellamy. "—Baby Jesus."

Mrs. Bellamy glanced at the logo on the spool. "From the Family Planning Center? I'm surprised, I must say. Their programs seldom require assistance of the sort we offer here."

"The fault is mine, I'm afraid. I made him grow too fast. He's become . . . reclusive. Also, his self-concept is very poor for his age."

"Which is?" Mrs. Bellamy inquired.

"Just turned six."

"Dear me." She checked the date on the spool. "You *have* been impatient. But still, six is a good age to start school, and the influence of other independently programmed children can do wonders. Now if I may ask you a few questions?"

"Certainly."

Mrs. Bellamy turned to the blackboard, took up a piece of chalk, and wrote a numeral 1. "First, your occupation?"

"I'm a housewife."

"Really! I always wanted to be a housewife when I was a girl, but—" With a martyred smile. "—I guess I just wasn't cut out for it." She wrote a numeral 2 on the blackboard. "Your husband's occupation?"

"Ordinarily, he's a data-flow coagulator for Honeywell, but he's been on sabbatical for most of this year, making mechanical music boxes. That's how we happen to have time available, on his supplemental banks, to program a child."

"Is this the first child you've had together?"

"Oh, he's not Howard's child."

"No?" Mrs. Bellamy hastily erased the 2 on the blackboard, and sat down on the floor.

Mrs. Manresa sat down beside her and unfolded the whole long tale, how she'd met Bobolink and fallen in love, how she'd flown to Rome and been converted accidentally to Catholicism, how Baby Jesus had been born, how Bobolink had abandoned her, and then, in simulation, abandoned his own son as well. "And so you see," Mrs. Manresa concluded, "why Baby Jesus is so important to me. He's all I have left."

"Yes, I see. May I ask—and please don't be offended—have you ever considered going back to conception and starting over? A new genetic mix can yield amazing results, and it would be much cheaper, you know, than entering him in the school. A separate tape must be developed for each of his classmates, each of which, like his own, must be coordinated with all the data currently available about the world he's growing up on."

"I realize it will be expensive, but I feel it would be like murdering him if I went back and started from scratch. And then, as IBM points out, I'm liable to make all the same mistakes over again. Most parents do."

"True, true."

"What I'm sure he needs most is just to meet other children. Children with other backgrounds. Children he can play with."

"Undoubtedly," said Mrs. Bellamy, though without notable conviction. "One final question: does your son understand, how shall I put it—" She patted her hair down in place over the socket in her neck. "—the facts of life?"

"As much as any other six-year-old, I suppose. He's not stupid. Just . . . untrusting."

"What I'm driving at, Mrs. Manresa, is that many imaginary children who grow up on planets far from Earth undergo a great shock when they realize that it would have been impossible for their parents to have met and, in the Biblical sense, known each other."

"Oh, that's not a problem with Baby Jesus. I'm a clone, you see. Ova of my exact genotype are available for transplantation at any office of the Human Bureau. All anyone would have to know in order to be able to have a child by me is my name."

"And your son understands that?"

"Yes, of course."

"Good. Then all that remains is to discuss what kind of classmates you'd like for Baby Jesus. And, by the way, I'd suggest that he adopt some more ordinary name when he does start attending. Children can be merciless teases. And, after all that, I'll show you our schedule of tuition fees."

VII

The spool came back from the School for Imaginary Children four weeks later. In those four weeks Baby Jesus had spent seven months, subjectively, at the Port Backside Military Academy. With a prayer to her favorite Pinturicchio Madonna, and crossing her fingers for good luck, Mrs. Manresa swallowed one of the last remaining wafers of Faith, inserted the spool into the simulator, and waited (scarcely a moment) for Baby Jesus to answer.

It was clear at a glance how great a change the school had wrought in the boy's self-concept. No more did he look like a puddle of finger paint. Every limb, every finger, every feature of his face was delineated with sharp black lines, and each area thus demarcated was filled in with bright, plausible colors. It was exactly the kind of self-concept the cassette said was to be expected from a child of his age.

"Darling," said Mrs. Manresa, feeling the delicious pressure of happy tears.

"Oh, it's you," said Baby Jesus.

"Yes, of course, dear. Who did you think? Oh, sweetheart, I'm so delighted to see you. It's been so long. Did you like your school? Were you happy there? Did you make a lot of friends?"

"I suppose so."

"You're *looking* so good, dear. I wish so much I could be there beside you. I'd pick you up and give you such a *squeeze*."

"Would you?" he asked.

"Yes, and then I'd take you to the best restaurant on Medea, and we'd have a lovely celebration to welcome you back home. Just the two of us. Would you like that?"

He shook his head.

She smiled. The school had not, after all, reformed him out of recognition.

"What *would* you like then?"

He shrugged his shoulders. "Nothing I can think of."

"Is something wrong?"

Baby Jesus regarded his mother coldly.

"If there is, don't you think you should try and talk about it? Maybe I can help you."

"No." He shook his head more emphatically. "You couldn't."

"Did something happen at the academy?"

"The academy?" he repeated scornfully. "*What* academy?" She deflected the question with a self-defensive smile.

"There *isn't* any academy. It doesn't exist. *I* don't exist. Nothing exists. Except maybe you. And I don't think you exist either. I hope you don't."

"Oh, Baby Jesus, darling—who *ever* told you such a thing?"

"*All* the other kids knew, all of them. And it's true, isn't it? We're just a lot of tapes spinning around inside some old computer. Aren't we? *Aren't* we?"

"No! No, you're my son. You know that."

"And that's why my father went away. Because *he* knew that's all he was. He was a grown-up, so it didn't take him long to figure out."

"Where is Octave, Baby Jesus? I'd like to talk with her a moment."

"She doesn't exist either."

"Why don't we let her decide that for herself? Now where is she?"

"You want to see?" Baby Jesus trundled the simulated receiver (his image on the screen swayed realistically) into the simulated houseboat. Octave was lying on the floor in a perfect ellipse of bright red blood.

"You've killed her." Somehow she knew Octave, even a simulated Octave, would not have had the courage to kill herself.

He nodded. "She asked me to." He pointed to a blood-stained bread knife lying on the kitchen table. "With that. She said she knew, when I told her, she was just the same as me. She knew she wasn't real."

"But she was real, and so are you. So is everything. Just look around you. Touch the bowl on the table."

"*You* touch it."

Mrs. Manresa switched off the simulator.

The Faith was doing terrible things to her system. She believed in Baby Jesus. She knew he was real. She had the evidence of her senses and the testimony of her heart. At the same time she knew he was only a simulation.

She advanced the tape four hours, and then, thinking that might not be long enough, another four hours.

No one answered her buzz.

She knew she'd been defeated. With a last regretful look at the white dots flickering on the simulator's screen, she locked the keyboard in the ALL position and pushed ERASE. With the pressure of a fingertip she murdered Baby Jesus.

I'm part of the last generation to have grown up largely outside the influence of television. By the time my family had moved within broadcast range, my twig was bent in other directions. In '57 I left the nest with a rooted elitist contempt for the boob tube, and I resisted owning one till the summer of '70, when I had to spend a month on my back convalescing from an operation. By the time I was back among the living I had developed an incurable addiction to the Evening News.

What I like about the Evening News is what responsible critics chiefly complain of—the way it turns everything it touches into entertainment. The Vietnam War, Watergate, or, this weekend, the incredible fire at the MGM Hotel in Las Vegas. Eventually, no doubt, Hollywood will add the needful trimmings to create a totally vicarious, wide-screen version: Al Pacino as the Mafioso who sneers away the demand for smoke detectors in every room; the scene where Helen Hayes loses her Social Security check in a slot machine (but later escapes with her life); the scene where the smoke comes curling with lyric vengeance under the door of the aforesaid comatose Mafioso; the last big Bingo winner's last hurrah before the fireball whooshes through the casino. A wonderful story, and all of it implicit, seedlike, in the Evening News.

The hard thing to bear in mind about the Evening News is the way it can impinge, sometimes, on our daily lives. The way, sometimes, it's real.

The Apartment
Next to the War

6-G, being a corner apartment in a ziggurat, had a terrace that measured fully twenty feet square. That, along with the view over the park, was what finally tipped the balance, even though at the time the rent was a little out of our category. It was a nice building, but not as nice as most of its neighbors, having gone up at a time when architects were lowering ceilings and reducing frills in general. There was myself and Dorcas, Betsy and Bill, and Dorcas's sister Rosemary. Later, for a while, Rosemary's boyfriend Gene moved in with us. Not exactly your average nuclear family, and if I add that we never really got in each other's hair you can begin to get an idea of the size of the place, and of the rent.

For a long time we didn't suspect anything unusual about 6-H. Sometimes we'd pound on the walls and yell things like, "Hey, pipe down in there!" But as our yelling never got any results, we learned not to bother. Anyhow, it never became so noisy you couldn't ignore it, so we ignored it. By comparison to a pianist friend of ours downtown, whose basement apartment abutted a printing press, we considered ourselves fairly lucky.

How we did find out at last who, or rather what, we were living next to was when one day Dorcas forgot her keys at home and had to wait in the hallway with her shopping bags till I got home from work. Two medics came out of 6-H with a casualty laid out on a stretcher, all bleeding and groaning, and went off without shutting the door so that it latched. Gradually it swung open until Dorcas could see the whole length of the apartment. There was a skirmish going on. She watched until she was too upset to watch any more, then went down and waited in the lobby, which is what she should have done in the first place, though I didn't say so, as Dorcas was half sick about what she'd seen and wouldn't have let me get a word in edgewise.

After that we were more careful coming out of the elevator, never being quite sure that the fighting might not spill over into the hall. For a time I started following the news a little more closely, trying to understand the issues involved, how it had all begun, etc., but by then the war had gone on so long and got so complicated that nothing you read ever made it make any more sense.

Dorcas, after that first eyeful, just looked the other way, and eventually, without ever meaning to, so did I. Wars aren't really very interesting, I think, unless you're a participant. They are also, if I may be permitted to generalize, very impersonal. That was our experience anyhow. We never got to know anyone from 6-H as individuals, though after a while, of course, we would recognize them going in and out of the building. They were all too much caught up in being part of their war and didn't have time or the inclination to be neighborly. A 'Hello' sometimes in the elevator, and that would be it. Actually, if you stop to consider, what's wrong with impersonality? In an urban environment, with everyone shoulder to shoulder with everyone else, it can be an actual plus.

So, for a couple years, it was live and let live with regard to apartment 6-H. Betsy went through a phase of horses (fortunately very brief) and then a phase of ballet. Bill disappeared into a private wonderland of electronic components, and we started worrying, quite prematurely, whether we had a genius on our hands. Dorcas gave up analysis and started reading Walter Scott. We had a week in Aruba, a week in the Catskills with the kids, another week in Aruba, and then Aruba once again. Aruba's lovely. Anyhow, two years.

Rosemary, meanwhile, had met Gene through the friend of a friend, and after a suitable period of looking before leaping, he moved in with Rosemary and, ipso facto, with us. Gene had good looks, good manners, and a good job at an airline ticket counter (which partly explains Aruba) and a disposition that allowed him to accept his good luck and enjoy it. Considering his age (twenty-three), that is rare good fortune indeed. Till I hit thirty-five I never knew what equanimity was. In short, the last person in the world you'd expect to become a fanatic.

Maybe it was nothing more than the fact that Rosemary's room was flush with 6-H (as were the living room and the larger of the baths), and so the sound of the war was more audible in there during the night. Whatever, Gene started to be interested, and from being interested he became concerned, and from concern he graduated to outrage and panic, until there was nothing he could talk about but casualty figures, and whether France should be selling its Sabres, and how one side was violating the Geneva Convention, and then how the other side was violating it too. It never became a matter, for Gene, of an Us and a Them, but that didn't prevent him from going on about it. Finally I told him, "Gene, goddamit, it isn't *our* war. If you've got something to complain about, all you have to do is go down the hall and complain to the people who are fighting it."

To make a long story short, that's what he did, and the result was that a week later there was a knock on the door, and when we looked out through the peephole there were the two medics Dorcas had seen before, only this time it was Gene laid out on the stretcher, bleeding and groaning. He'd had his stomach torn apart by shrapnel during an attack on an anti-aircraft emplacement. It was a lucky thing, really, that he wasn't killed.

A month later he moved out. Though he claimed the war had had nothing to do with his leaving, that it was strictly a matter between himself and Rosemary, I have always had my doubts as to that.

After Gene's accident the whole neighborhood seemed to fall to pieces all at once. It used to be you couldn't go into the park at night. Now, with all the refugees, you couldn't go there in broad daylight. Obviously it wasn't just in 6-H that the war was going on. It had taken over half the building. The regular tenants protested, with the usual result—zero. Naturally, no one dared to go up to the people fighting the war and say, "Hey, what's this all about?" You could read in the papers what happened to the foolhardy few who tried that.

The last straw came this past November, right on top of the Energy Crisis. The Tenants Against the War had been driven to the extremity of pinning up a petition outside the elevators asking for a ceasefire. That was in the morning. When I got home from work that night, the lobby had been gutted. Lamps busted, sofas shredded, the big mirror smashed. Obscenities scrawled all over the wallpaper mural. The brass fittings stripped off everything. Not one elevator left in working order. Going up to our floor, I passed four bodies they'd just left lying on the stairs.

"Thank God," Dorcas said, when I came in the door. "Oh, thank God we're all alive!" Then she became completely hysterical.

The management was unusually prompt about putting the building back into shape, but that was it for us. We did what we had always told ourselves we wouldn't do. We moved to the suburbs. Which are not, I've since discovered, all that bad.

Time again to turn down the lights. Here is horror story number two. I tip my fright-wig this time not to Poe, but to Hollywood and its decade-long pact with the devil. Actually, I never really got off on the movies that made the biggest diabolic splash. Despite some fine interiors, *Rosemary's Baby* didn't chill my blood or tingle my spine. *The Exorcist,* though it tried its damnedest, seemed silly, while *The Omen* was unremittingly dumb. (Dumb, in my private lexicon, is several degrees worse than silly.)

Anyhow here is my contribution to the genre. With Sissy Spacek in the starring role, I think it could be genuinely nasty, though if it's to achieve feature length, the incidents in the Baltimore part of the story would have to be spun out at greater length. But then, what else are screenwriters for? Possibly the ending would have to be a little more explicit. Though possibly not. Montage can do wonders, and there is plenty of stock footage that would fit.

The Foetus

The devil, as his familiars have many times revealed, cannot create. Creation is reserved to God and, in a lesser way, to Man. The devil imitates, negates, denies; he is the father only of lies. In this regard we may cite the case of Magdalena Hunziger of Wilmersdorf in the principality of Liegnitz in lower Silesia. Magdalena, having been discovered to be pregnant, was examined by a learned Dominican and declared that she believed herself to be carrying the devil's own child. Put to the rack, Magdalena—or rather the demon with whom she had had sexual congress—revealed that the sperm by which her child was conceived had been taken from the gibbeted body of a felon, which sperm the demon had introduced into Magdalena's womb by means of his own sterile genitals, which she described as extremely thin and cold. The infant so unnaturally conceived was burnt at the stake with its mother in the square before the Cathedral of St. John in Liegnitz on the 24th of February, 1386, for there is no doubt that such progeny, though not the children of Satan's body, are nevertheless fated to be his minions. Their only hope of salvation, according to the noted inquisitor, Nicholas Savin, who has written extensively on this and similar cases, is baptism followed immediately by death.

The following narrative traces a series of events in some respects similar to those referred to above, but taking place in our own time in the city of New York, one of Satan's favorite habitations—favored for its atheism and disbelief as much as for its sinfulness. The devil, like other celebrities of an infamous kind, is most comfortable where he is least likely to be recognized. There would be no examination on the rack for Agnes Brill, however; no auto-da-fé for her or her child; by the same token there could be no hope for her of winning free of the fiend's designs, which were, accordingly, formed on the largest possible scale. But of that in due course.

First a word concerning Agnes Brill's character and circumstances at the time of her original misfortune in the spring of 1969. To say only, as Richard Sullivan had said in his final leave-taking, that Agnes was a prickteaser scarcely does justice to Agnes's own distressful sense of her situation. Like many young women of the lower middle class, she was at once obsessed with sex and ignorant about it. She held on to her virginity as a timid investor would hold on to his portfolio of blue-chip stocks, and all the while her mind was filled with the shadows of imagined raptures, as that same investor might have dreamed of speculating in gold mines, wildcat oil rigs, or Broadway hits. She wanted quite desperately to get laid, and she resisted, just as desperately, every attempt. She was your average Irish-Catholic sexpot—half ripe tomato and, already at the age of twenty-four, half fading rose—one of those rare beauties of whom it could actually be said that her eyes were *not* her best feature, for her eyes, unless animated by a spark of calculation, were rather lackluster and tended, unless she were very careful, to squint.

Twenty-four and still, for all her careful preservation of

her technical virginity, not a prospect in sight, not a nibble on the hook. She might as well have lived in the Mohave Desert as here at the center of Western Civilization. What, she often wondered, was the use? At such times she liked to go into churches and kneel in prayer, so as to remind God of her grievances. It wasn't fair, certainly, that her well-hoarded virtue should have no better reward than a job at a watch importer's that paid a miserable $87.50 a week and a room that she had to share with two younger sisters.

At last, one April day in 1969, Agnes's prayers were answered, though not by God. She had gone on her lunch hour into the Franciscan church of Christ the King on East 37th Street to present her case once again to God's deaf ear. There were grains of rice scattered across the rubber mat at the entrance, and the altar was heaped with the most extravagant floral arrangements money could buy. Agnes felt as bitter a disappointment as if she'd been jilted by the unknown and absent bridegroom. She walked down the aisle to the flower-decked altar in a state of indignation and bleak despair. Only as she reached the first pew did she realize that she was not alone in the church. There was a priest standing in the shadowed recess of a side-altar devoted to the adoration of the Infant of Prague. He was watching her, and Agnes, accordingly, knelt down on the padded kneeler, folded her hands, and began to recite Hail Marys. The priest continued to watch her, and she continued to pray. There was something peculiar about him, she could not have said what.

He approached her. She knew somehow that he was not just crossing to the other side of the church. She felt uneasy, but he was, after all, a priest. She hoped he wouldn't ask her if she wanted to go to confession, since she was in a state of mortal sin. In addition to sins of impurity, she had done quite a lot of shoplifting on her lunch hours, to the degree that she didn't see how she would ever be able to make restitution to the stores she had plundered. Indeed, she had no intention of doing so. No one can dress decently on a take-home of $62.59. But a priest would not have understood that.

He stopped in front of her.

"My child," he said.

She looked up at him. He was holding a knife. "Don't make any noise," he whispered. "If you resist me in any way I'll kill you."

Agnes did not resist.

After the priest had raped Agnes he rose from the wooden pew, straightened his cassock, and quickly and deftly slit his throat from side to side. In the weeks that followed, when Agnes would relive this scene in her dreams, the priest's suicide would precede her rape rather than follow it. In this transposition Agnes evidenced an instinctive understanding of demonology, for the devil is known to be able, for brief periods, to reanimate the corpses of the damned. In any case, it was only a matter of moments separating the two crimes of rape and of suicide, and they were hatched, so to speak, from a single submission to the sovereignty of evil. The Dominican who had examined Magdalena Hunziger would not have been in any doubt: the child conceived that day was the devil's own, as surely as Magdalena's little brat had been.

The diocesan clergy, naturally, were anxious to keep such a potentially troublesome scandal out of the press, and Agnes, no less naturally, was happy to cooperate. She was given a job at a much improved salary in the office of a major Catholic charity, and when there was no longer any doubt as to her being with child, she was transfered to the Baltimore office of the same organization, where, as the secretary of the director, she had her own office and a rent-free apartment in the same building. Her rape had begun to seem a kind of blessing in disguise. She continued to be troubled by dreams of a progressively more unwholesome nature, but these were not really so entirely unlike the dreams she had innocently enjoyed in the days of maidenhood. In any case, when she woke from them they ceased to have power over her, for she put them out of her mind. Agnes had the gift of forgetfulness.

She had become, possibly as a result of her pregnancy, more appetizing and lovelier than ever, and she had the wherewithal now, at her new salary, to make a larger capital investment in her charms. Lou Donovan, the director of the Baltimore office, began to take notice of his new employee, and Agnes, no longer under the onus of preserving her status as a virgin, was able to encourage his interest actively. This interest ripened into what they both agreed was love. Marriage became a real possibility.

Agnes had promised her benefactors in New York, as a condition of their benevolence, *not* to get an abortion, but that had been before the prospect of matrimony. Abortion was, of course, a deadly sin, but fornication was no less deadly, and she was fornicating, on the average, two or three times a week. At least an abortion, once it had been performed, would not have to be repeated and repeated like a hit record.

Agnes didn't struggle long against the temptation, but even so she was reluctant to commit herself to anything so drastically unpleasant as surgery. Though already in the fifth month of pregnancy, she decided to trust to the modern miracle of chemistry. Through a friend in New York who knew of her misfortune, she purchased an abortifacient, which came with the friend's personal endorsement. Agnes took three times the recommended dosage, and was ill for many days. She spent that time locked up in her rent-free apartment, suffering spasms of the most acute nausea, and hemorrhaging violently.

The foetus, however, remained in her womb, for the devil (who has an expert knowledge of medical anomalies, and great skill in the manipulation of basic genetic materials) contrived it so. The foetus was neither dead nor alive. It belonged to the demon who had so patiently tempted, corrupted, and finally possessed the pastor of Christ the King, and who had by this means brought it into being. And it shared that demon's power. It was evil, and its evil grew, though the warped tissues of which it was formed could not.

Agnes, when she had recovered and some further time had passed, believed she had accomplished her purpose. She told Lou she had had a miscarriage—to his considerable relief, for now he was able to introduce her to his family as his intended without the awkwardness of accounting for a pregnancy so far advanced.

They were married in April, on the anniversary of her rape. It was, everyone agreed, a lovely wedding. Agnes wore white. The church was full of Lou's relations and associates, among whom were numbered some of the mid-Atlantic states' highest-ranking leaders in the fields of sports, politics, and organized crime. They honeymooned in the Bahamas.

The devil looks after his own.

The foetus did not grow, but its evil grew, and the power of that evil.

Agnes, in her new role as Mrs. Donovan, paid little heed to the first premonitory signs—a cat that had to be put away for its recurring fits of ill temper; a maid caught stealing; a neighbor's child diagnosed as schizophrenic. But the foetus's most signal accomplishment in those early years was such that Agnes could not possibly have suspected its agency at work, and if she had she could only have been grateful. For its power was greatest when Agnes made love. Then, indeed, its shriveled brain could reach out and veritably touch the soul of whoever had trespassed so near its dark demesne—touch it and turn it towards its own hidden purposes.

Lou never understood why, even before his marriage, he found himself impotent with all other women. Nor did he greatly care. He lusted after his own wife with a passion he could only suppose testified to the sincerity of his conjugal love. (Though that worthy theologian Xystus Pithagoricus has witten: *Omnes ardentior amator propriae uxoris adulter est.* That is, Passionate love of a man's own wife is adultery.) It embarrassed him at times to be so infatuated with Agnes that he couldn't even be aroused by a beaver shot in a magazine, but it did allow him to give more of his attention and energy to his work. He had always skimmed off a proportion of the money that came in to the charity he directed, but now, under the influence of his unwittingly adopted (and unborn) son, he accomplished more daring peculations. With the funds embezzled in this way he branched out, aided by his many excellent connections, into other areas of endeavor. He showed himself to be resourceful, imaginative, and increasingly ruthless.

On the night he received his party's nomination to run for the office of governor of Maryland, Lou Donovan committed suicide. He had just had intercourse with Agnes in their suite at the hotel where the convention was being held. The foetus, now eight years old, reached into Lou's reeling mind and gave its last command to him. He rose from the bed on which Agnes lay in a daze of torpid satisfaction, went into the spacious bathroom, and returned with a straight-edged razor, which he'd bought on a sudden impulse only four days before. Then, as Agnes watched, quickly and deftly he slit his throat from side to side.

Agnes had no desire, once she had recovered from the shock of this second tragedy, to remain in Baltimore. After many indecisions she decided to move to Phoenix, in which city she had inherited considerable holdings in real estate. There, in a great modern glass box of a mansion filled with the perpetual purr of air conditioning, she lived a reclusive and, as she believed, luxurious life.

The foetus, sated for the time being, was content to wait for Agnes to recover. It needed her in the same way that she needed a car, as a means of transportation, the only one available. And it was wonderful, truly, how quickly Agnes was back in working order.

She could not understand—she never would—why Lou, at the very pinnacle of his success, should have behaved so vilely and unreasonably. The coroner's verdict had been temporary insanity, and Agnes, for lack of any better explanation, had to leave it at that. Perhaps men are just like that. Or else it might be that Lou's death was a punishment for the sin of her abortion. Agnes thought it punishment enough that their marriage had never been blessed with children. There was simply no fathoming it, but then there was so much one could never hope to understand. She decided to put it out of her mind, and with the foetus's help she succeeded.

Even so, she continued to lead a life apart. An obscure sense of foreboding made her fight shy of even the most innocuous proffers of friendship. When a neighbor invited her to play bridge, she declined, though in Baltimore bridge had been the mainstay of all her afternoons. She watched television, especially the quiz shows. She looked after the house. She went shopping. But she made no friends, and her evenings, especially the weeknights when TV was dull, were desolations of loneliness.

The foetus became impatient. It missed Lou quite as much as Agnes did—missed the exercise of its irresistible authority. It knew its strength now, but unless Agnes could be made to bestir herself, it could not exercise that strength.

At last it took the initiative. Agnes had got into the habit of driving out on the desert highways about Phoenix as a form of recreation. The car—a cream-colored behemoth of an Imperial—seemed to rush forward under the power of the music that blasted from its radio, and Agnes had nothing more to do than hold onto the wheel and be borne along in the swift current.

It was easy for the foetus to arrange an accident. Agnes simply wasn't conscious of the car that attempted to pass. The next thing she knew, the Imperial's back wheels were hanging over the shoulder of the road. The other car was demolished, its front end accordioned into a concrete culvert that passed under the highway. Amazingly, its driver wasn't hurt, though he was, predictably, quite angry. Agnes tried to be mollifying. She admitted her fault, and offered to take the man wherever he was going.

There was little point in standing about in that heat and arguing with her: he agreed.

Agnes ceded the driver's seat to the man she had so nearly killed. In those first raddled moments she hadn't taken in even the most salient features of his person, but now, caught up again by the resistless current of the empty highway, she had nothing to do but observe him. She thought him rather handsome in a weathered, southwestern way. He wore a conservative chalk-stripe suit, and his hair was clipped so close that the deep tan of his face could be seen through the iron-gray bristles of his crewcut. Something about him, a glint in his eye, reminded her of Lou. But then, most of the men she found herself admiring did remind her of Lou. He was about the age Lou would have been now, and had Lou's intent, committed way of handling a car. Though he would, for all that, turn to look at her from time to time, and in just the way that Lou had looked at her when he was beginning to court her.

The foetus exerted its full strength. It knew that the moment was at hand, the moment for which it had drudged at so many lesser evils, the moment of its consummation.

"I'm sorry about my cussing back there," the man said. "Sometimes my temper runs away with me."

"Oh, that's all right," said Agnes. "It *was* my fault."

She reached into her purse for her cigarettes. They were in a Cartier case with her initial on it in diamond chips. She took out a cigarette, then thought to offer one to him.

"Thanks, but I don't smoke. Gave it up two years ago."

"I should give it up too." She lit a cigarette, inhaled, and heaved a sigh. "But I can't seem to."

"On second thought," said the man, turning toward Agnes and smiling, "maybe I will. I'm still a little shaky."

Agnes lit his cigarette for him and handed it to him.

"My name is Agnes. Agnes Donovan."

"Mine's Sam. Sam Winchester."

She could tell, just from the way he said his name, that he was already thinking of how he could get into the sack with her.

They were stopped at the gate of the missile complex by a uniformed guard. Sam had a long argument with the guard about whether or not Agnes was to be allowed in. Except for the high fence and the guardhouse, there was nothing in sight but asphalt road winding across the dun desert sand.

When he returned to the car Sam appeared to have lost the argument. "Fucking hell," was all he would say. He backed the car around and returned to the main highway.

"You certainly do have a temper," said Agnes, approvingly.

"Oh, he was right—that's the hell of it. If he had let me in, I'd have had the bastard court-martialled. If you want tight security, you can't make exceptions."

"Really. It must be very secret, whatever's in there."

Sam laughed. "You better believe it."

"Do you work there?"

"It's my baby."

"Really." She wondered what it might be, this baby of his, and what kind of job he did there. Something important by the sound of it. "Are you in the Army?" she asked.

"Mm."

"I'm starting to feel like some kind of spy."

He turned to look at her and grinned. "Well, I'll tell you, Agnes—you'd be a good one."

"What do you mean?" she knew perfectly well what he meant.

"I mean you're a damned fine-looking woman."

"I'll bet you say that to all the spies you meet."

He laughed, and leaned sideways as far as the seatbelt would let him to kiss her cheek.

"You live in Phoenix?" he asked.

"At 1385 Crestwood Lawn Gardens."

In no time at all they had passed his wrecked car alongside the road. A pickup had pulled up beside it, and two teenagers were stripping it clean. Sam didn't even slow down to swear.

"Can I offer you a drink?" she asked, as he followed her into the living room. Even with all the curtains drawn, the house was flooded with the late afternoon light.

"Never touch the stuff."

"A Coca Cola, then?"

"Keep offering."

She turned round, once she'd finished unbuttoning her blouse, and let it slip from her shoulders. The way she did it, it was just like a movie, and the way he reacted, too.

They made love three times without stopping to catch their breaths. Then, when Sam was finally played out, they returned, both of them naked, to the living room. It was still daylight.

Sam sprawled on the couch. He had a body like the photographs of old statues, with every little ripple of muscle crisp and neat. Agnes felt pleased with herself, with Sam, with life in general. Everything was going to be all right again.

"What time is it?" Sam asked.

"Six on the dot. I hope you're not thinking of going already."

"No, but I'd like to see the Channel 6 News, if you don't mind."

Agnes was a bit taken aback, but, obligingly, she turned on the news. Though usually she never paid much attention to the news, since it was either depressing or didn't make any sense, this time, to be polite, she sat down at the other end of the sofa from Sam and pretended to watch it while she smoked a cigarette. The president had said something about the economy, and a businessman didn't agree. A big strike was still going on somewhere, and then another announcer stood in front of a map of throbbing, garish colors with arrows on it. At first Agnes thought it might be the weather and started to pay attention, but she ought to have known better. Phoenix didn't have weather, just sunshine. The map was of Asia, and the arrows were troops.

"Fucking hell," Sam said, when an ad for Exxon replaced the announcer's face. "God *damn!*"

"What's the matter?" Agnes asked.

"What's the matter! Weren't you listening to him? Don't you realize what they're *doing?*"

"Who?"

"The fucking Reds. They're taking over the whole goddamned continent, piece by piece. I'll tell you, though— they're not going to get away with it. They'll . . . Hey, what's wrong?"

"Excuse me just a minute, Sam." Agnes got up carefully from the couch, afraid she wouldn't be able to make it to the bathroom in time. "I'm feeling a bit . . . peculiar. I'll be right back."

After one good heave she felt all right again. Wiping the mess from the sides of the toilet, she remembered those days of nausea in Baltimore, when she had literally lived in the bathroom. For just a moment, sitting there on the couch by Sam, the pain had been as intense as back then. But now she was better.

She returned to the living room. Sam had turned off the TV and was lying on the sectional. He was getting a hard-on all over again.

Again she felt a spasm in her stomach. Not so much nausea this time, but more as though . . .

"That's strange." She stopped a few feet from the sectional.

"What's strange?" Sam asked, gazing, entranced, at the sliding shifting planes of flesh that, once again, seemed to be taking his mind over, seemed to become the whole of existence.

"I felt something . . ." She laid her hand on the smooth, slightly drooping undercurve of her stomach, just at the focus of Sam's fascination. ". . . here. It seemed to move."

Sam smiled. "Maybe you're pregnant."

"No, I don't think so. I wonder what it was."

It was the foetus, squirming with impatience and delight, as it scanned, in General Winchester's thrilled unconscious, a vision of magnificent, unstoppable flowering clouds, clouds of raw power that could, that would, that must, that will annihilate the world.

Once upon a time there was an old woman who wanted to get her pig home from the market, but the pig refused to cross a stile. So the old woman asked a dog to bite the pig by way of persuasion. But the dog refused. So she asked a stick to beat the dog, but the stick also wanted persuading. So she asked a fire, etc. I forget how the problem was finally solved, but a first cause was found, the dominoes all tumbled, and the old woman got home.

That synopsis in case you didn't know the story that gave this story its title and its pattern. When pattern takes over from plot, whether in poetry or prose, the results can be more surprising than a surprise that's been planned for right along. For instance, that most sinister of nursery rhymes, which I first encountered in William Gaddis's *The Recognitions* and which I can't resist passing along (with the excuse that it's at least a second cousin to the pattern traced in the stories above and below).

> There was a man of double deed
> Sowed his garden full of seed.
> When the seed began to grow,
> 'Twas like a garden full of snow;
> When the snow began to melt,
> 'Twas like a ship without a belt;
> When the ship began to sail,
> 'Twas like a bird without a tail;
> When the bird began to fly,
> 'Twas like an eagle in the sky;
> When the sky began to roar,
> 'Twas like a lion at the door;
> When the door began to crack,
> 'Twas like a stick across my back;
> When my back began to smart,
> 'Twas like a penknife in my heart;
> When my heart began to bleed,
> 'Twas death and death and death indeed.

The Fire Began to Burn the Stick, The Stick Began to Beat the Dog

It was neither the best nor the worst of times, and it certainly wasn't the French Revolution. After most things were legalized, America had moved in more or less the opposite direction, away from struggle and towards accommodation, toward what we generally think of as niceness. As the president put it in one of his poems, "It's where we've always been headed and it's where we've always been."

Of course the world is usually nice to presidents, so let us take as an example of the general drift to serenity Ormond Brown, a brevet lieutenant in New York City's Urban Reclamation Corps, and let us take him on the specimen morning of December 14, a Sunday. On second thought, the 15th would probably do better, since Ormond's Sundays, like most people's, are largely given over to spectator skills, and wouldn't show him in a light that is distinctive of the future's *new* niceness. Television, after all, is one of those things, like cold water or warm breezes, that's *always* made life bearable. It is fine, isn't it, to lie back and let yourself be lifted up into the roiling turbulence of yet another shattering story?

Such as (returning just briefly to the aforementioned Dec. 14) NBC's BARDS IN FEALTY, now in its third award-winning and ratings-busting year. This particular 90 minute segment (being lapped up in the lounge by Ormond and four other cadets) alternated between an account of poor mad John Clare in the Northampton Lunatic Asylum and poor mad Hölderlin locked up in his tower in Tübingen, with occasional glimpses of burnt-out, doddering Wordsworth pacing the hills of Patterdale, waiting for the old sublimity to make a farewell performance. . . .

Meanwhile, on Channel 5, unwatched by Ormond and his coterie but beloved and believed by millions of their fellow viewer-Americans, the wonderful Lawrence Welk did his utmost for Sominex and Geritol. Though these products no longer existed, due to a government crackdown eight years before, the National Endowment for the Arts, who funded the show, felt that these ads were an essential part of the Welk esthetic, and so the lovely names and sweet advertisements endured even when the products were defunct. Among the elderly throngs who followed the program's gently bouncing ball on this Sunday night was a nonogenarian named Mrs. Wasserman. This Mrs. Wasserman was in some distress, because her set wouldn't bring in Channel 5 unless she sat beside it and exerted a steady clockwise pressure on the channel selection dial. It may not sound like much, but Mrs. Wasserman found it fatiguing to both eyes and hand. A sense of unmerited injury mounted in her breast, and then, as Susan and Billy joined their voices in "Don't Sit Under the Apple Tree", that sense crystallized into an act of will, into a resolution: Tomorrow she was going to do something!

And so—moving forward again to the 15th—there was Mrs. Wasserman at her neighborhood welfare center, and there, at the same time was Ormond Brown, downtown to pick up his U.R.C. check and to do the rounds of the various community labor lounges where he advertised his specialty. Ormond was a kind of electronics bricoleur of middling competence and proportionally low rates, a trade he'd picked up in the Army and which he'd improved by the necessity of keeping his dorm's own TV functioning happily. Mrs. Wasserman punched out the code number of her need, the board lighted up with a bright red 47-D, and in a little while Ormond noticed that his number was flashing, and went up to the desk to offer his services.

Out in the lobby Mrs. Wasserman told Ormond her sad story, a story that could never be too often repeated. Oh, her wrist, and the strain on the eyes was worse, if that could be possible! Ormond was sympathetic, but business-like. It sounded like a simple replacement of the selector—a couple hours waiting at a parts window, and then fifteen minutes of actual work.

This diagnosis was confirmed at Mrs. Wasserman's apartment, where a giant plastic palm of a hand three feet in height projected from the living-room wall, as Ormond could not help but notice. They sat down on cushions under this palm to negotiate over a cup of what tasted to Ormond like plywood tea. Mrs. Wasserman wanted to pay by check, being of that generation. Ormond explained that he had no use for checks or even cash, since the I.R.S. seemed to have bugged every dollar bill you tried to spend. No, Ormond would only be interested in items that were strictly *hors de commerce*, which is French for *sub rosa*. Such as, he suggested, three ounces of grass? Mrs. Wasserman, who naturally had known all about the I.R.S. and the problems it could cause individuals, thought that three was rather steep. She pointed out that she'd have to pay forty dollars on top of Ormond's wages just for the new whachamacallit. They settled on two-point-four ounces, but the problem remained for Mrs. Wasserman, how was she going to get it?

The only real possibility was her downstairs neighbor, Ms. Horner, who had helped her through previous barterings in return for services rendered. Ms. Horner was an original, second-generation member of the famous New York School of Poetry, not an especially prominent member back then, but becoming more significant nowadays, thanks to sheer longevity. Her apartment was a little museum of vintage photo-offset magazine covers and snapshots of other famous-long-ago poets and poetesses. Ms. Horner kept her head above water (barely) by a combination of grantsmanship and re-publishing her old work in extremely limited, if very frequent, first editions. If she could have given readings or taught, she'd have done a lot better, of course, but alas she was an invalid, the rheumatic prisoner of 2½ rooms, which she shared with a family of very smelly cats and her ponderous life-support system, the mimeo machine.

Mrs. Wasserman, who was hyperkenetic for someone her age, did all of Ms. Horner's absolutely necessary errands into the outer world, and therein (in Ms. Horner's sense of debts never to be liquidated) lay the possibility of fixing the TV. They went down the busy stairs and knocked. Ormond was introduced (as "my young friend"), and Ms. Horner was propositioned. "Oh, I'm so sorry, Mrs. Wasserman, believe me, I would really like to help, but I just don't have any." She was able to extend this much hope: that she knew someone who very well *might* have some, and who, if he did, would probably be overjoyed to exchange some of his stash for . . . Ms. Horner rummaged in a stack of papers under her bed . . . for this first issue of *Thtruggle,* a West Coast gay socialist magazine from 1976. In fact, Ms. Horner thought an asking price of two-point-four was something less than such a relic was worth, and so she stipulated that Ormond or Mrs. Wasserman, whichever one did the bargaining, should also bring back a gallon of yogurt, since the same party made very good yogurt in his hotel room. It was a kind of cottage industry.

Ormond and Mrs. Wasserman set off together for Hotel Dixie, where this party lived. Strictly speaking, Ormond didn't have to trail along, but he had nothing better to do, and besides, he was beginning to be interested in the microcosm of living literature into which he'd stumbled. At the Dixie, when they asked for the party by name (Marvin Maloney, Room 1423), the desk clerk said he was sorry but the gentleman wasn't answering. He really did seem sorry, too. He was a nice desk clerk.

While they waited in the lounge, Mrs. Wasserman watched the various people screwing in the various rooms, over the hotel's closed-circuit TV. It felt good just to see a screen you didn't have to hold in focus by brute force, and then, too, it was always nice to see young people fucking. As one of the couples flashed by, the desk clerk said he thought that was the boy they were looking for. It was reassuring, at least, to know he was in the hotel.

Ormond, meanwhile, was leafing through *Thtruggle,* even reading bits of it, which for Ormond was a change of pace, since generally he considered himself post-literate. It was odd and rather awful to think of the past as something real that people had once actually been stuck in, like mafiosi in cement or knights locked into suits of armor. In the barbarous past where, according to *Thtruggle,* you could be

arrested for making out in the privacy of a filling station
toilet in Berkeley, California, where you could be thrown
into prison for five years for possessing an ounce of grass,
where apparently the only *legal* thing you could do was get
married and read books. (A lot of which got scathing reviews
in the back pages.) Guilt? Anxiety? Guilt was no stranger
to Ormond (who once had murdered a friend of his, in one
of his moments of insensate rage), but still, think of feeling
guilty for something you needed each and every day, like
dope or sex or dinner? How did they bear it, those people
of the past?

The other peculiar thing about them, to Ormond's way
of thinking, was the way they seemed to assume that the
government was their enemy. It went beyond just complaining about taxes and such to a point of downright
disloyalty that Ormond found a little shocking. He was, if
not exactly a patriot, then an average good citizen. He'd
done basic training in Arizona, fought in Colombia, and
learned TV repair at West Point, no longer the elitist preserve of the privileged few. Last election he'd helped to
re-elect Senator Calley. He was proud of his pink-and-
black Reclamation Corps uniform, and enjoyed marching
in his neighborhood parades. In short, without actually
loving his country, he saw no reason to bite the hand that
wrote his bi-monthly checks, certainly not so long as that
hand did not molest him otherwise. He would admit, to
some of his more left-leaning friends, that there were some
government policies that he didn't entirely agree with,
such as nuking Buenos Aires, but such decisions were best
left in the hands of the president, who, whatever you
might think of his ideas, you had to admire for his style.
And anyhow, he was probably right when, in another poem,
he'd called the Argentine expedition "a forced march to the
grocery store."

All trains of thought must finally pull into the station,
even marathons like this one. Ormond gradually surfaced
from the moldy magazine, becoming aware that he was
under surveillance. By, as it happened, Marvin Maloney.
Maloney, in the tight white jeans of the U.S. Coast Guard,
was back at work cruising the johns in the Dixie's lounge,
looking for his next meal or movie ticket. He seemed to

have set his hopes on Ormond, but before Ormond could begin to consider the case on its merits Mrs. Wasserman had recognized Maloney from the TV. She asked him if that's who he was, and he was.

Once again business was discussed. Maloney was, as expected, greedy for Volume One, Number One, the asking-price of which he allowed to be more than fair. However, and sad to say, he didn't have any grass, none at all. Pointing out that December has always been a dry month for dope, he tried to persuade Ormond to settle for seven gallons of yogurt.

Ormond, having no idea where he could unload so much yogurt, stuck by his original demand, two-point-four ounces.

"And," Mrs. Wasserman insisted, sticking on her own little surtax, "a gallon and a half of yogurt."

Maloney didn't even argue the point. Obviously, he had overproduced. "Alright," Maloney agreed, "there's one place I might score. Perhaps."

The quest continued. While Mrs. Wasserman, in possession of the heirloom magazine, waited in the lounge, Maloney and Ormond set off for the corner of 57th and 5th, where they found the fellow Maloney was after, a decrepit Santa Claus, identical to at least a dozen others on that corner, ringing his bell for contributions. Not, as Santas rang their bells in the past, ringing it for some anonymous, doubtful charity, but proudly and loudly for himself. Since it was almost Xmas, and since the economy had been spiraling upwards that year, Santa's pot was brimming over, and among the various offerings there was indeed the requisite quantity to fix Mrs. Wasserman's TV.

There was a catch. Santa affected to think he might get twofers. Ormond could have shat. He explained politely as possible that he was straight as Gibraltar and that, in any case, he would never think of making it with a Santa. Santa wheedled, and Ormond became ungracious. The deal was on the brink of falling through, but Maloney cajoled and felt up the old geezer, and at last Santa was won over.

A time was fixed for Santa to rendezvous at the Dixie, and Maloney got the grass. He was elated: that first issue of *Thtruggle* would be worth a box of mints from the right dealer. Some day, he promised himself, he'd have his own catalogue, and life would be simpler. Meanwhile he was learning the trade.

Arriving back at the Dixie, they found Mrs. Wasserman reading the Tarot for one of Maloney's colleagues. This, it turned out, was the lady's profession, along with horoscopes and palmistry, and that explained the giant plastic palm in her living room.

The grass and the magazine changed hands, and Maloney, after a bit of small talk, said good-bye. Ormond and Mrs. Wasserman made their way to Sam Goody's. The line only took fifty minutes.

Two hours later, Channel 5 was coming in as if the set had just been born. Mrs. Wasserman was so pleased that she offered to share her yogurt with Ormond. He accepted.

No money had changed hands, and so no crime had been committed. Everything was strictly *hors de commerce*, and everyone got what he wanted. As the President had put it in one of his very earliest poems, "Aren't you glad it's legal at last to be alive?"

Liberals and libertarians tend to take a dim view of the Authorities' abiding need to regulate the pleasures of those who are not Authorities. Throughout the '70's drugs were the central symbolic focus of the regulatory impulse, but there are few pleasures so innocent that they haven't been interdicted sometime or somewhere. The statute books are full of rules governing who may have sex with whom. The consumption of alcohol has inspired almost as many laws. Jews and Moslems are denied the pleasures of pork and bacon, and Weight Watchers gather periodically to ritually torment those members who've exceeded their caloric limits. Name a pleasure, and somewhere there is certain to be an organization devoted to its rationing or extirpation.

However debatable any particular regulation, the regulators have a powerful argument for the principle of regulation in the example of those laboratory rats who, given a choice between food and direct stimulation of their brains' pleasure centers, choose the pleasure center every time, until they've starved to death. (If only all city sewers could be supplied with such devices, the problem of pest control could be solved in a single deliriously happy generation!) Are people, the regulators might ask, different in this respect from rats?

So long as there are regulators to ask that question, so long shall we be able to answer: Yes, *people* are regulated.

At the Pleasure Center

Years ago the pleasure center had been something monumental and beside the point. A parking lot, or maybe a theater. In any case, the ceiling was high and the floor tilted. If Gloria had been a perfect sphere, she could have rolled from Room 348 to the exit. In fact, she was thin and angular, and walking served her purpose just as well. Most of the door-plates indicated either VACANT or IN USE. When you need a policeman he's never there.

Except in one cubicle, where a very young, very homely cop chewed on a cud of gum. Their eyes tangled and she thought—*No, not this one*. She was not the slave of passion: she could wait. Appetite would be her sauce. Hungrily, she imagined the ideal policeman: fortyish, graying at the temples and wilting at the edges of his spirit; friendly, wistful, uncomprehending, and willing (above all) to accommodate her needs.

The same rooms were still empty or being used, so on her second go-round she went into 111, where in the meantime he'd got everything ready. She signed his form, he punched her card, she lifted the quiff of hair that covered the socket in her forehead. Without teasing or delay, he unzipped his pocket, took out the plug, connected it to an outlet, and plugged her in. It almost went too fast.

He went to the wall where the panoply of dials on the console trembled in sympathy with her psyche's least electric twitter, and his finger paused above the button—paused, while their eyes skirmished once again. There was just time enough to wonder if he wanted her to beg.

Then he pressed the button.

From the intrinsic center of her being a seed of light swelled into endless flowering. Cerise and lovely, leaf after leaf of radioactive lettuce wrapped themselves around the grateful lobes of her brain. Bells rang. Her cells absorbed a perfect nectar. The swift, elusive meaning of all existence slowed, stopped, and glowed with a yummy clarity. Heaven!

Then it stopped.

"How was that?" he asked, after a just barely decent interval.

"Oh, wonderful."

"Yeah?"

"Really, really terrific."

"What did you see?"

"It's not like seeing, exactly. It's hard to describe."

She was disconnected now. The policeman was wrapping the cord around the three-pronged plug. He no longer seemed homely or hostile. She could see him perishing in his own humanity, a Prometheus self-immolated and self-consumed, and she wanted to reach forward and undo the tight little black bow tie that was strangling him.

"Do you mind if I ask you a question?"

"Ask," he said.

"Why do you do this? I mean, it should be clear why *we're* here. But what does it feel like for you?"

"I don't know."

"Just a job like any other?" she suggested.

"There's a lot of other jobs I don't think I'd care for. What do *you* do?"

"Programmer."

"You like that?"

She shrugged one bony shoulder. "I like *this*."

He laughed. "I'll tell you, Dorabella, there's one part I like."

"Gloria," she corrected.

"Dorabella," he insisted, with a shift down the spectrum toward those wave-lengths she first remembered. "Can you guess what part that is?"

"Now? Us, here, talking?"

"No. I don't usually care to talk. Tonight's the exception. Some guys do, but for me what I like is the same, really, as for you. It's when I'm holding down the button. I like to see what happens in your face."

"What happens?"

"I don't know. Something disappears."

"Is it like flushing a toilet?"

He laughed again. "You said it, lady, not me."

"Don't you ever wonder what it feels like for ordinary people?"

"I can guess." He pulled down the steel shutters over the console.

"You can't."

He turned off the lights.

"Where are you going?"

"It's ten o'clock. I'm off duty."

She followed him down the tilting corridor, linked to him by the hopeless desire that he might be corruptible. It was her dream that some day, somewhere, she would meet a policeman who would yield her more than what she was allotted by her card; who would have his own power sources (a battery?); and who would never take his finger from the button, who would hold it down forever. But she could not say this to him, and in any case there was no policeman so guileless that he didn't understand this.

"Will I see you tomorrow?" she asked him as they neared the exit. It was as far as she could venture toward the dream.

"If you come back to the same room, you will."

"One more question?"

His feet were already planted on the mat that opened the door. "Shoot."

"When you *imagine* what it's like, what do you imagine?"

"Oh, colors, music. That sort of thing."

"And you don't want it for yourself?"

"I'm not wired."

"You could be."

"So? You could have yours ripped out."

She cringed. "No way!"

"That's just how I look at it, Dorabella. I got what I need. My hand is on the button, I make you jump—that's all right."

"I don't understand you."

"If you did, Dorabella ... if you did, you might not come back tomorrow night." He grinned, and the streetlight underlined every lesson scrawled in the young, painful flesh.

He strode out into the street, where she could not follow him. He reached the bus stop at the same moment the bus did. When the bus pulled away he was gone.

Gloria walked to the corner and waited for the green light.

144

Herewith, my rendition of one of the great daydreams. Suddenly you're not yourself. Suddenly, instead, you're Someone Else. Faust is a youth. The Prince is a Pauper, and vice versa. Wife suits up and goes to the office, while hubby in a frilly apron wreaks havoc in the kitchen. The moral of the story is usually that it isn't as easy as it seems to take over Someone Else's role. But I don't think that's quite the moral of this story. Indeed, does a daydream have to have a moral? So long as you can keep from waking up, a daydream is for having fun. Forget all that stuff about responsibilities beginning in dreams. In *some* dreams you leave your responsibilities at the door.

The Grown-Up

Always we awake to our metamorphosed condition, to the awareness that the strange body in the bed is our own. Women awake and discover, after centuries of dreaming, that they are men. Worms awaken into birds, and music bursts from their astonished throats. An elderly business-man awakes and knows himself to be a plane tree: his leaves reach for the light and swell with growth. Often the amazement is too much 'to bear, and our awakening is brief. We slip back into being the rudimentary creatures that we were. We become less, and sleep resumes its old sovereignty, until once more, without warning, we awaken.

So it was when Francis awoke, one morning in July. He had gone to bed a ten-year-old; he woke twenty-six years older. Even before his eyes were open the shock of the transformation had wiped out the particulars of his old identity. He was free, therefore, simply to glory in this enormous fulfillment: the mass of his arms, the breadth of his chest, his sheer immensity. He stood up. He stretched, and touched, with his fingertips, the plaster nubbles of the room's low ceiling. So big!

And there, in the mirror mounted to the closet door, was the proof of his transformation and its benediction. His, the moustache, the smile, the teeth. His, the legs and arms, the muscled neck, the . . . His mind, abashed, refused to name it, but it was his as well, with all the rest.

He thought: I must get dressed.

In clothes he was even more amazingly a grown-up. Tieing a tie had proved to be beyond him, but there was, in the same drawer as his socks, a single clip-on bow, white polka-dots on maroon.

And in the closet, on a shelf, a straw hat.

He clattered down the fire stairs, twenty flights, each flight a full clockwise rotation through the four points of the compass, and arrived in the lobby giddy and out of breath, but still exultant, like a painter on the day of *vernissage*. Here he was, for all the world to see!

An older man than himself, in the most magnificent of uniforms, approached. His heart poised at the edge of panic, but the man in the uniform was (though curious) entirely deferential.

"Good morning, Mr. Kellerman. Isn't the elevator working? It was just a moment ago."

"Oh. Yes, right. The elevator." He smiled.

His name was Mr. Kellerman!

There were mirrors all over the lobby, and as he made his way before them, he couldn't keep from grinning. The name—*his* name—repeated itself inside his head like the tune of a solemn but still pretty spirited march.

The man in the uniform slipped round him and opened the plate-glass door.

"Thank you," he thought to say.

The scalloped edge of the building's blue marquee brushed his hat as he walked beneath it. Walking along, he could see *over* the tops of the cars parked on the street. What a difference it made, being tall! His muscles all worked so much harder. He felt like Frankenstein, giant hands swinging like counterweights to the crashing of his feet. He flexed his thick fingers. On the middle finger of his right hand was a ring, a square black chunk of something encased in gold. Smash, crash, smash, crash, he crossed the street, passing a woman being wheeled in a wheelchair by another younger woman. He tipped his hat to them and said, "Good morning, ladies." He was thrilled by the resonance of the voice that boomed from his chest.

A grown-up . . .

One by one, he thought of all the dirty words he knew, but didn't say them aloud, even in a whisper. He *could* have, though, any time he wanted to. He could be a dirty old bum, if that's what he wanted. Was it? he wondered. Probably not.

At first the neighborhood had been nothing but tall brick apartment buildings, but now he was on a block of small businesses. In front of one store was a bench with newspapers on it. He wondered if they'd make any sense to him. They never had, before.

He picked up a paper and took it inside the store, which also sold candy and cigarettes. He must have been a foot taller than the boy behind the counter.

"How much is this?" he asked, holding up the paper.

The boy bent his head sideways, conveying, in some indefinable way, a sense of unfriendliness. "Quarter."

He reached into his back pocket, where he had had the foresight to place that most essential item of the clothes that grownups wear, his billfold. It was stuffed full of money, more than he could imagine spending all at once. He took out a dollar bill, handed it to the boy behind the counter, and waited for his change. The boy rang the register, took out three quarters, and handed them to him. A shiver went up and down inside his body. He felt as though he'd done something irrevocably adult.

There was a cafe further down the block, called Lenox Cafe, where he sat down at a table next to the front window. While he waited for the waitress, he read the newspaper's headline:

CARTER ARRIVES
AND ESTABLISHES
CONVENTION BASE

The Man Who Had No Idea

Aides Have All Preparations

Ready for a First Ballot

Nomination Wednesday

He read on a while longer, but it was all the same sort of thing and made no more sense than it ever had. He wasn't stupid—he knew what the words meant—but he really couldn't see why grown-ups ever got interested in the things newspapers wrote about. So, in fact, he *wasn't* a grown-up, completely.

He was and he wasn't. It was strange, but he didn't find it upsetting. After all, lots of things are strange.

When the waitress came from the back of the cafe, she said, "Hello, Frank."

"Oh. Hello there."

"Hello there, Ramona," she insisted.

"What?"

"My name: Ramona. Remember?"

"Oh, sure."

She smiled, in not a nice way. "What'll it be?"

"Uh." He knew he didn't like coffee. "How about a beer?"

"Schaeffer's. Miller's. Bud. Heineken."

"Heineken."

She raised an eyebrow, tightened and tilted the side of her mouth. "That be all?"

"Yes."

Now that he'd ordered, he realized he didn't want to stay in the cafe, where the waitress seemed to know him and he had to pretend to know her.

She flipped the pink order-book closed and put it in the pocket of her apron. Under the apron she was wearing a very short and shimmery black dress with a white collar, and under the dress tight stockings that made her legs look black and featureless. In some way he couldn't put his finger on, she seemed all wrong. Yet there wasn't anything that unusual about her. She looked like almost any other waitress. And very strange.

In fact, *all* the grown-ups he could see on the sidewalk outside the restaurant looked strange. Uncomfortable and dazed, as though, like him, they were all having to *pretend* to be grown-ups and didn't enjoy it. Himself, he loved it. Loved *being* a grown-up, that is. The pretending wasn't especially fun. He hadn't considered that there might be people who knew him, knew his name and maybe more important things, like where he worked. Assuming that he already had some kind of job, the way he already had a name.

Mr. Kellerman. It seemed a reasonable enough name. Mr.—he looked inside the wallet again—Francis Kellerman. There it was, spelled out a dozen times: on his Master-Charge card, and on similar cards for different stores; on his Social Security card; on a card that said he was a member of something; and, yes, on a driver's license!

The waitress, Ramona, came back with a bottle of beer and a glass. She poured some of the beer into the glass and set it down in front of him.

"Thank you, Ramona," he said. "Here—" taking it from the billfold. "—is a dollar."

She took the dollar and gave him a funny look. He decided he must have said the wrong thing.

"Keep the change," he suggested.

"Prick," she said flatly, and walked to the back of the cafe.

He tasted the beer, but he couldn't swallow any. He spit a mouthful of it back into the glass.

"Blaigh!" he said, loud enough for Ramona to hear, and left the restaurant, leaving the worthless newspaper behind. As soon as he was out the door he got the giggles, and couldn't stop till he was halfway back to the apartment building where Mr. Francis Kellerman lived.

When he got there, though, he couldn't get in. The big glass door was locked and there was no one in the lobby, so knocking wasn't any help. He knocked anyhow. No one came. If he'd had a set of keys . . . But (he looked in all his pockets) he didn't. He'd forgotten that grown-ups always use keys.

Finally a lady came along who lived in the building, and

she let him in. This time he used the elevator. He'd forgotten the apartment number, but he knew where it was along the hall.

The door was open (the way he'd left it probably), which was good, and someone was inside, which wasn't. A bald man with sunglasses was putting things into a suitcase spread open on the unmade bed.

"Hey!" Francis said.

The man looked up. He was holding stereo earphones.

"Mister, you're in the wrong apartment." What had begun as a cautious rebuke ended up as out-and-out anger. The man was a burglar—he was robbing his apartment!

The man backed away toward the kitchen. The spiraling wire of the earphones followed, bobbling.

"Hey, you better get out of here. Right now!" His voice boomed incredibly. "Do you hear me—right *now*!"

The man dropped the earphones and ducked through the open door of the kitchen. Francis could hear him rummaging around in the silverware. Looking (Francis realized with alarm) for a knife.

He acted quickly. Fighting, after all, is still a natural accomplishment for most boys his age. He unplugged a floor lamp, upended it, and stood poised beside the kitchen door. When the man came out, armed with a butcher knife, Francis let him have it. The lamp base raised a large lump on the man's bald head, but he hadn't been cut or, fortunately, killed. Francis didn't know what he'd have done with a dead body, but this one, which was only unconscious, was no problem. He dragged it out to the stairwell (where there was a *second* suitcase, packed and ready to go) and left it, the body, on the landing. He brought the suitcase back to his apartment. Then, feeling vengeful and mischievous, he went back, undressed the burglar (even took his underpants), and threw all the clothes down the incinerator chute. Serves him right, he thought.

This time when he left the apartment he didn't forget to take his keys and to lock the door behind him.

"That son of a bitch," he said aloud, when he was alone in the elevator. "Trying to steal my things. *Son* of a bitch." But he was basically over feeling upset or angry or anything but tickled over the idea of the burglar waking up without his clothes. What would he think? What could he do?

Returning to the breezy freedom of the street, where he could go in any direction he wanted, and where no one could tell him what to do or what not to, he began to realize how totally lucky he was, something that most of the other grown-ups around didn't seem to understand at all as clearly. He would go into stores and buy something, anything at all, just for the fun of spending his money. He bought flowers in a flower shop, and a book called *Reassessments*. He bought a bottle of perfume, an electric popcorn popper, another ring (for his left hand), a telephone that you could see the insides of, a $150 backgammon set (after the salesman had explained the basic rules), and twenty Marvel comic books. Which was about as much, even with a shopping bag, as he could easily lug around.

Then, as he was going past a church, it occurred to him that God must be behind the whole thing that was happening to him. It was a Catholic church. He didn't know if he were a Catholic, or what, but it seemed logical that his not knowing that was as much God's doing as his, so it ought not to matter if he prayed here rather than some other church. The important thing was to stay on God's good side.

There was no one else inside, so he went right up to the front and knelt down on one of the padded kneelers and started praying. First he thanked God for having made him a grown-up, then asked, with a good deal of feeling, not to be changed back. After that there didn't seem to be much else to say, since he didn't have friends or relatives to ask favors for, or enterprises to be concerned about. He did remember to ask to be forgiven for the dirty trick he'd played on the burglar, but he wondered if God would really have been angry with him for that, since after all he *was* a burglar. Before he left he unwrapped the flowers and put them in a vase on the altar. Beside the vase he placed the copy of *Reassessments*. Even though he wasn't sure that this was exactly the right offering, it seemed more appropriate than perfume or a popcorn popper or his other purchases (which were all things, moreover, that he'd like to have for himself). Anyhow, God would like the flowers. There were two dozen of them, and they were the most expensive kind they'd had in the shop.

He was driving the car he'd rented at Hertz Rent-a-Car, a bright red '76 Dodge Charger, driving it slowly and carefully on the least busy streets he'd been able to find. Ten blocks on a one-way street going north, then a right, and another right, and then ten blocks in the other direction. You only had to push the button marked Drive, and steer. It was easy. Around and around, in and out of traffic. It was easy, but it wasn't as much fun as he'd thought it would be beforehand, so after only an hour of practice, he pulled up in front of an Army Surplus Store into a space that didn't require a lot of complicated parking.

While he was locking the door, one of the girls who'd been leaning against the store-window came over and asked him if he wanted to score.

"Hey, Cowboy," she said, "you want to score?"

She'd called him Cowboy, because of the hat and the boots he was wearing, which he'd bought just after he'd come out of the church that afternoon.

"What?" he said.

She pushed her tangly red hair back from her eyes. "Do you want to fuck?"

He was so astonished he couldn't think what to say. But, really, why should he be surprised? He was a grown-up, and this was one of the most basic things that grown-ups did. So why not?

"Why not," he said.

"It's twenty bucks," she said. She was able to talk without quite closing her mouth entirely.

"Fine," he said.

Her mouth opened a little wider, and her tongue moved forward over her lower teeth, retracted, and came forward again. It seemed strange, but friendly even so.

"Where do we go?" he asked.

"You don't want to use the car?"

"Oh. Right." He unlocked the door, and they got in. "Now what?"

She told him where to drive, which was to a kind of parking lot beside a river. On two sides were broad brick buildings without windows. On the way here he'd gone through a red light and nearly run down a pedestrian. The girl had only laughed. She didn't seem at all concerned about his driving, which was reassuring.

When they were in the parking lot, she opened up his trousers and reached inside his underpants to take hold of his thing. He wondered if he weren't supposed to be doing the same to her. He knew girls didn't have anything there but a crack. The idea was for the man to get his thing inside the woman's crack, and then to move around until some kind of juice squirted out. He started looking for buttons or a zipper on her shorts.

She wiggled around and in no time her shorts were on the floor of the car.

He bent forward so he could see where her crack was. She spread her legs helpfully. "You like that?" she asked.

"I guess so." Then, because that didn't seem adequate, or even polite, "Sure." But it lacked conviction.

She took hold of his thing again and started tugging at it. It felt quite satisfying, like scratching poison ivy, but somehow it didn't seem right that he should be making love to this girl who didn't know the first thing about him. She seemed so nice, and was trying so hard.

"I believe in being honest," he announced.

"Oh boy." She let go of his thing and pushed back her hair. "Here we go. What is it?"

"You probably won't believe this," he began tentatively, "but I think I should tell you anyhow. I've got a kind of . . . problem, I guess you'd say."

"Yeah? What's that?"

"I'm only ten years old."

"No kidding. Ten years old."

"I said you wouldn't believe it, but it's true. This morning when I woke up I had this grown-up body, but my head, inside, is only ten years old."

"I believe it."

"You do?" He couldn't tell from her tone of voice if that was true, but she seemed no less friendly than before. "It doesn't bother you?"

"Listen, Cowboy, your age doesn't matter, not to me. What the hell—*I'm* ten too."

"You are? Really?"

"Sure. You could say we all are. In a way. You know?"

"No. I mean . . ."

"Look here, in my eyes." He looked in her eyes. "You see?"

"What am I supposed to be seeing?"

"Me, age ten."

"You don't *seem* any different, or— Oh."

"You saw."

"Maybe. But it wasn't . . . what I thought it would be."

"How's it different?"

"Sadder, I guess. If that's what you meant I should be seeing. I mean . . . I mean it isn't as though your age is *printed* there, like on a driver's license."

"Have you *got* a driver's license?" she asked.

"Oh, yeah. They wouldn't let me have this car till I showed it to them."

"Listen, Cowboy, time flies. You want to do something, or don't you?"

"Sure." He braced his mind against the words, and said them: "I'd like to fuck you."

"Then come here."

He was already beside her, but she scrunched round into a different position and made him do the same.

"Comfortable?" she asked.

"Fine. Sure."

"Okay. Now just relax. Close your eyes. Now tell me, what does it feel like when I do this?"

"Warm," he said, after concentrating on the exact sensation. "But not right there. In my stomach, more."

"Then there's no problem. Just think about some little girl-friend of yours, and leave the driving to me. All right?"

"All right."

The feeling in his stomach started to spread everywhere in his body. There were little bubbles of color fizzing in the darkness of his head. They became faces, faces of women whose names he almost remembered. It started to hurt.

And then he could see the building where he would have to go to work tomorrow—a gigantic office building with gray glass walls. His back bent. His hands flexed in the air. His left boot pressed into the accelerator. His right was up on the seat of the car.

He could see his whole life, clear as day. There was his desk, his telephone, a calendar that showed a single day at a time. And his secretary, Miss Applewhite. His back bent in the other direction. There was a paper full of numbers, stacks of papers, and he understood them with a persistent clarity and there was also a cloudy pain everywhere inside him, a sorrow beyond the reach of his mind, which was now, again, as the child within fell back into its long, long slumber, the mind of a grown-up only.

He came.

Always we awake to our metamorphosed condition, to the awareness that the strange body in the bed is our own. Women awake and discover, after centuries of dreaming, that they are men. Worms awaken into birds, and music bursts from their astonished throats. An elderly businessman awakes and knows himself to be a plane tree: his leaves reach for the light, and swell with growth. Often the amazement is too much to bear, and our awakening is brief. We slip back into being the rudimentary creatures that we were. We become less, and sleep resumes its old sovereignty.

Flying, like falling in love, is wonderful. The combination of ecstasy and competence, of doing something and knowing *how* you're doing it . . . can't be explained, can't be compared, almost can't be described. Of course, I only fly in my dreams, but what of that. My flying dreams are not low-budget productions. They're wide-screen Technicolor spectaculars shot on location in Sequoia National Park and under the dome of St. Peter's. *Exultate, jubilate* is the sense they convey. Admittedly, they're infrequent, but how often is anyone invited to heaven? I'm grateful for the times I've been there, and thank the agency that sponsors them. (I write this, as it happens, on Thanksgiving Day.)

Though the circumstances vary from flight to flight, I can't resist interpreting each flying dream as an endorsement of whatever opus is presently in the works or on the runway. *You're doing okay,* my dream would seem to say. *Fly with it.*

Given such dreams and the practical importance I attach to them, it occurred to me that I should write about my experiences aloft. Writers are always looking about for subjects to which they can bring some special competence or expertise, and here was one in which the sense of conscious know-how was central and glorious. But how to write about flying without trivializing it into a Superman fantasy? I didn't want to end up looking like Dumbo. After some pondering, I came up with the following very short flight of fancy. While it may register (I hope) as a modest, amusing instruction sheet, it is much too brief and too self-deprecating in its irony to suggest the power and the glory of in-body flight. I think of "How to Fly" now rather as an I.O.U. written to myself against the day that I would deal with this theme seriously. Seven months later, at the end of '75, the pledge was redeemed, and the catalyst for that long-waited Eureka was so specific that I can't resist making a formal acknowledgement.

I was reading the title essay of John Berger's collection, *The Moment of Cubism.* That essay is a paean to Cubism as a specifically political vision of the liberations unleashed by the new technologies of the 20th century. Berger quotes the Cubist poets, Cendrars and Apollinaire, who salute the dawning age in poems that use the airplane as a metaphor for transcendence. Then Berger writes:

"At the moment of Cubism, no denials were necessary. It was a moment of prophecy, but prophecy as the basis of a transformation that had actually begun."

Apollinaire:

Already I hear the shrill sound of the friend's voice to come
Who walks with you in Europe
Whilst never leaving America. . . .

Right then, reading those lines in that context, with the intention already established of writing about flying, the idea for my novel, ON WINGS OF SONG, and most of the plot came to me.

How to Fly

Basically, nothing is easier. The one absolute essential is perfect self-confidence. As in swimming, one must take the leap. Then, for most people, instinct takes over: they flap their arms, they draw up their legs into a semi-kneeling position, they rise into the air.

Just because it's so easy, however, beginners often make mistakes. They believe that loose, flowing clothes, such as capes and evening gowns, are useful for attaining and sustaining higher altitudes. In fact, nudity is always to be preferred. Fabrics only interfere with maneuverability. So *don't* try and be a kite.

Similarly, don't imitate airplanes. Remember, they're only machines. Their source of power, though ultimately organic, is far inferior to the pure act of will that enables people to fly. Except for the awkward motions of their rudders and ailerons, the metal bodies of airplanes are rigid. Though they continue to be useful, both for rapid transit over large distances and for the postal system, as a model for human flight they are more than worthless—they're harmful.

Obvious, you say? Yes, and yet among beginners there is no more common error. Invariably, a novice flyer will assume the Superman, or Up-up-and-away, position once he reaches an air current in which it is possible to glide. A cruciform, spread-eagle stance is little better, for in both positions the torso and legs are locked stiffly into a bow shape that may look well in snapshots but contributes nothing aerodynamically. No other style of flight so swiftly and so drastically depletes those inner energies that the flyer must draw upon. It is as though a boxer were to assume the fighting style of a V-8 engine: possible, perhaps, but very wearying.

As important as fluidity of movement is pliancy of rhythm. Don't be an aerial metronome. Fly as the great pianists play, as singers sing. Indeed, for people as for birds, the most certain way to achieve unstrained, integral movement is to accompany flight with song. It's amazing what a few bars of *Swan Lake* can do for the average 'Ugly Duckling', while even the most accomplished flyer still has something to learn from the likes of Chopin or Albeniz.

In the first flush of enthusiasm we're all liable to go aloft every day without reckoning the cost. We forget—or we don't care—that every minute in the air draws heavily on a finite supply of Life Energy. After a certain age most of us learn to budget our flying time to one or maybe two flights a week. This is entirely natural, and nothing to be ashamed of. True, there are those who manage to continue short daily flights to the age of sixty and beyond, but as with other professional athletes, there isn't room in the lives of these zealots for very much else. The price they pay is great, but who shall say that any price is too great for what is surely life's supreme pleasure?

The first readerly reaction to this story I ever received was a severe reprimand from a woman who refused to believe it was meant as a lampoon on male chauvinism. She thought it was a sincere wish-fulfillment fantasy in the spirit of John Norman's Gor. On cross-examination it became clear how this confusion had arisen. People of refined (or squeamish) tastes are liable to mistake the grossness of a gross-out for the grossness of the object under attack. In the more inspired moments of *Saturday Night Live* (before NBC changed it to *Buried Alive*) there was a savagery of ridicule that genteel critics often mistook for bad taste. But when laughter's at issue, taste is beside the point. Claims to the contrary are usually made by the butt of the joke.

So now that you understand that the following is *satire,* and not a blueprint for utopia, let me fill out this intro with part of a poem I started two years ago, when *Saturday Night Live* was in its heyday. The poem went off the rails halfway through, and now with the show so completely gone to the dogs, I foresee I'll never get it back on the rails. So, in a spirit of string-saving thrift, and by way of a satirical credo, let me copy out those lines I'm loath to lose to the triumph of entropy:

Through all the nights of the week we await you
With nothing to watch but the news and the Late Show.
How we rejoice
At the voice
That announces that, live from New York, it is Saturday Night!
What bliss it is to believe there are those
Like to oneself similarly disposed,
Who prefer to the pabulum of earlier hours
A cannibal humor that rends and devours,
The laughter of Saturday Night!
And while we view you and watch your destruction
Of all of the leaders and liars and fools
Who run for our offices and teach in our schools

We're at one and the same time receiving instruction
In how to survive in a world where the rules
Are either unspoken
Or made to be broken
And nobody knows what is wrong and what's right—
Except you! Only you, our droll, our adorable,
Our darling, our horrible
Saturday Night!

Planet of the Rapes

Colly felt, and felt very strongly, that she was too young to be raped. With only weeks left till she took her degree, it seemed nothing short of genuine unkindness to be scheduled for a jump to Pleasure Island. A person is more than a fertility index, as she wrote in her letter of protest to the Federal Procreation Council. A person has feelings, plans, priorities. A person deserves some consideration. She pleaded for just two more weeks of virginity.

Then, after thinking some more about it, she tore the letter up. After all, as Mama Joey had pointed out more than once, 'Duty is duty.' Babies don't grow from radish seed, and if girls didn't go to Pleasure Island to be raped, there would *be* no more babies, and eventually no people at all. Surely a few hours of fleeting agony wasn't too great a price to pay for the survival of mankind?

If only she had a better idea of exactly what happened on Pleasure Island. The other members of her utopia would tell her nothing except that, painful and disgusting as the rape process undoubtedly was, you got over it. To do them credit, they *couldn't* remember their own rapes anyway, except in the most disconnected way, because at the very beginning of the rape process they'd all taken the amnesia drug. Their time on Pleasure Island passed under the drug's influence, and when they came home their memory of the experience consisted of nothing more than lurid flashes, like the isolated images remembered from a long nightmare.

"Which is a mercy, you must admit," Mama Joey had pointed out, during their one serious discussion of the subject. "Why, think if I could still remember *all* of it! I'd always be dwelling on it. It would drive me crazy, worrying about the next time I had to go back. No, thank you."

"But you do remember something surely," Colly objected. "Or else how would you know it's so awful?"

"I remember enough to know *that*, believe me," Mama Joey replied with deep conviction.

"Is it as awful as childbirth? Our civics class saw a childbirth last year, and I really can't imagine anything more . . ." As there were no words to express the horror of what Colly's civics class had witnessed, she shook her shoulders in a mock shiver, stuck out her tongue, and gurgled in her throat by way of approximation. In some ways she was still a little girl.

"It's much, much worse than that," Mama Joey declared. "It's the men, you see. They're so vile."

"Vile in what way?"

Mama Joey looked down at her knitting needles and pursed her lips, as if to say that she had reached the farthest limits of indiscretion.

It was so frustrating to be left in the dark. Colly had never seen a man, hadn't even thought about them much, unlike some girls her age (a few weeks short of 17). Those girls would stay up late in their dorms, spinning gruesome tales about men. Men without feet and arms who rode about in little wheeled boxes. Men with blue snakes growing from their stomachs. Men with metal eggs instead of faces, and other men covered with hair from head to toe, and even on their tongues. It was impossible to know which of these stories might be true and which made-up, since all the men who did exist, existed in Outer Space. There *was* a difference between the sexes, that much was certain, but just what it was, and precisely how awful, no one was sure. No one who hadn't been raped.

"Anyhow," Mama Joey said, with deliberate good cheer, "why should we dwell on the gloomy side? After a month, at the most, you'll be back here in your own utopia and everything will be back to normal."

Colly sighed and shook her head. "Everything except me. I'll be a Mama instead of a Miz."

"Is that such a cruel fate, my dear? Aren't I a Mama? Isn't Mama Mimosa? And Mama September? And Mama Cherelle? Believe me, it's a lot nicer being a Mama. For one thing, you'll be able to vote in elections. And run for office."

Colly smiled wanly. She'd never been interested in politics.

"*And* you'll be able to join whatever orgasm club you decide to. For what it's worth, Colly, I hope it's ours."

Colly didn't have the heart to tell her old friend that she had no interest at all in either trout fishing or sanitation arts, the two main avocations of Mama Joey's orgasm club. Indeed, she didn't have many outside interests at all, having majored in General Traditions, which, since there were so many, had taken every moment of her time for the past four years.

On the appointed day, Colly cycled to the nearest jump-port, in New Jerusalem, and reported to the duty officer, Sergeant-Major Mama Conifer, a brisk and businesslike octogenarian. There were forms to be filled out, and a medical exam, followed by a slide show explaining one's rights as a rape victim. Then, one by one, the girls bound for Pleasure Island were zipped into their jumpsuits and jumped to their destination.

A man was there, waiting for her, when Colly arrived. He was unthinkably ugly. In part it was an inescapable ugliness, for his body was misshapen, his skin rough and matted with hair. The other part of his ugliness seemed the natural consequence of an evil character. Through the aperture of the metal ovoid that covered his head, his blue eyes gleamed with demented intensity.

"Hubba, hubba," he said by way of greeting. Colly replied with a single piercing scream, and fainted dead away."

Ensign 73-J Hardscrabble of the Space Marines was on his way to his mother planet Earth, some 20,000 or so lightyears from his post aboard the S.S. *Gestapo Melody* at the far edge of the Milky Way. Despite recent improvements in jumpsuit technology, it was a devilish'y tiresome trip. For 14 solid hours he'd been doing backwards somersaults past a series of bright blue flashes, each of them a unique paradox of the hyperspace through which he gyrated homeward. He was halfway there. Sometimes, to pass the time, he would hum the tune of a popular new march, but the somersaulting made it hard to hold fast to any rhythm but the rhythm of his own head-over-heels revolutions. Other times, being rather religious, he would chant a prayer, or meditate on the inspiring adventures of one of his favorite gods—Buddha, Krishna, Hercules, or Jesus Christ. Ensign 73-J was not programmed to turn his mind off when not employed on the official Space Marine business of conquest and domination. Not only did Ensign 73-J possess his own practically original thoughts, but he had a range of feelings besides, ranging from curiosity to vague regret and on to muddled aspiration, which he cultivated, like so many hybrid flowers, for their own sake. In a word, Ensign 73-J was a dilettante, but not so that it had ever interfered with his capacity to perform his duty with gung-ho dedication. He was the kind of soldier who would have thrown himself on a live grenade, in the days when there were such things, in order to save the buddies in his platoon. He was a Space Marine.

After many more somersaults and a small infinity of blue paradoxes, Ensign 73-J arrived at the Green Hills Decompensation Station on Luna, where he had to spend a time equivalent to the time of the jump being decompensated, lacking which precaution he would have bounced back all the way he'd come in the form of a random, extremely rapid flux of quarks and pi-mesons.

After an hour in a sleep accelerator, he spent his remaining time at Green Hills wondering whether the reality of his first rape would measure up to the long-cherished dream. Not that he let on to any of the other decompensating Marines at the station that this was his first taste of R-and-R, and that the closest he'd ever come to seeing the bonafide blue skies, scudding white clouds, and soft sensuous cunts of his native Earth was in the thought-reels of porn that unwound through his head during his daily trip to the Men's Room. No, he could swap tales with the best of them, and nobody the wiser, since (as he suspected) they were all faking it too, the Green Hills station being used exclusively for the decompensation of ages 15 to 19, the jerkoff brigade.

Not all of Ensign 73-J's time in this lunar waiting room was spent gassing about apocryphal exploits. As always, he toned up with a session in the gym, starting off with ten minutes of incline sit-ups, seventy-five pushups, and a nice sprint eight times around the quarter-mile track. Considering the moon's low gravity, even with the station's boosters, he should have done better than that, but he was feeling too frisky to concentrate. He missed the weight room, and did four rounds with a Norelco Electropuncher, winning three and drawing one, following which, without even a zap of the toner, he went straight to the Men's Room and threw a quick fuck into the Polly Doll. Whap-Blap. Exactly 12 strokes, whereupon he shot his load with a satisfying sense of despatch.

The Green Hills Men's Room was built on a scale and appointed with an opulence that exceeded any Men's Room Ensign 73-J had ever visited. Just the range of fetishes was amazing, and some of them were of so exaggerated a character as to seem nearly grotesque to the young Marine, who, naturally, only had eyes for his own sweet Polly. Polly Dolls were British Leyland's answer to Ford's prize-winning Susie Tawdry model. They had red hair, red hoopskirts, and blue tits with little tassels—the so-called Queen Victoria look. Ensign 73-J had done his Erotic Training on a Polly all through boot camp—between the ages of 11 and 15. After that much behavioral conditioning it would have been strange, indeed, if anything but these precise specifications should turn him on.

Ensign 73-J had not always been such a lady-killer as to climax in just 12 swift plunges. In his first months of boot camp he'd had to drill an extra hour every day, plugging into god only knows how many reels of remedial porn until the stuff seemed to come out his ears, at which point, crazed with desire, he'd slip his very best hard-on into the fetish and pump for dear life, since if he didn't come within the allotted two minutes he would get a punishing jolt of electroshock direct to the cerebral cortex instead of the lollipop of orgasm. Many the day that he'd overstayed his welcome and had to suffer the consequences, but eventually he got it down pat. The human organism is, after all, a pretty reliable piece of engineering.

Even after a shower and massage, there were three hours of decompensation to get through before the jump down to Earth; so he decided to take in a mind-flick. He went to the public library, found himself an empty console, and connected the jacks to his brain stem. The choice was between "Kiss of Fire," a saga of World War III, a gladiatorial combat direct from Wimbledon, and an art movie, "Cylinders in Space," on the educational channel. He chose the art movie. Made in Shanghai, it featured, as its title promised, various kinds of cylinders moving through space. Some were pricks; some were missiles; some were just plain computer-generated cylinders in primary colors. They rotated, vibrated, wobbled, and pulsed, but mostly they just plunged straight ahead into the roseate glow of a space that unfolded endlessly to receive the cylinders' endless zoom ahead. Very abstract, very intellectual, and very ennobling, thought Ensign 73-J, as he zoomed along with the movie unwinding in his brain. Every so often, like the launching of some incredible religious rocket of inspiration, his own real-life reality would grab hold of him, and he'd shiver all over, thinking, "O Lord, O Baby, I'm about to rape a real live woman, yes I am!"

He'd never been so nervous in his life.

The man who had given Colly such a turn was not, after all, the man who was going to rape her, but only the beautician who was going to make her ready. While he took blood tests, urine samples, and the rest, he chattered away, burbling at his own incomprehensible jokes, and asking a lot of useless questions, the answers to which were all there in the packet of forms that Colly had brought with her.

"Well, Fresh-Face," he announced cheerily, when the tests were done, "What did you say your name was? Colly?"

"Yes. It's short for Ecology."

"You'll be a Colly no more, my little lady. For I am going to turn you into . . ." He paused for effect, eyes gleaming within the ovoid casing of his head. ". . . a Polly! What do you think of that?"

"Not anything, really. I don't know what you mean."

A snicker emerged from the ovoid. "Oh yes, we've heard *that* story before! And I suppose you think your cunt is a changepurse, too! Ha! You'll find out what a Polly is soon enough, and I can guarantee it's a lesson you won't forget!" Abruptly his manner changed. "Good God in heaven, I almost forgot!"

He went over to the cabinet of medical supplies and returned with a bottle labeled "Amnesty". He uncapped the bottle, rolled out a capsule and pushed it into Colly's mouth with a peremptory, "First things first. Swallow."

But Colly, who had studied General Traditions long enough to guess the pill's purpose from its name, did not swallow. She was feeling so aggrieved at the uncaring way her rape was being processed that she decided then and there *not* to forget a single demeaning moment. So, while the beautician's back was turned, she quickly removed the amnesia-producing capsule from her mouth, and stuck it as far inside her left ear as it would go.

After strapping Colly into a body-brace that would have been suitable to the treatment of a broken spine, the beautician began to dress her for her new role as a living, breathing Polly Doll. First a floor-length, hemispherical bustle was slung from the body-brace. Then the bustle was draped with a red skirt, across whose vast circumference a multitude of pink ribbons formed a brief message of sexual invitation. Her bare breasts were coated with a kind of plastic, and placed into moulds, from which they emerged a few minutes later, firm as eggplants and blue as the noses of two baboons. Tiny silver tassels were hung from the nipples. Her face was painted the same Day-Glo pink as the ribbons on her skirt, while her temporarily enlarged lips, her wig, and her blindfold picked up the skirt's shimmery red. Her shoes were a size too small, and had heels so absurdly high that every step she took in them seemed an unreasonable risk—until she discovered, stumbling, that the bustle not only supported her skirts but held her upright. As a final touch, to emphasize her feminine delicacy and defenselessness, her hands were snugged into a pair of fingerless, thumbless, shoulder-length mittens, and her

wrists were weighted with heavy gold bracelets with winking red lights.

With a parting pinch of her tasseled tits, the beautician
led his latest creation down a corridor and through a tall
glass door into a hall where several gigantic carousels
revolved. On the carousels stood the women of Earth,
attired and bedizened to provoke the lusts of the space
warriors home on leave. The warriors themselves milled
about on the floor of the hall, comparing the wares being
offered and, here and there, leaping aboard the carousels
to sample them.

A small cheer went up as Colly was ensconced in her
own little niche on a carousel, but this proved to be only a
formal courtesy, for no one immediately approached her.
None of this scene, of course, was visible to the blindfolded
girl. For her there was just a varying rumble of voices that
was largely drowned out by the ear-splitting waltz being
broadcast through the hall. She stood, balancing precari-
ously on her heels, her weighted arms dangling at her
sides, while the carousel joggled slowly round and round.
Sometimes hands would squeeze her breasts. Sometimes a
finger would wiggle into her cunt. But none of these inti-
macies were pursued any farther. The carousel turned,
and Colly waited, wondering where she was, not daring to
remove the blindfold.

Earth was nothing like Ensign 73-J Hardscrabble had imagined it during all those years growing up at the edge of the
galaxy. Its famous blue sky was no different from the blue
skies of a dozen other planets he'd been to. The water was
blah, and very expensive. Except on a few streets set apart
for the top brass, the buildings looked old and worn-out,
while the widely advertised natural beauties—the trees and
grass and other forms of vegetation growing wild in the
ancient bombsite at the heart of Old London Town—all
these left Ensign 73-J completely cold. If Pleasure Island
were a fair sample of the planet, then the best thing to do
was move the personnel out, scrape it down to bedrock,
and terraform it into some sort of order.

The real source of the young marine's distress lay elsewhere, however. It lay in the fact that after three hours on

Pleasure Island he had yet to score. Part of it was plain bad luck. The women he'd seen were all built along the wrong lines. They were Blonde Venuses or African Queens or some other off-turning variety. A Space Marine responds to a doll just like the doll he does his Erotic Training on, and to no other. Thus, by the simple means of matching a girl's genotype to her style of attire, the government guaranteed that every seemingly free encounter between rapist and rapee resulted in an optimum genetic match. God himself could not more cleverly have concealed His predestining hand.

There had been some Polly Dolls about, of course, but all those he'd seen seemed to be spoken for. So, unless he picked a fight over someone else's Polly, which he was not feeling prime for, the only thing to do was to go, as the Official Pleasure Island Guidebook recommended, to the source, which was the YWCA on Oxford Avenue, and that is where, eventually, he went, and where he saw Colly, as we left her, mounted on the carousel. With her bracelets winking and blinking and the tassels on her blue breasts jingling a delicate song of romance, she seemed, to the smitten Ensign, to have stepped right out of his dreams. He almost came, just looking at her.

Now he understood what had been so disconcerting about all the other Earth women he'd seen so far. Despite the best efforts of the Quartermasters Corps to deck them out like familiar Men's Room fetishes, they all looked human! Particularly when their escorts allowed them, in open violation of the S.M. Code of Conduct, to remove their blindfolds, since the blindfold of a real fetish was not removeable. Of course, theoretically, women *are* human beings, for if they didn't belong to the same species, how could you breed with them? But some of the women he'd seen had seemed human in a really ugly and threatening way, as though a *man* had been trapped inside the machinery of a Polly Doll and all that could be seen of him were his eyes rolling around desperately in a doll's pink face.

Not, however, this one! This one was a goddess. Ensign 73-J had to have her for his very own, and as there was no one else just then who was in the market for a Polly, nothing could be easier. He clambered onto the revolving platform, grabbed a boob in each hand, squeezed hard, and bit down passionately on the puffy red lips. The goddess screamed, but he went right on kissing, certain that her .joy was equal to his own. She raised her weighted, mittened hand as though to push him from her, and as she did so the velvety tip of a mitten brushed against the hairtrigger source of all his joy, which required no more. Semen gushed all over the pink ribbons that formed the 'F' on his Polly's skirt. The marines who had been spectators at this brief performance burst into sincere, admiring applause. A Space Marine was expected to be quick on the draw.

Proudly, eagerly, and all a-tremble, Ensign 73-J Hardscrabble led his captive off to the De Sade Hilton, where in the privacy of a forty-credit Deluxe Dungeonette he fastened his beloved to the wall and proceeded to screw the daylights out of her. Once, twice, a third time, and a fourth. Then, after a mess of resimulated steak and Gallowbird Burgundy, he did it all over again. Eight times he had raped her on their first day together! You can't do better than that.

"O Polly, juicy Polly, I want to fuck you forever and ever and ever," he whispered into her ear, when he had finished with her for the last time that night.

He'd chosen the ear with the pill in it, and she never heard him. If she had, it doesn't seem likely that she could have made an appropriate response. After so many hours of screaming, there was nothing left of her voice but the driest husk of a whimper. But to Ensign 73-J that little whimper was dearer far than another victim's most anguished screams. Truly, he'd fallen in love.

The third day after she'd been brought to the Hilton, Colly broke down and begged to be fed.

Ensign 73-J set aside his copy of *Martial Love*. "Darling! I was beginning to wonder if maybe you *couldn't* talk. But I figured if you can scream, you can talk." He chucked her under the chin affectionately. "So what'll it be, sweety?" He picked up the variety pack of Femme-Food ampules he'd bought at the deli downstairs. The pack included a free syringe and mouth clamps for rapid forced feeding.

"There's meat flavor, cheese flavor, lemon-lime, and red-hot mexicana," he explained.

Colly burst into helpless tears and shook her head. Raised, as she had been, on wholesome organic foods, this stuff was like being offered a choice of motor oils for an aperitif. Better, after all, to starve herself to death, as she'd been meaning to. If only, if only, *if only* she could have freed her hand and reached the pill that was still lodged inside her ear! Ah, but it was too late now! How would she ever return to her old utopia with the memory of this experience?

While Colly was thinking such melancholy thoughts, Ensign 73-J had returned to his manual, where the author was explaining the fierce sexual pleasure to be shared with a woman who was suspended upside-down from a system of chains and pulleys designed by Peckinpah's of Bond Street and available at most good department stores. An enticing notion, but Ensign 73-J was just too fucked out to take such initiatives.

What he really wanted to do was talk. Polly was so beautiful, so warm, so soft, so womanly, and he was so in love with her, and therefore curious. There was so much he didn't know about women. What were their lives like when they weren't here on Pleasure Island?

According to *Martial Love,* by using the right combination of threats and promises, any woman could be made to carry on an intelligible conversation. There were sample dialogues in the book, but much as he enjoyed them, Ensign 73-J somehow didn't like the idea of his Polly memorizing someone else's words. He wanted her to use her own words to tell her secret, innermost thoughts.

Threats he could come up with easily enough, and when his own were used up there were whole chapters in the manual to refer to. The problem was what to promise. His Polly no longer screamed and struggled with the same passion as when they'd first made love. This seeming list-lessness might simply be caused by hunger, but it seemed just as possible that she wasn't enjoying it as much any more. Women were known to be easily jaded.

Then it came to him—he could *ask* her!

"Polly?" He tweaked her nose affectionately. She whimpered. "Polly, isn't there something I could do for you? Something I haven't thought of myself yet? Just tell me, darling, and I'll do it." He bent close to her lips to hear her whispered request. "What's that again, dearest? You'll have to speak louder."

She wanted him to remove her blindfold and take off her mittens.

At first he refused. Much as he loved her, he didn't entirely *trust* her. Furthermore, he thought that fingers and thumbs were a desecration of any woman's true beauty, which is her helplessness. But there was nothing she could be persuaded to accept as a substitute, so after explaining what he would want in return—her absolute honesty—he removed her blindfold and mittens.

She was not the same Polly. Her bare hands, which she began to flex and rub, seemed especially unnerving, even repulsive. Yet at the same time she became more fascinating than ever. Those eyes! Like tiny portholes peering out into the depths of space. They were alive. They regarded him, Ensign 73-J Hardscrabble, and sent detailed reports about him to her brain. Jesus, how he'd have liked to read those reports.

He was about to ask her whether she thought he was particularly good-looking or only average, when she started playing with her left ear—sticking her finger in and wiggling it round energetically. Surely, this was an example of one of those unpredictable erogenous zones talked about in *Martial Love*. Being too shy to tell him about her desires outright, Polly had asked to have her mittens removed so she could show him in this silent fashion.

Taking the hint, he pinioned her naked wrists above her head and began to lick and tickle her left ear. She struggled with new energy. Mounting her, he took her whole ear in his mouth and sucked for all he was worth. At the moment that he came, so did, amazingly, her ear.

Unless a woman's anatomy were even more peculiar than he'd supposed, it must have been wax—a great gob of wax that slid down his throat before his reflexes could chuck it back up. Not that a Space Marine would ever get squeamish over a little thing like earwax. Even so, he decided that for the future he would leave ears alone.

A month went by.

At last the time came for Colly and for Ensign 73-J to say farewell to Pleasure Island. He was to be jumped back to his post on the S.S. *Gestapo Melody* on the outskirts of the galaxy. She would go home to her utopia. As they left the De Sade, Ensign 73-J gave her a parting fuck, then draped the symbolic blue mantle of motherhood over her slender shoulders. From now till they clocked in at the jump station Colly would be off-limits, even to himself.

As they walked down the cracked pavements past the crumbling hotels of the old city, Ensign 73-J was overcome by an emotion compounded in equal parts of sadness, relief, and guilt. He was sad for the obvious and ageless reason that his holiday was now definitely at an end. His relief stemmed from a sense, dim but powerful, that his love for Polly had grown out of hand. Once in their final week together, berserk with delight, he had completely disrobed her, making her, in effect, not his Polly at all, but something ancient and solemn, an Aphrodite. Then, naked himself, he had deliberately prolonged his lovemaking, timing himself with a stopwatch to see just how exquisitely far he could drag it out. His best time, after four tries, was a nerve-racking three minutes, 48 seconds. This was insane, even subversive behavior, but Ensign 73-J was beyond caring about right and wrong when it came to the dictates of the heart. Love was his excuse.

The guilt he felt now had less to do with his sexual misconduct than with the fact that he had revealed certain vital military secrets to his Polly. It had seemed natural at the time. They had been lying side by side on the little mattress on the floor of the dungeonette, and she was telling him about the life she'd led here on Earth in her utopia. It all seemed so lovely, a life made of music and talcum powder. She told of milking cows and watching sunsets, of gathering rosebuds and sitting by the fire on long winter nights. Then she asked him about his life in the Space Marines. What did they do out there in outer space? How had the Marine Corps come into being? And though it had been stressed in all the briefings that it was strictly forbidden to speak of such classified and top secret subjects in the presence of women, even when they were presumed to be asleep or unconscious, and though this was tantamount to collaborating with the enemy, he *had* answered all her questions to the best of his ability, which was, admittedly, limited. What harm could it do, after all? Her memories of the entire month she'd spent on Pleasure Island would soon be randomized out of recognition, including her memories of his act of treason.

Including (and this thought turned his knees to jelly) all her memories of *him*!

"Will you miss me, Polly darling?" he asked, in a burst of fervor.

"How can I, if I have no memory of you, Sir?" She had adopted the suggestion in *Martial Love* that he was always to be addressed as Sir.

Ensign 73-J sighed. He wished she would have stooped to an occasional accommodating lie. He would have, in her shoes.

"I'll miss you, Polly." That, certainly, was no lie. "I'll miss you something awful."

They walked on in silence. Since they were on the street, Polly was wearing her blindfold and so she couldn't know how near, how very near they were to the jump station. The guards outside had already seen them. There could be no turning back. He stopped. He groaned. He grabbed her mittened arm, and she stumbled to a halt, swaying in the rigid basket of her skirt. He looked at her for a long moment, but so little of what her costume left visible suggested the girl of legs, fingers, eyes, and toes that he'd learned to adore.

"Oh Polly, Polly, Polly," he began in a tone of ardent valediction.

"Oh Colly, Colly, Colly," she corrected. Ever since she'd begun to talk to him, the matter of her name, that single consonant of difference, had been a bone of contention between them. "Sir."

"Colly," he repeated in a whisper. The name sent shivers through him. Truly, love had made him mad. "Colly, tell me one thing before we part forever. Tell me—do you love me? Really love me from the bottom of your heart?"

Whenever her rapist went off on one of these tangents,

Colly was unsure what would serve to put him off. Some of her expedients had worked very well, others not at all. Her ordeal was so near an end. For all she knew they might be standing on the threshold of the jump station. She dare not make a mistake now! So to answer him she fell back on her oldest standby. It was a kind of monologue she'd learned by heart from *Martial Love*. "Oh, oh, oh, stick it in me now, I'm so hot, oh, oh, fuck me, fuck me, yes, oh, shove that big cock right up there, oh yes, oh!"

It was more than mortal flesh could bear. With a strangled cry he lifted her up in his arms and ran the rest of the way to the station.

Due to an unexpected supernova in the vicinity of Procyon, the journey returning to the edge of the galaxy took much longer than it had in the other direction. Procyon was nowhere near the straight line that would have connected the two points of Earth and the S.S. *Gestapo Melody*, but in hyperspace straight lines don't count for much. Ensign 73-J arrived at his ship's decompensation station after 32 uninterrrupted hours of tumbling headlong through the violet (due to the supernova) void.

During these 32 hours he had reached a decision. He was going to approach his commanding officer, Admiral 99-A, and make a clean breast of it. Never before had he allowed the slightest infraction of the S.M. Honor Code to remain on his conscience, but had always gone straight to the authorities to confess before a single one of his friends had been able to report him. That's what he'd do now. No doubt there would be repercussions. At the very least a black mark would be entered on his record. Possibly he'd be broken in rank, or even sent to the brig. But for a Space Marine duty comes before any personal considerations, and it was clearly his duty to report the wrong that he had done.

He would confess, but not this very moment, since there was no way he could communicate with his officers. In terms of their reality, Ensign 73-J was still in hyperspace until he had finished decompensating. He'd have to wait another 32 hours, and since there were no amusements or amenities on the ship's decompensation chamber, he decided to catch up on his sleep.

He went to sleep with a clean conscience, and while he slept the Amnesty did its work. He woke with every experience and thought of the last 30 days wiped from the slate of memory. The last thing he could remember was his beautiful Polly sticking her finger in her ear. Then—but this was impossible, perhaps it was a dream—they were walking together, at sunset, through a meadow towards a cow with gigantic blue udders . . .

The Chairperson of the Federal Procreation Council removed her reading glasses and put on the other pair so as to see the face of the girl who'd been waiting eight days to speak with her. Her records identified her as Mama Ecology of the Butterberry Utopia in the 4th Administrative District. She had recently returned from her first tour of duty on Pleasure Island; so recently that her body as yet gave no sign of her altered condition.

Doubtless she had come to protest the established policies of the Council. The situation was not unusual, but it was never easy to deal with. So often her meetings with these poor guileless zealots had repercussions that were most unfortunate for those who refused to come to reasonable terms with the Council. The Chairperson did pity them, but there was no better way, alas, to dispose of the danger they represented to the civil order than to follow the procedures already laid down and known to be effective.

"I see your name is Ecology," the Chairperson said, with professional warmth, "and that you live at the Butterberry Utopia. One of my dearest friends lives at Butterberry . . ." This was so, but for the life of her the Chairperson could not remember her friend's name. She concluded lamely, "One of my *very* dearest friends."

Colly nodded gravely. After all the inner turmoils of the days of waiting, she felt strangely calm now. It was too late to turn back. She would speak out, regardless of the consequences.

"When I was on Pleasure Island," she began cautiously, "I learned something I didn't know before."

The Chairperson patted her hand. "Of course you did,

my dear. I daresay we *all* do. But then, thank goodness, we forget it."

"I didn't forget it." There! It was out in the open.

"No? I am sorry to hear that. But there have been other cases of this sort. Whether they came about by accident or oversight is no concern of ours, here at the Central Office. Indeed, your case is much more common than you would think. Now, I suppose, you'd like to be able to forget what happened—and you can't."

"Well, yes, that too. I mean, I *would* like to forget my rape. But what I learned . . . what I came to tell you . . . is something much more important than . . . what happened to *me*. It's something that no other woman on Earth is aware of—a vital military secret."

"Dear me. And how did you come to ferret out this secret?"

"I was told by the man who raped me. He thought I'd forget it along with everything else that happened to me then."

"Well, my dear, spit it out, spit it out."

"The world," Colly explained carefully, "wasn't always the way it is now. Men and women didn't always live apart. At least not to the same degree."

"I've had four years of General Traditions myself, and I'm aware that there were eras and eras of darkness and injustice. History is something of a speciality of mine."

"Then do you know about the Hyperboleans?"

"The Hyperboleans?" The Chairperson removed her glasses and pinched the bridge of her nose. "Not the Hyper-*bor*-eans? No? Then I don't believe I ever heard such a name in *my* years at school."

Colly, anxious to set forth her astonishments, did not notice the Chairperson's equivocation.

"You see, Mama Chairperson, the Hyperboleans are the reason that things are the way they are today. A long time ago, hundreds of years probably, there was a war on Earth, the most destructive war there'd ever been, and the only reason it didn't wipe everybody out is that at the last moment these people from outer space, called Hyperboleans, stepped in and stopped it. Apparently Hyperboleans had always been around, watching us and interfering now and then with history to make it go according to their plans. They looked like ordinary human beings. The men did, anyhow. No one ever saw the Hyperbolean women. And so it was easy for them to be pharaohs and prime ministers and kings and such."

"And Chairpersons?" asked the Chairperson archly.

Colly looked startled. "There could have been male Chairpersons, I suppose. But the thing is, there aren't *any* Hyperboleans any more. That's the secret I discovered."

"Really? What became of them?"

"We killed them. I mean, men did. You see, they were what once was called 'warlike'. That was why they hung around Earth for all those centuries, pretending to be human. One group of them would join a war on one side, and another group on the other side. It was all a game for them, like checkers, only immensely more complicated, of course. Then, after they'd stopped World War III, they decided it would be more fun to teach us to fight a war by *their* rules. With their weapons, which were exponentially more powerful. So they trained us. There weren't many human beings left at that point. Just a few Mormons in some caves in Utah, some Italians in the Dolomites, and the odd survivor here and there. The Hyperboleans rounded them all up, put them in a training camp, and taught them a new kind of mathematics and some other things. And at the same time—and this is what is so shocking—they made them adopt their own peculiar social and . . . and sexual customs."

"And what were those, Ecology?"

"Their women lived completely separate lives back on their home planet, Hyperbole. Once every three years they had to prostitute themselves at a kind of sex resort, like Pleasure Island. They kept their own female children, but the males were raised as warriors. We adopted their system, lock, stock, and barrel."

"Don't you think there may be something to be said for the system?"

Colly shook her head. "Nothing whatever. It's as degrading for the men as for the women."

"That's as it may be. But in a practical sense, my dear, it

179

seems to me it might be a very effective way to breed a race of warriors. Or Space Marines."

"But that's just it! There's no *need* for warriors any more. We conquered the Hyperboleans ages ago. First we atomized their home planet, with all the Hyperbolean women, and then we wiped out the men. There isn't a DNA molecule of Hyperbolean flesh left in existence."

"Fancy that! It makes one proud to be human, doesn't it?"

"But don't you see what that means? We're a warrior culture without any wars to fight. The nearest thing to an actual enemy that the Space Marines have found in centuries is a kind of aquatic dinosaur on the fourth planet of Aldebaran. There simply isn't very much intelligent life in the universe. That's why the Hyperboleans needed us for an enemy. We were all there was, except for themselves."

"And now we're all there is, in the absolute sense. How ironic."

"It's more than ironic. It's wrong."

"How so, my dear?"

"The wrong is in the way they treat *us*."

The Chairperson smiled a superior smile. "I thought so! Sex. It always comes back to that."

"But the way we live, as a result of all this, is unnatural. And unnecessary."

"But just think—what if we had to cohabit with our men the way women used to? Do you think *they'd* be any better for having us about all the time? On the contrary, *we'd* become worse. Believe me, dear, things are much better as they are now. We've reached a kind of equilibrium, and I think it would be most unwise to tamper. Yes? So what I would suggest is a nice course of hypnotherapy, so that you can put all these distressing details out of mind. That's what the Central Office is here for, you know—to handle details."

"But, Mama Chairperson, there's something else. But it's so . . . so awful . . . so incredible. You'll think I'm crazy, but . . . Oh, I don't know how to *say* it!"

"In as few words as possible, my dear. I'm already late for an important conference on glanders."

"You see, rape is . . . quite awful . . . at first. But then, after a while, you get used to it. And when you've got used to it . . ."

"You mean to say, my dear, that you enjoyed being raped."

Colly looked away from the Chairperson's piercing gaze. Her shame was boundless.

"But of course, my dear! Of course. We *all* enjoy it. That's what I thought you meant to tell me when we first sat down. It's what most girls discover their first time out."

"But if you understand all that . . ." Colly didn't understand at all.

"You mean to ask—why do we bother? Why do we maintain Pleasure Island, et cetera? The drama, my dear—that's why. One returns, each time, with one's entire maiden innocence. One re-learns, each time, the same inspiring lesson. Sex is a very dull habit. But it is a wonderful adventure."

"So you don't mean to do anything?"

"Well, my dear, something must certainly be done about *you*. You can't be allowed to return to your utopia in your present frame of mind. So, I can offer you this choice. Either you may choose to undergo a course of treatments that will erase the trauma of your rape . . ."

Colly shook her head decisively. "I'm sorry, but that would go against my principles."

"Then you may prefer to stay on here at the Central Office. We can always find room for a young lady of your initiative."

"There's no other possibility?"

"There is, but I'm not at liberty to mention it till you've determined whether you'd like to work in the office."

"I'd like some time to consider."

"Naturally. As long as you like. Till you've made up your mind, my dear."

When Colly had left her office, the Chairperson breathed a sigh of relief. Her nose was simply killing her. Catching hold of the bridge between her thumb and forefinger, she peeled it off. Then, able to breathe again at last, she sat down to write a recommendation, in the ancient script of Hyperbole, that Mama Ecology of the Butterberry Utopia be sent back to Pleasure Island for a permanent tour of duty.

Sometimes a story will say everything on a particular subject that I can think of saying. For instance, this story. I started an introduction for it, got suspicious, reread the story, and, just as I'd suspected, found I was repeating myself.

To recount the circumstances in which the idea arose—a convivial dinner with Chip Delany and Frank Romeo—does not add much to the sum of human knowledge, even the small subcategory of human knowledge filed under Me.

So how about a recipe? A recipe, what's more, with a strong connection both to conviviality and to Chip Delany, since it is his family's recipe for an egg nog compared to which all other egg nogs are mere gruel.

Pour a quart of bourbon in a bowl, add two cups of sugar, cover it loosely and let it sit around overnight. (The sugar ferments, and the proof rises.) As the hour approaches beat 18 eggs (no need to separate them) to a smooth but not yet foamy yellow. Then dribble the beaten eggs in the thinnest of trickles into the bourbon, continuing to beat the mixture all the while. (This takes two people.) Whip a quart of heavy cream and fold it in. Dust with nutmeg. Be merry.

The Revelation

Ingman Bergmar was a wretched man. Not for any of the workaday reasons you or I or Job might have offered, such as unrequited love or insufficient funds or boils, but for what seemed to some of his critics a secondary sort of complaint—God's silence. Bergmar wanted God to talk to him the way He'd talked to Moses and Abraham and Adam in the Bible. Not that he believed there'd ever been a historical Moses or Abraham, much less an Adam. He didn't, and that was part of the problem. Actually, he would have settled for an angel, even a small Sign, so long

183

as it was genuinely miraculous and not just a bit of luck. He'd always thought the story about Hemingway turning Catholic as a thank-you for being cured of impotence reflected poorly on that author's intellectual equipment, nor did he have much respect for Pascal and his wager. If God were up there he should speak out. Nothing less would satisfy Ingman Bergmar.

This challenge to the Almighty had been a recurrent theme in Bergmar's films. From the first frame of the Arctic Tetralogy in the late '40's down to the last anguished whisper of Senta in *The Wolves Are Howling*, Bergmar had been making the same non-negotiable demands: speak now or forever hold Your peace. He had repeated Ivan Karamazov's famous poser—how could a just God allow innocent children to suffer? There was no answer. He'd confronted Him with Auschwitz, Hiroshima, the statistics for highway fatalities and terminal cancer. God did not choose to reply. His mistress, two-times Academy-Award-winning Una Thorwald, had committed suicide at the height of her career, and still not one word of consolation or reassurance from on high. Bergmar had come to believe that God didn't exist, that there was nothing but a meaningless mulch of atoms and energy bubbling around in the void utterly indifferent to questions of human fate.

Then God spoke to him.

He spoke to him out of the center of a canolle that Bergmar had brought home from the one good Italian bakery in Stockholm. "Okay, Bergmar," God said (in Swedish), "let's talk."

"Lord!" said Bergmar, putting down his fork on the homey embroidered tablecloth and staring at the canolle in dismay. He knew with *a priori* certainty that it *was* the living God talking to him out of the canolle, but even so he felt compelled to ask: "Is it You?" After a lifetime of taking nothing on faith, Bergmar wasn't about to trust to mere intuitions, however powerful.

God assured Bergmar that He was indeed the Everlasting God, Creator of Heaven and Earth, the One and Only King of Kings and Lord of Lords.

Bergmar didn't know how to continue. Somehow it didn't

seem either polite or entirely safe to return to such subjects as suffering children or atomic holocaust. Undoubtedly God, since He evidently did exist, had His own
inscrutable reasons for letting such things happen.

."Well?" God insisted.

"I'm not worthy of this," Bergmar ventured, always handy
with an appropriate quote.

The canolle seemed to accept this as its due. "So? Neither were the others." Meaning (Bergmar understood) Moses
and Abraham and Adam.

"Is there something you'd like me to do, Lord?" Bergmar
asked, perhaps a touch too eagerly.

"I think you could eat a more balanced diet," God
answered. "Cut out the cholesterol, and reduce your starches.
Get more roughage. And Vitamin C, at least five hundred
milligrams a day. Vitamin C is great stuff."

Bergmar nodded respectfully but also a bit impatiently.
Dietary regulation, though a traditional benevolence of the
Diety, was not the area he'd hoped for guidance in. "I'll do
that. Anything else?"

"I think you *might* start observing the Sabbath. It's only
one day out of the week, after all."

"Absolutely! Anywhere in particular?"

"Wherever you feel comfortable."

"Is that all, Lord? Isn't there some message I could pass
on to the world at large?"

"I doubt the world at large would believe you, Ingman.
In any case, My prophets have said most of it before. People
don't listen. They're iniquitous. *You* know that."

."Yes, of course, Lord. But I—"

"Iniquitous," the canolle muttered in grieved tones. "And
I'll tell you *this*—I don't intend to put up with it much
longer! The fornications and false gods! The additives! The
things they show on TV even during the hours when
young children might be watching!"

"It is a disgrace, Lord, I know."

"And *you're* one of the worst offenders, Ingman!" He
bellowed so that the canolle seemed in danger of exploding
all over the breakfast nook.

Then, in a twinkling, He was once again all sweetness

and light. "But that's all one. I'll forgive you your tres-passes if you'll promise to put an end to them. If you must make movies, make ones the whole family can enjoy watching."

Bergmar promised, though at the same time he wished God would be explicit as to just which aspects of his film-making He objected to. The nudity? Hadn't He cre-ated us male and female, and was it sinful to pay a certain respectful attention to the results? Or was it rather the general emotional *tone* he was objecting to, what one critic had referred to as 'the typical Bergmar blend of stoic dis-tress and quiet, unassuming despair'? That might be harder to remedy, even now. There were still aspects of human existence to complain of, regardless of the long Silence being finally broken. Bergmar wasn't sure he'd ever be able to make a film entirely to his own and the Almighty's liking. The Lord God seemed to have a rather old-fashioned outlook, not to say reactionary. He put Bergmar in mind of his own father, Ole Bergmar, a timber merchant in Sveg. Noting this resemblance didn't lead Bergmar to doubt the objective reality of the manifestation. When God talks to you, you *know* who He is.

God, being all-wise, had followed the drift of Bergmar's thoughts, and His next words were spoken in an admon-ishing but not unkind tone. "So, what did you think—that I'd sound like Soren Kierkegaard?"

Bergmar shook his head. "No, no. It even makes sense, when you think about it. I just wish—"

"You wish I were more like you. Everyone does, it's human nature. Now you're probably wondering if I'm really like this or just putting on an act to tease you. Haven't you read the Book of Job? Don't you know better than to question My Judgment?"

"Lord, my name is mud: what can I say?" Bergmar replied contritely, though not without a dash of pride at his quick paraphrase of Job's answer to a similar challenge.

God seemed mollified. He continued in a milder vein. "Would you like to know a secret?"

There was nothing in the world Ingman Bergmar wanted more than to know one of God's secrets. He bowed his head reverently, scarcely daring to look at the pastry on the dish before him.

God said, "Lo, in two years this world will come to an end."

"Completely?" Bergmar insisted, astonished. He'd expected a much smaller secret.

"Completely and irrevocably. Kaput—forever!"

"If you don't mind my asking . . . how will it happen?"

"By an entirely natural cataclysm that will satisfy both a moral and a poetic sense of justice."

"A collision with another planet?" Bergmar guessed, when it appeared the canolle would not elaborate on these very abstract hints.

"No."

"The Bomb?"

"Not that either."

"Some kind of ecological catastrophe, then?"

"No more guessing, Ingman. When the time comes, it will all be clear. Till then, remember: eat right, keep the Sabbath, and love your neighbor while you can."

God said no more.

Bergmar went on looking at the canolle the rest of the afternoon, but the Divine Presence had definitely absconded. The canolle was no more now than an ordinary canolle with a slightly soggy crust. Needless to say, Bergmar found it impossible to consider eating it. He put it into the refrigerator, where gradually, over the course of the next three weeks, it developed a fuzzy green mold. Finally, with a sense of grief and of relief in equal parts, Bergmar put the canolle out with the morning garbage.

Given the more than two year time-lag between the initial inspiration and the final release of any movie, there didn't seem to be much point in starting a new production, even if he'd been able to think of something suitable in the apocalyptic circumstances. Bergmar announced his retirement and returned to his native Sveg. He ate sensibly, attended church every Sunday, learned the names of his neighbors, and tried his best to love them.

As the allotted time wore on he did sometimes wonder whether his revelation hadn't been something in the nature of a hallucination. Without God present and actively inspiring his faith, Bergmar tended to fall back in his old rut of materialistic doubt and ordinary common sense. Could he ever be certain it had really been God who'd spoken to him out of the canolle, and not just some quirk of his subconscious? Had the Silence truly been broken?

When the world did come to an end, exactly on the day God had predicted, Bergmar knew for a fact that his doubts had been unfounded. It had been God who'd talked to him. He was annihilated a happy man.

When the following serious proposal appeared in *Harper's Magazine* early in '74, it drew (I'm told) a larger reader response than anything they'd published in years. Most of the letters were from people volunteering to join the proposed corps of pyramid builders. One of the letter writers, a citizen of Austin, Texas, summed up the main difficulty that then beset this noble undertaking: "Unfortunately, many people are not responding to your article because they think it is, while a worthy idea intrinsically, nevertheless a put-on." The same correspondent concluded his letter, even so, with a commitment "to contribute labor and money when I believe the project is on a sound footing."

What chiefly was lacking to get the project off the ground (or on it) was a benevolent, public-spirited millionaire, foundation, or government agency similarly taken with the idea and willing to fund it. If any such are now reading this, let me assure them that *this is a serious proposal*. It is not a put-on. I would like to get together with other like-minded people, and build some pyramids. On the evidence of the response from *Harper's* readers, thousands of people would contribute their labor to such an undertaking, and only lack leadership and cash.

For my part, while I'm perfectly willing to stump for recruits and appear at fund-raising dinners and such as that, I don't think of myself as a leader. On the other hand, I don't think of most leaders as leaders, so if people want to elect me as pharoah or whatever, I would think about it. I can promise there'll be no mass suicides, no rattlesnakes in the mailbox, no l.p.'s to distribute at airports, and no dumb ideas you'd be indoctrinated into believing. Nothing but an opportunity to pile block on massive block for the erection of . . .

Pyramids for Minnesota

A Serious Proposal

Q. Does Minnesota need pyramids?

A. No. Pyramids transcend the notion of "utility". This, indeed, is their special merit. If they could be put to any use whatever, people would not be interested in them. Why do people go to Europe? Not to see its magnificent grain elevators and factories, but to climb the ramparts of indefensible forts and stroll through the palaces of defunct monarchs. Above all, they visit churches—hundreds of churches, thousands of churches, ever more and more churches!

Q. Why not build churches, then?

A. It would confuse too many people. They would want the church to belong to a religion or express a style; they would complain of the expense, insisting that so much money and effort were better spent feeding poor children or searching for a cure for leukemia. Pyramids elude such controversies. They stand outside the flow of History. It is the very inexpressiveness of a pyramid, like that of a corpse or a crystal, that is so awesome.

Q. Why Minnesota, then? Why not in a desert?

A. There too, by all means. But, really, why *not* Minnestoa?

Q. Should they all be the same size?

A. Yes. Especially if there are to be several in one area.

Q. And of the same degree of steepness?

A. Yes—45°. As there will not be steps, this will dispel any lingering doubts as to their usefulness. One should never be prompted to climb a pyramid for the sake of a view. This is principally what is wrong with mountains.

Q. Passageways?

A. Absolutely not! No time capsules, either. Rock-solid throughout. If they are to be vandalized, it should be from motives as disinterested as those that led to their formation.

Q. Who will build them?

A. All of us who want to. Volunteers must enlist for at least one year, but for no longer than three, thus steering a course between the Scylla of amateurism and the Charybdis of expertise. All volunteers must spend at least half their workweek in the actual labor of construction. Those who have clearly shirked or malingered must forfeit the bond they posted upon enlisting.

Q. Why would anyone volunteer?

A. For the reason one does anything—the experience promises to be congenial to one's temperament. Undoubtedly the slaves who hewed and moved and fit in place the blocks of the first pyramids felt a secret gratification at taking part in the erection of such great monuments. Who can read of the building of Chartres without a smart of envy? By enlisting in the Pyramid Corps, one becomes part of a community devoted to a high and selfless goal, and yet there is no danger, in this case, of unwittingly furthering less worthy aims while pursuing one's own enlightenment. The CIA will have as little patience with pyramids as the church of Rome, but no great animus against them either. Pyramids, being all alike, do not excite the imagination, and so even the least competent of painters, architects, or interior decorators should be able to view their construction with equanimity. What other undertaking could be at once so strenuous and so little self-deluding? This is a purer form even than working for an insurance company of modern, secular monasticism.

Q. Where will they be located?

A. Outside the towns of Fairmont, Pipestone, Moorhead, Bemidji, and Aurora. Anyone who wants to see them should have to make a special effort.

Q. How can I help *now*?

A. Send your name and address to PYRAMIDS, c/o this publisher, indicating whether your interest is in contributing funds or your own labor. When sufficient interest has been demonstrated, a nonprofit Pyramid Foundation will be established, and you will be notified.

I live in a building in which five of the 16 floors are given over to dormitory residences for a nearby art school. For a long time one elevator served all 16 floors, and it frequently happened that students from the art school would, in a spirit of mischief or malice, push *all* the buttons on the elevator panel just before they got off at their floor. Say the student got off on 5, and you were on 10 waiting to go down: you would have to wait while the elevator stopped at 6, 7, 8, and 9, and then you'd have to continue in the wrong direction all the way to 16, stopping at every floor (remember, this was a *slow* elevator), and stopping at 4, 3, and 2, as well, on the way down. This could be aggravating, and one day, as I was once again taking this long detour to the lobby, I thought of the ideal corrective action to be taken in such circumstances. By the time I'd reached the lobby I had written the first page and a half of the following cautionary tale.

Let all irresponsible and inconsiderate button-pushers be warned: you are being observed. If you don't mend your ways, *this may happen to you!*

Josie and the Elevator:

A Cautionary Tale

"You shouldn't do that," said the elevator, closing its doors in Josie's face and keeping her fast within its cage, for it meant to teach her a lesson. "You can't be going to 14 *and* 15, especially if you're getting out here on 13. You're simply causing *me* to do extra work—and I don't like it!"

It waited for the little girl to speak, and when she wouldn't, prodded her: "Well? Speak up."

"Elevators aren't supposed to talk," said Josie, without seeming confounded, only a bit surprised. After all, she'd often been in elevators that played music.

"Never mind Supposes. I demand an apology—and a promise that you'll stop punching all my buttons every time you leave. You've been doing that for weeks. Don't think I haven't noticed. It's wrong, and it must stop."

Josie made no reply, but stared up at the numbers over the door, none of which was lit. Then, taking thought, she jabbed the button for the first floor.

"Don't bother pressing buttons, young lady. I'm not letting you out of here till you apologize politely."

Josie pushed the alarm. It didn't ring. She pushed it again. Still the elevator wouldn't budge.

"*Why* have you been pushing those buttons, I should like to know?"

"It's none of your business why I do anything. You're an elevator, and you should just go up and down. I didn't ask you to talk to me."

"I don't need *your* permission, child. I go where I like, at the pace I like. As that also happens to be where my passengers want to go, there's no conflict. But I can keep *you* here as long as ever I like, so you'd best not be surly. Now answer my question."

"I punched the buttons because I wanted to," said Josie, not at all in an accommodating tone.

"And why did you want to?"

"Because I don't like living in this building! This building stinks!"

"And so you'd take out your resentment on me? And on all the people who have to wait for me? Do you think that's fair?"

"I don't care if it is or it isn't. So there."

"Oh, really?" said the elevator in a tone partly sarcastic and partly ominous. "I think it would be well if you were *made* to care!"

"I never *asked* to live here, did I?"

"You should be glad you do. This is a fine building. It keeps you warm in winter, and dry when it rains. Where would you sleep at night if you didn't sleep here? What would you eat for dinner if you didn't have a kitchen to cook in?"

"It's an *awful* building," Josie insisted petulantly. "I *know* what nice buildings are like, you can't fool me. My father lives uptown in a penthouse, and when I'm with him I have my own bedroom *and* my own bathroom, and the tub isn't old and yellow, and the walls don't have cracks, and there aren't any cockroaches, and there's a doorman at the front door who always says, 'Good morning, Miss Hardwinter, how are you today?' "

"Those are advantages, surely, but they all cost money. People who can't afford such luxuries must make do with what they can afford. What is the doorman's name?"

"How should I know that? He's only a doorman."

"It sounds like you're just as rude when you live with your father as you are here. What sort of things do you talk about with him?"

"He's usually too busy to talk with me. He's a famous businessman. He had his picture in the newspaper, you know."

"I didn't mean your father: I meant the doorman—what do you talk about with *him*?"

"I don't talk with the doorman!" Josie said indignantly.

"You should. Doormen get very bored sitting about in their uniforms; they'd like some company. They're much like elevators in that regard."

"Poo on doormen, and poo on elevators too! I want to get *out* of here. Right now."

"Not until you apologize."

"I'll scream."

"No one will hear you."

Josie, who by now was genuinely distraught, began to stamp on the scuffed linoleum-tiled floor, but the elevator was not stirred except to become angrier itself. Josie had never understood that this was the invariable result of her temper tantrums.

True to its word, the elevator did not give in. Even when Josie carried out her threat and screamed and threw herself down on the floor and pounded on it with her fists— even through all that, the elevator remained unmoved.

It was then that Josie made a most unwise decision. She took off her left shoe and threw it with all the force she could muster at the elevator's mirror. That mirror, up in the corner of the cage, was the elevator's proudest possession. No other elevator (it believed), however superior in other respects, could boast a mirror of such bright distinction. When it shattered, the elevator shivered along the length of its whole cable and then, with a terrible roar, began a wild descent. Down it plummeted, down past the first floor without a stop, and still it fell—ever deeper down to those dark regions only elevators know how to reach. Down to the very floor of hell, where it opened its doors with a shudder and shouted at the astonished child, "Get out!" Josie got out.

She didn't realize that she'd been taken to hell, for it looked nearly the same as the ground floor lobby of her own apartment building. There was the big aluminum ashtray, beside the elevator door, looking just as it had looked in the world above. Josie didn't notice that it was overflowing with cigarette butts and other refuse, nor did she notice, when she went out upon the street, that the cars all drove much faster and honked their horns at the least provocation.

Hell, you see, is exactly like the world we all live in, the only difference being that everyone you meet there is completely inconsiderate and rude. Judging by appearances, they are the same people you knew above, but they behave quite differently, as Josie was soon to discover.

Naturally she did not want to go back inside the elevator she had just escaped from. As little did she want to climb thirteen flights of stairs. Her father had told her that if she were ever in an emergency she must call him or come to his apartment, and this must surely count as an emergency. So that's where she decided to go. The problem, however, was how to get there. Her father lived in another neighborhood far on the other side of town, and though Josie knew how to get there on the number 12 bus, the bus driver wouldn't let her into the bus without paying. The fare was a quarter, and she had spent her last quarter just an hour ago on a Mounds candy bar.

She knew that it would be wrong and shameful to beg for the money she needed from passersby, and in any case all the people on the streets looked crazy or hostile or dangerous.

But how was she to *walk* so far, even supposing she

could find the way? Her left shoe, the shoe she had thrown at the mirror, was still inside the elevator.

For a long time she just sat on the curb, trying to cry. People, she had discovered, will often help you if you are crying. But that was in the world above. In hell no one notices your tears very much. In any case, she wasn't able to produce more than a bit of dampness about her eyelids, for the air of hell makes it harder to cry.

When looking forlorn produced no results, Josie decided she must ask a policeman to help her. That is what she'd been told to do if ever she were lost. Taking off her one shoe and both stockings, she set off in search of a policeman, taking care not to step on the shattered glass that covered the sidewalk and the street. At the very first corner she came to, she didn't see the light was about to change from green to red, and she was almost run over by an enormous white Cadillac. She jumped back just in time, and the driver shouted a dirty word out of the window.

Josie scarcely noticed the driver's bad language however, for she had just cut her foot on a large sliver of glass. Hell, you see, is full of non-returnable bottles, which people throw from the windows of their apartments just for the satisfaction of hearing them smash.

It would take much too long and be much too distressing to give a full account of all the sufferings that Josie underwent in hell, for, sad to say, she lived there many years, each one a little more miserable than the year before. It had never been the elevator's intention to leave her there so long, but once Josie had gone off to her father's apartment, the matter was beyond its control. Josie, not wanting to explain to her father about her disagreement with the elevator, led him to suppose that the reason she'd suddenly appeared on his doorstep, barefoot and bleeding, was because her mother had locked her out of the apartment as a punishment. Naturally, when Mr. Hardwinter called his ex-wife on the phone and yelled at her, she was not a little angry with her daughter for telling such a lie and with her husband for believing it and for yelling so. The argument became embittered, and the final result was that Mrs. Hardwinter threw over her job with the life insurance company (there are life insurance companies in hell, just as there are here) and went away across the ocean to the island of Ibiza (yes, hell even has its own version of Ibiza), which she had been threatening to do ever since the divorce. Because of this Josie never had occasion to return to her mother's apartment, which had been sub-let to a complete stranger. And so the elevator couldn't take her back to the world above. (For only the elevator that takes you down to hell can take you up again.) The elevator felt very sorry, but there was nothing it could do till such time as Josie should re-enter its cage.

Though she knew that her life had become, of a sudden, drastically unhappier, Josie never suspected she was in hell. At school she was always made to sit in the front row. Her teachers were boring, stupid, and either weepy or very mean. Her classmates teased her mercilessly for being fat. At home her father ignored her, and she spent her afternoons and evenings all alone watching mind-numbing programs on TV and eating junky desserts, which made her still fatter. These desserts were poisoned, as all the food in hell is poisoned, so that when she was in school she couldn't think clearly. She flunked fourth grade, and seventh grade too. By then her father had become an alcoholic. They moved to a cheaper apartment in a neighborhood filled with muggers, where even on summer afternoons it wasn't safe to go outside to play. No longer could she brag about having her own bathroom, or even her own bedroom, for the room she had to sleep in now was also a kind of office. There was an awful smell in the kitchen that never went away.

Josie became a teenager, and then a grown-up, and still each year was more rotten and dismal than the year before. But really, there's no need to go into details. Enough to say that by the time she was 24 she had been married three times and raped twice—once, when she was 15, in the locker room of her high school, and the second time when she was 22 by her first ex-husband, who very nearly killed her. She had also made two suicide attempts, with pills, but in hell suicide attempts are never allowed to succeed. Otherwise everyone could just kill themselves and be done with it.

Despite everything that had happened to her in hell, Josie still somehow believed there was a way things might get better. She believed, in the words of one of her favorite songs, that *somewhere* there was a place for her, a place she could at last be happy in. But where? She would never have believed that that happier place was no farther off than the other side of town, for by now she'd forgotten everything that had passed between her and the elevator, the way you forget the things that happen in nightmares. In hell there are so many nasty things happening all the time that if you kept track of every one of them you'd soon go quite insane.

That, in fact, is what had happened to Josie's mother in Ibiza. First she had come down with infectious hepatitis, and then while she was recovering from that something went wrong inside her head and she was able to see all hell's usually invisible devils. For years she had to live in mental hospitals, jeered at by these devils the way poor Josie was jeered at by her classmates. Even in our world mental hospitals are nowhere anyone would want to live, but in hell, naturally, they're much, much worse. Nevertheless, one day Mrs. Hardwinter's insanity disappeared as inexplicably as it had come. That is to say, she stopped being able to see the devils around her. After she'd convinced the examining doctors that she wasn't crazy any more (which took rather a long while), they let her out of the hospital. Having no other idea where to go, she returned to the apartment building she used to live in, and asked if there was an apartment she could rent. As the building was scheduled to be demolished in two more years (a fact of which the renting agent didn't bother to inform her), there were several vacant apartments to choose from, and so, twenty years after she'd left it, Mrs. Hardwinter returned to apartment 13-D.

When Josie got her mother's postcard inviting her to visit her at the old address, her first reaction was simply to be furious. The nerve of her, after running away and leaving her with her old soak of a father! After twenty years of almost unbroken silence! (There had admittedly been Christmas cards, for even in hell one is obliged to send Christmas cards.) After locking her out of the apartment without her shoes! (For Josie had come to believe her own long-ago lie.) To send a *postcard* after all that! "I'll send *her* a postcard," she thought. "See how she likes *them* apples!"

But then (for Josie led a very lonely life in hell) she decided, after all, that a single visit could do no harm. Her mother might actually have become a nice person. And if she hadn't, Josie would at least have the satisfaction of telling her off. So, donning her brightest pants suit and arming herself with a purse containing a spray-can of Mace (a standard precaution in hell), Josie set off on the number 12 bus and arrived in her old neighborhood in a little less than an hour.

The years had not been kind to the old apartment building. Its stone doorway had been vandalized, and its remains covered over with yellow formica, part of the decoration of the pornography shop that had moved in on the ground floor. The buzzer system didn't work, and inside the lobby half the mail boxes looked like they'd been broken into. The aluminum ashtray had disappeared, and the floor now served in that capacity. Graffiti covered every surface with irrefutable evidences of the hatred, lust, and imbecility so prevalent in hell.

Josie regarded the elevator button doubtfully, unable to believe that in such a derelict building the elevator might still be working. But even in hell one hopes against hope. She pressed the button, and lo and behold, there was a rattling of chains and then a long, deep groan, and the doors of the elevator opened.

Suddenly it all came back to her—everything the elevator had said to her, and how she had replied.

"Oh, elevator!" she cried out, falling to her knees and pressing her hands and then her lips to the scuffed, unswept linoleum tiles. "Elevator! Dear elevator, I'm sorry! I'm so sorry—please, please forgive me! I'll replace the mirror I broke. And keep you clean. And— And I *promise* never, never to do such a terrible thing again."

Without a word (being too moved to attempt a reply), and without waiting for Josie to press 13, the elevator hurtled upwards, up past the boundaries of hell, up past the ground floor of the world above, up in a single glad rush to where Josie's mother lived on the thirteenth floor. There it stopped and opened its doors, and Josie got off with a sense, irrational but nonetheless unshakable, that her life had taken a turn for the better.

And of course it had. Josie found that she liked her mother better than she'd ever liked her before, and her mother, though a little suspicious at first and inclined to believe Josie crazy (for she could not be kept from conversing with the elevator whenever she was in it), eventually came round to liking her, too. They decided to live together there in the old apartment building, which wasn't torn down, after all, but renovated instead. Josie, true to her promise, replaced the mirror she'd broken, and the poor old elevator was so overcome that it was stuck for four days on 13. But after the repairman came and tinkered with it, it seemed as good as new.

Josie's life, too, took a turn for the better. With a bit of friendly bullying from her mother, she got her weight down to a comfortable 130 pounds. Nicest of all, she found a job that didn't drive her crazy with boredom, and paid a decent wage beside. (In fact, she became a teacher, but that is another story.)

All in all, Josie could not complain, or at least she preferred not to. If this wasn't heaven (elevators, alas, cannot go *there*), it was clearly an improvement on hell.

Though critics rarely examine its nuts and bolts, visualization is as crucial to the craft of story-telling as character, plot, or (in the prosodic sense) style. Often, when prose is praised for being 'poetic', it is not for its aural properties but for its power to project images on the camera obscura of the reading mind. J. G. Ballard, for instance, might as well have been born deaf, but few writers *paint* so persuasively with a typewriter.

The reason critics are so leery of the subject is that it borders on epistemology. It's easier to talk about the characters and events of a story as though they were established facts than to sail close to the reefs of solipsism and semiology. This note, therefore, is only an I.O.U. against the day my own thoughts on the matter are better formulated, and as an admonition to readers to make a small adjustment in the viewing apparatus as they attend . . .

An Italian Lesson

She knew, before he'd even entered, that she would fall in love with him—or with someone—just as starlings know, with annual infallibility, that they must begin to collect the straws that will become, with a bit of poking and prodding, their cozy little nests.

This would be her first ball, and she was dressed all in pink—pink shoes and pink stockings, a pink ball gown trimmed with a sash of a more vivid pink, pink feathers in her hair, and, clutched in her lovely fingers, a pink *fazzoletta,* or handkerchief.

The violins were whirling about her with a kind of gentle violence, leaves by the wild hurricane tossed. Some, growing tired, nestled on the chandelier; others, more reckless, floated in fountains of recirculated champagne. And still the waltz went on: one two three; one two three: Vienna, Paris, Hollywood! Where *was* he?

But even before she could think that thought, before one scintilla of her first girlish exhilaration could dim, a servant approached with a crystal goblet brimming with champagne. "Signorina?" he enquired. She accepted the enchanted beverage, and even as she drank it he whispered in her ear the legend of the Blessed Giulietta—how she had slept three days and three nights, how she had cured the beggar simply by the passage of her shadow over his shadow. A strange and rather ominous tale, which she listened to with every fiber of her being.

What was happening to her? Too late to ask! Even before the waiter had finished relating this legend, before he had vanished into the throng with his tray of drinks, she realized that her forebodings had been realized: she had fallen in love! And with him! With a waiter in a starched white shirtfront and a black bow tie. A waiter, moreover, who, unless she were mistaken, had just stolen her pink handkerchief and one of her pink gloves. She didn't even know his name. There was nothing she could do except to hide her naked hand behind her back and hope she had not been observed.

The Prince approached her. He asked her to dance. She had no choice but to refuse, and he offered his hand, next, to one of the infuriating Arditti sisters. They were so full of themselves, those Ardittis! Not that it could possibly matter, now, to her, for she was already in love, for ever. She could have cried, she could have spat, she could have died there on the spot, but worse was still in store.

A *zingara* approached her, a gypsy girl with cheap imitation shoes and a cardboard sign demanding that she adopt her as her own daughter. "Nonsense," she told the zingara. The girl prodded her with the piece of cardboard, forcing her, step by step, backward through the crowd. In its way it was as though they were dancing. She'd never been one to say no easily, so she gave excuses to the girl why she couldn't adopt her. The girl told her she was being insincere. And it was true! She started to cry.

"This is not my life," she insisted as the waiter led her by the elbow out of the ballroom. "I was meant to lead a nicer life than this."

He put her into a cab with the zingara and told the driver their address. It was in the poorest quarter of the town. She was only eighteen. Her life was over. All her clothes would be black.

Hegel said that when history repeats itself, the tragedy of round one changes to comedy in the replay. History may resist such a neat pattern, but I can't, and halfway through the following story, with the end already well in view, I realized that I'd slipped into Hegel's paradigm. "Understanding Human Behavior" is clearly an upbeat, comedy-toned version of "The Asian Shore," one of my darker tales, which I'd written 11 years earlier, in 1968. The hero is in the same rudderless situation. He encounters a woman who presents him with a theory about who he is that tends to contradict his own (rather shaky) theory. There is, as well, in both tales a waif who thirds their pair. Further, both stories are set in exotic locales which had recently bowled me over. In "The Asian Shore" it was Istanbul, in this story the Colorado Rockies.

The defining difference, though, is not between dark city streets and wide open spaces, nor between the East of ancient history (with all its horrors) and the West of a hopeful Tomorrow. The difference is mainly the distance, internally and externally, between 1968 and 1979. Quite simply, I'm happier these days, and on that mellow note let me say *Ave atque* (I'm leaving now, before the feature starts) *vale*.

Understanding Human Behavior

I

He would wake up each morning with a consciousness clear as the Boulder sky, a sense of being on the same wave length exactly as the sunlight. Innocence, bland dreams, a healthy appetite—these were glories that issued directly from his having been erased. Of course, there were some corresponding disadvantages. His job, monitoring the terminals of a drive-in convenience center, could get pretty dull, especially on days when no one drove in for an hour or so at a stretch, and even at the busiest times it didn't provide much opportunity for human contact. He envied the waitresses in restaurants and the drivers of buses their chance to say hello to real live customers.

Away from work it was different; he didn't feel the same hunger for socializing. That, in fact, was the major disadvantage of having no past life, no established preferences, no identity in the usual sense of a history to attach his name to—he just didn't *want* anything very much.

Not that he was bored or depressed or anything like that. The world was all new to him, and full of surprises: the strangeness of anchovies; the beauty of old songs in their blurry Muzak versions at the Stop-and-Shop; the feel of a new shirt or a March day. These sensations were not wholly unfamiliar, nor was his mind a *tabula rasa*. His use of the language and his motor skills were all intact; also what the psychologists at Delphi Institute called generic recognition. But none of the occasions of newness reminded him of any earlier experience, some first time or best time or worst time that he'd survived. His only set of memories of a personal and non-generic character were those he'd brought from the halfway house in Delphi, Indiana. But such fine memories they were—so fragile, so distinct, so privileged. If only (he often wished) he could have lived out his life in the sanctuary of Delphi, among men and women like himself, all newly summoned to another life and responsive to the wonders and beauties around them. But no, for reasons he could not understand, the world insisted on being organized otherwise. An erasee was allowed six months at the Institute, and then he was dispatched to wherever he or the computer decided, where he would have to live like everyone else, either alone or in a family (though the Institute advised everyone to be wary at first of establishing primary ties), in a small room or a cramped house or a dormitory ship in some tropical lagoon. Unless you were fairly rich or very lucky, your clothes, furniture, and suchlike appurtenances were liable to be rough, shabby, makeshift. The food most people ate was an incitement to infantile gluttony, a slop of sugars, starches, and chemically enhanced flavors. It would have been difficult to live among such people and to seem to share their values, except so few of them ever questioned the reasonableness of their arrangements. Those who did, if they had the money, would probably opt, eventually, to have their identities erased, since it was clear, just looking around, that erasees seemed to strike the right intuitive balance between being aware and keeping calm.

He lived now in a condo on the northwest edge of the city, a room and a half with unlimited off-peak power access. The rent was modest (so was his salary), but his equity in the condo was large enough to suggest that his pre-erasure income had been up there in the top percentiles.

He wondered, as all erasees do, why he'd decided to wipe out his past. His life had gone sour, that much was sure, but how and why were questions that could never be answered. The Institute saw to that. A shipwrecked marriage was the commonest reason statistically, closely followed by business reverses. At least that was what people put down on their questionnaires when they applied to the Institute. Somehow he doubted those reasons were the real ones. People who'd never been erased seemed oddly unable to account for their behavior. Even to themselves they would tell the unlikeliest tales about what they were doing and why. Then they'd spend a large part of their social life exposing each others' impostures and laughing at them. A sense of humor they called it. He was glad he didn't have one, yet.

Most of his free time he spent making friends with his body. In his first weeks at the halfway house he'd lazed about, eaten too much junk food, and started going rapidly to seed. Erasees are not allowed to leave their new selves an inheritance of obesity or addiction, but often the body one wakes up in is the hasty contrivance of a crash diet. The mouth does not lose its appetites, nor the metabolism its rate, just because the mind has had memories whited out. Fortunately he'd dug in his heels, and by the time he had to bid farewell to Delphi's communal dining room he'd lost the pounds he'd put on, and eight more besides.

Since then fitness had been his religion. He bicycled to work, to Stop-and-Shop, and all about Denver, exploring its uniformities. He hiked and climbed on weekends. He jogged. Once a week, at a Y, he played volleyball for two hours, just as though he'd never left the Institute. He also kept up the other sport he'd had to learn at Delphi, which was karate. Except for the volleyball, he stuck to the more solitary forms of exercise, because on the whole he wasn't interested in forming relationships. The lecturers at the halfway house had said this was perfectly natural, and nothing to worry about. He shouldn't socialize until he felt hungry for more society than his job and his living arrangements naturally provided. So far that hunger had not produced a single pang. Maybe he was what the Institute called a natural integer. If so, that seemed an all-right fate.

What he did miss, consciously and sometimes achingly, was a purpose. In common with most fledgling erasees, there was nothing he *believed* in—no religion, no political idea, no ambition to become famous for doing something better than somebody else. Money was about the only purpose he could think of, and even that was not a compelling purpose. He didn't lust after more and more and more of it in the classical Faustian go-getter way.

His room and a half looked out across the tops of a small plantation of spruces to the highway that climbed the long southwestward incline into the Rockies. Each car that hummed along the road was like a vector-quantity of human desire, a quantum of teleological purpose. He might have been mistaken. The people driving those cars might be just as uncertain of their ultimate destinations as he was, but, seeing them whiz by in their primary colors, he found that hard to believe. Anyone who was prepared to bear the expense of a car surely had somewhere he wanted to get to or something he wanted to do more intensely than *he* could imagine, up here on his three-foot slab of balcony.

He didn't have a telephone or a TV. He didn't read newspapers or magazines, and the only books he ever looked at were some old textbooks on geology he'd bought at a garage sale in Denver. He didn't go to movies. The ability to suspend disbelief in something that had never happened was one he'd lost when he was erased, assuming he'd ever had it. A lot of the time he couldn't suspend his disbelief in the real people around him, all their pushing and pulling, their weird fears and whopping lies, their endless urges to control other people's behavior, like the vegetarian cashier at the Stop-and-Shop or the manager at the convenience center. The lectures and demonstrations at the halfway house had laid out the basics, but without explaining any of it. Like harried parents, the Institute's staff had said, "Do this," and "Don't do that," and he'd not been in a position to argue. He did as he was bid, and his behavior fit as naturally as an old suit.

His name—the name by which he'd christened his new self before erasure—was Richard Roe, and that seemed to fit too.

II

At the end of September, three months after coming to Boulder, Richard signed up for a course in *Consumership: Theory and Practice* at the Naropa Adult Education Center. There were twelve other students in the class, all with the dewy, slightly vulnerable look of recent erasure. They sat in their folding chairs, reading or just blank, waiting for the teacher, who arrived ten minutes late, out of breath and gasping apologies. Professor Astor. While she was still collecting punchcards and handing out flimsy Xeroxes of their reading list, she started lecturing to them. Before she could get his card (he'd chosen a seat in the farthest row back) she was distracted by the need to list on the blackboard the three reasons that people wear clothing, which are:

1. Utility,
2. Communication, and
3. Self-Concept.

Utility was obvious and didn't need going into, while Self-Concept was really a sub-category of Communication, a kind of closed-circuit transmission between oneself and a mirror.

"Now, to illustrate the three basic aspects of Communication, I have some slides." She sat down behind the A/V console at the front of the room and fussed with the buttons anxiously, muttering encouragements to herself. Since the question was there in the air, he wondered what her black dress was supposed to be communicating. It was a wooly, baggy, practical dress, sprinkled with dandruff and gathered loosely about the middle by a wide belt of cracked patent leather. The spirit of garage sales hovered about it. "There!" she said.

But the slide that flashed on the screen was a chart illustrating cuts of beef. "Damn," she said, "that's next week. Well, it doesn't matter. I'll write it on the board."

When she stood up and turned around, it seemed clear that one of the utilitarian functions of her dress was to disguise or obfuscate some twenty-plus pounds of excess baggage. A jumble of thin bracelets jingled as she wrote on the board:

1. Desire,
2. Admiration,
3. Solidarity.

"There," she said, laying down the chalk and swinging round to face them, setting the heavy waves of black hair to swaying pendulously, "it's as simple as red, white, and blue. These are the three types of response people try to elicit from others by the clothes they wear. Blue, of course, would represent solidarity. Policemen wear blue. French workingmen have always worn a blinding blue. And then there's the universal uniform of blue denim. It's a cool color, and tends to make those who wear it recede into the background. They vanish into the blue, so to speak.

"Then white." She took a blank piece of paper from her desk and held it up as a sample of whiteness. "White is for white-collar workers, the starched white shirt wearable only for a single day being a timeless symbol of conspicuous consumption. I wish the slide projector worked for this: I have a portrait by Hals of a man wearing one of those immense Dutch collars, and you couldn't begin to imagine the work-hours that must have gone into washing and ironing the damned thing. The money. Basically that's what our second category is about. There's a book by Thorstein Veblen on the reading list that explains it all. Admittedly there are qualities other than solvency and success we may be called upon to *admire* in what people wear: good taste, a sense of paradox or wit, even courage, as when one walks through a dangerous neighborhood without the camouflage of denim. But good taste usually boils down to money: the good taste of petroleum-derived polyesters as against—" She smiled and ran her hand across the pilled cloth of her dress. "—the *bad* taste of wool. Wit, likewise, is usually the wit of combining contradictory class-recognition signals in the same costume—an evening gown, say, trimmed with Purina patches. You should all be aware, as consumers, that the chief purpose of spending a lot of money on what you wear is to proclaim your allegiance to money *per se,* and to a career devoted to earning it, or, in the case of diamond rings, the promise to keep one's husband activated. Though in this case we begin to impinge on the realm of desire."

To all which he gave about as much credence as he gave to actors in ads. Like most theories, it made the world seem more, not less, complicated. Ho-hum, thought he, as he doodled a crisp doodle of a many-faceted diamond. But then as she expounded her ideas about Desire he grew uneasy, then embarrassed, and finally teed-off.

"Red," she said, reading from her deck of three-by-fives, "is the color of desire. Love is always like a red, red rose. It lies a-bleeding like a beautiful steak in a supermarket. To wear red is to declare oneself ready for action, especially if the color is worn below the waist."

There he sat in the back row in his red shorts and red sneakers thinking angry red thoughts. He refused to believe it was a coincidence. He was wearing red shorts because he'd bicycled here, a five-mile ride, not because he wanted to semaphore his instant availability to the world at large. He waited till she'd moved off the subject of Desire, then left the classroom as inconspicuously as possible. In the Bursar's Office he considered the other Wednesday night possibilities, mostly workshops in posture or poetry or suchlike. Only one—*A Survey of Crime in 20th Century*

America—offered any promise of explaining people's behavior, so that was the one he signed up for.

The next day, instead of going to work, he went out to New Focus and watched hang-gliders. The most amazing of them was a crippled woman who arrived in a canvas sling. Rochelle Rockefeller's exploits had made her so famous that even Richard knew about her, not only on account of her flying but because she was one of the founding mothers of New Focus, and had been involved in sizable altercations with the state police. The two women who carried her down from New Focus in the sling busied themselves with straps and buckles and then, at Rochelle's nod, launched her off the side of the cliff. She rose, motor-assisted, on the updraught, and waved to her daughter, who sat watching on the edge of the cliff. The girl waved back. Then the girl went off by herself to the picnic table area, where two rag dolls awaited her atop one of the tables.

He walked over to the table and asked if she minded if he shared the bench with her.

She shook her head, and then in a rather dutiful tone introduced her dolls. The older was Ms. Chillywiggles, the younger was Ms. Sillygiggles. They were married. "And *my* name is Rochelle, the same as my mother. What's yours?"

"Richard Roe."

"Did you bring any *food?*"

"No. Sorry."

"Oh well, we'll just have to pretend. Here's some tuna fish, and here's some cake." She doled out the imaginary food with perfunctory mime to her dolls, and then with exaggerated delicacy she held up—what was it?—something for him.

"Open your mouth and close your eyes," she insisted.

He did, and felt her fingers on his tongue.

"What was that?" he asked, afterward.

"Holy Communion. Did you like it?"

"Mm."

"Are you a Catholic?"

"No, unless that just made me one."

"*We* are. We believe in God the Father Almighty and *everything*. Ms. Chillywiggles was even in a *convent* before she got married. Weren't you?" Ms. Chillywiggles nodded her large, wobbly head.

Finding the subject uncomfortable, he changed it. "Look at your mother up there now. Wow."

Rochelle sighed and for a moment, to be polite, glanced up to where her mother was soaring, hundreds of feet above.

"It's incredible, her flying like that."

"That's what everyone says. But you don't need your leg muscles for a hang-glider, just your arms. And her arms are very strong."

"I'll bet."

"*Some* day we're going to go to Denver and see the dolls' Pope."

"Really. I didn't know dolls had a Pope."

"They do."

"Will you look at her now!"

"I don't like to, it makes me sick. I didn't want to come today, but no one would look after me. They were all *building*. So I had to."

"It doesn't make you want to fly someday, seeing her up there like that?"

"No. Some day she's going to kill herself. She knows it, too. That's how she had her accident, you know. She wasn't always in a wheelchair."

"Yes, I've heard that."

"What's so awful for *me* is to think she won't ever be able to receive the Last Sacrament."

The sun glowed through the red nylon wings of the glider, but even Professor Astor would have had a hard time making that fit her theory. Desire! Why not just Amazement?

"If she does kill herself," Rochelle continued dispassionately, "*we'll* be sent to an orphanage. In Denver, I hope. And Ms. Chillywiggles will be able to do missionary work among the dolls there. Do you have any dolls, Mr. Roe?"

He shook his head.

"I suppose you think dolls are only for *girls*. That's a very old prejudice, however. Dolls are for anyone who *likes* them."

"I may have had dolls when I was younger. I don't know."

"Oh. Were you erased?"

He nodded.

"So was my mother. But I was only a baby then, so I don't remember any more about her than she does. What I think is she must have committed some really terrible sin, and it tortured her so much she decided to be erased. Do you ever go in to Denver?"

"Sometimes."

Ms. Sillygiggles whispered something in Ms. Chilly-wiggles' ear, who evidently did not agree with the suggestion. Rochelle looked cast down. "Damn," she said.

"What's wrong?"

"Oh nothing. Ms. Sillygiggles was hoping *you'd* be able to take them to Denver to see the dolls' Pope, but Ms. Chillywiggles put her foot down and said Absolutely Not. You're a stranger: we shouldn't even be talking to you."

He nodded, for it seemed quite true. He had no business coming out to New Focus at all.

"I should be going," he said.

Ms. Sillygiggles got to her feet and executed an awkward curtsey. Rochelle said it had been nice to make his acquaintance. Ms. Chillywiggles sat on the wooden step and said nothing.

It seemed to him, as he walked down the stony path to where he'd locked his bicycle to a rack, that everyone in the world was crazy, that craziness was synonymous with the human condition. But then he could see, through a break in the close-ranked spruces, the arc of a glider's flight—not Rochelle Rockefeller's, this one had blue wings and his spirits soared with the sheer music of it. He understood, in a moment of crystalline levelheadedness, that it didn't make a speck of difference if people were insane. Or if he was, for that matter. Sane or insane were just stages of the great struggle going on everywhere all the time: across the valley, for instance, where the pines were fighting their way up the sides of the facing mountain, hurling the grenades of their cones into the thin soil, pressing their slow advantage, enduring the decimations of the lightning, aspiring (insanely, no doubt) toward the forever unreachable fastness of the summit.

When he got to the road his lungs were heaving, his feet hurt, and his knees were not to be reasoned with (he should not have been running along such a path), but his head was once again solidly fixed on his shoulders. When he called his boss at the Denver Central Office to apologize for absconding, he wasn't fired or even penalized. His boss, who was usually such a tyrannosaurus, said everyone had days when they weren't themselves, and that it was all right, so long as they were few and far between. He even offered some Valiums, which Richard said no-thank-you to.

III

At Naropa the next Wednesday, the lecturer, a black man in a spotless white polyester suit, lectured about Ruth Snyder and Judd Gray, who, in 1927, had killed Ruth's husband Albert in a more than usually stupid fashion. He'd chosen this case, he said, because it represented the lowest common denominator of the crime of passion, and would therefore serve to set in perspective the mystery and romance of last week's assassinations, which Richard had missed. First they watched a scene from an old comedy based on the murder, and then the lecturer read aloud a section of the autobiography Judd Gray had written in Sing Sing while waiting to be electrocuted:

"I was a morally sound, sober, God-fearing chap, working and saving to make Isabel my wife and establish a home. I met plenty of girls—at home and on the road, in trains and hotels. I could, I thought, place every type: the nice girl who flirts, the nice girl who doesn't, the brazen out-and-out streetwalker I was warned against. I was no sensualist, I studied no modern cults, thought nothing about inhibitions and repressions. Never read Rabelais in my life. Average, yes—

just one of those Americans Mencken loves to laugh at. Even belonged to a club—the Club of Corset Salesmen of the Empire State—clean-cut competitors meeting and shaking hands—and liking it."

There was something in the tone of Judd Gray's voice, so plain, so accepting, that made Richard feel not exactly a kinship, more a sense of being similarly puzzled and potentially out of control. Maybe it was just the book's title that got to him—*Doomed Ship*. He wondered, not for the first time, whether he might not be among the fifteen percent of erasees whose past has been removed by judicial fiat rather than by choice. He could, almost, imagine himself outside the Snyder bedroom in Queens Village, getting steadily more soused as he waited for Albert to go to sleep so that then he could sneak in there and brain him with the sash weight in his sweaty hand. All for the love of Ruth Snyder, as played by Carol Burnett. He couldn't, however, see himself as a more dignified sort of criminal—a racketeer or an assassin or the leader of a cult—for he lacked the strength of character and the conviction that those roles would have required, and he'd probably lacked it equally in the life that had been erased.

After the class he decided he'd tempt Fate, and went to the cafeteria, where Fate immediately succumbed to the temptation and brought Professor Astor of *Consumership: Theory and Practice* to his table with a slice of viscid, bright cherry cheesecake. "May I join you?" she asked him.

"Sure. I was just going anyhow."

"I like your suit," she said. This close she seemed younger, or perhaps it was her dress that made that difference. Instead of last week's black wool bag she was wearing a dull blue double-knit with a scarf sprinkled with blurry off-red roses. One glance and anyone would have felt sorry for her.

His suit was the same dull blue. He'd bought it yesterday at the Stop-and-Shop, where the salesman had tried to convince him not to buy it. With it he wore a wrinkled Wrinkle-Proof shirt and a tie with wide stripes of gray and ocher. "Thanks," he said.

"It's very '70's. You're an erasee, aren't you?"

"Mm."

"I can always tell another. I am, too. With a name like Lady Astor I'd have to be, wouldn't I? I hope I didn't offend you by anything I said last week."

"No, certainly not."

"It wasn't directed at you personally. I just read what it said in my notes, which were taken, all of them, practically verbatim, from *The Colors of the Flag.* We teachers are all cheats that way, didn't you know? There's nothing we can tell you that you won't find expressed better in a book. But of course learning, in that sense, isn't the reason for coming here."

"No? What is then?"

"Oh, it's for meeting people. For playing new roles. For taking sides. For crying out loud."

"What?"

"That's an old expression—for crying out loud. From the '40's, I think. Actually your suit is more '40's than '70's. The '40's were *sincere* about being drab; the '70's played games."

"Isn't there anything that's just here and now, without all these built-in meanings?"

She poised her fork over the gleaming cheesecake. "Well," she said thoughtfully, then paused for a first taste of her dessert. "Mnyes, sort of. After you left last week someone in the class asked if there wasn't a way one could be just anonymous. And what I said—" She took another bite of cheesecake. "—was that to my mind—" She swallowed. "—anonymity would come under the heading of solidarity, and solidarity is always solidarity *with* something—an idea, a group. Even the group of people who don't want to have anything to do with anyone else—even they're a *group.* In fact, they're probably among the largest."

"I'm amazed," he said, counterattacking on sheer irresistible impulse, "that you, a supposed expert on consumerism, can eat junk like the junk you're eating. The sugar makes you fat and gives you cancer, the dye causes cancer too, and I don't know what else, and there's something in the milk powder that I just heard about that's lethal. What's the point of being erased, if afterwards you lead a life as stupid as everybody else's?"

"Right," she said. She picked up a paper plate from an abandoned tray, and with a decisive rap of her fist squashed the wedge of cheesecake flat. "No more! Never again!"

He looked at the goo and crumbs splattered across the table, as well as on her scarf (there was a glob on his tie, too, but he didn't notice that), and then at her face, a study in astonishment, as though the cheesecake had exploded autonomously. He started to laugh, and then, as though given permission, she did, too.

They stayed on, talking, in the cafeteria until it closed, first about Naropa, then about the weather. This was his first experience of the approach of winter, and he surprised himself at the way he waxed eloquent. He marveled at how the aspens had gone scarlet all at once, as though every tree on a single mountain were activated by one switch and when that switch was thrown, bingo, it was autumn; the way, day by day, the light dwindled as his half of the world tilted away from the sun; the way the heat had come on in his condo without warning, and baked the poor coleus living on top of the radiator; the misery of bicycling in the so much colder rain; and what was most amazing, the calmness of everyone in the face of what looked to him like an unqualified catastrophe. Lady Astor made a few observations of her own, but mostly she just listened, smitten with his innocence. Her own erasure had taken place so long ago—she was evasive as to exactly when—that the world had no such major surprises in store for her. As the chairs were being turned upside down onto the tabletops, he made a vague, semi-enthusiastic commitment to hike up to New Focus some mutually convenient Sunday morning, to which end they exchanged addresses and phone numbers. (He had to give his number at work.) Why? It must have been the demolition of that cheesecake, the blissful feeling, so long lost to him, of muscular laughter, as though a window had been opened in a stuffy room and a wind had rushed in, turning the curtains into sails and bringing strange smells from the mountains outside.

* * *

.In the middle of November the company re-assigned him to the central office in downtown Denver, where he was assistant Traffic Manager for the entire Rocky Mountain division. Nothing in his work at the convenience center had seemed to point in this direction, but as soon as he scanned the programs involved it was all there in his head and fingers, lingering on like the immutable melody of $1 + 1 = 2$.

The one element of the job that wasn't second nature was the increased human contact, which went on, some days, nonstop. Hi there, Dick, what do you think of this and what do you think of that, did you see the game last night, what's your opinion of the crisis, and would you *please* speak to Lloyd about the time he's spending in the john. Lloyd, when spoken to, insisted he worked just as hard in the john as in the office, and said he'd cut down his time on the stool as soon as they allowed him to smoke at his desk. This seemed reasonable to Richard but not to the manager, who started to scream at him, calling him a zombie and a zeroid, and said he was fired. Instead, to nobody's great surprise, it was the manager who got the axe. So, after just two weeks of grooming, Richard was the new Traffic Manager, with an office all his own with its own view of other gigantic office buildings and a staff of thirty-two, if you counted temps and part-timers.

To celebrate he went out and had the famous hundred-dollar dinner at the Old Millionaire Steak Ranch with Lloyd, now the assistant Traffic Manager, with not his own office but at least a steel partition on one side of his desk and the right, thereby, to carcinogenate his lungs from punch-in to punch-out. Lloyd, it turned out, after a second Old Millionaire martini, lived up at New Focus and was one of the original members of the Boulder branch of the cult.

"No kidding," said Richard, reverently slicing into his sirloin. "That's fascinating. So why are you working here in the city? You can't commute to New Focus. Not this time of year."

"Money, why else. Half my salary, maybe more now, goes into the Corporation. We can't live for free, and there sure as hell isn't any money to be earned building a damned pyramid."

"So why do you build pyramids?"

"Come on, Dick. You know I can't answer that."

"I don't mean you as a group. I mean you personally. You must have *some* kind of reason for what you're doing."

Lloyd sighed long-sufferingly. "Listen, you've been up there, you've seen us cutting the blocks and fitting them in place. What's to explain? The beauty of the thing is that no one asks anyone else *why* we're doing what we're doing. Ever. That's Rule Number One. Remember that if you ever think of joining."

"Okay, then tell me this—why would I *want* to join?"

"Dick, you're hopeless. What did I just *say* to you? Enjoy your steak, why don't you? Do I ask why you want to throw away two hundred dollars on a dinner that can last, at the longest, a couple hours? No, I just enjoy it. It's beautiful."

"Mmn, I'm enjoying it. But still I can't keep from wondering."

"Wonder all you like—just don't ask."

IV

With the increased social inputs at work, he had gradually tapered off on his visits to Naropa. Winter sealed him into a more circumscribed routine of apartment, job, and gym, as mounds of snow covered the known surfaces of Boulder like a divine amnesia. On weekends he would sit like a bear in a cave, knitting tubes of various dimensions and looking out the window and not quite listening to the purr of KMMN playing olden goldens in flattened-out, long-breathed renditions that corresponded in a semi-conscious way to the forms of the snow as it drifted and stormed and lifted up past the window in endless unravelling banners.

He had not forgotten his promise to Lady Astor, but a trip to New Focus was no longer feasible. Even with skis and a lift assisting, it would have been an overnight undertaking. He phoned twice and explained this to her answering machine. In reply she left a message—"That's okay."—at the convenience center, which got forwarded to the central office a week later. His first impression, that Destiny had introduced them with some purpose in mind, was beginning to diminish when one Saturday morning on the bus going to the gym he saw a street sign he'd never noticed before, Follet Avenue, and remembered that that was the street she lived on. He yanked the cord, got off, and walked back over unshoveled sidewalks to the corner of 34th and Follet, already regretting his impulse: fifteen blocks to go, and then he might not find her home. It was 8 degrees below.

In the course of those fifteen blocks the neighborhood dwindled from dowdy to stark. She lived in a two-story clapboard shopfront that looked like an illustration of the year daubed in black paint over the entrance: 1972. The shop windows were covered with plywood, the plywood painted by some schizophrenic kindergarten with nightmarish murals, and the faded murals peered out forlornly from a lattice of obscene graffiti, desolation overlaying desolation.

He rang her bell and, when that produced no result, he knocked.

She came to the door wrapped in a blanket, hair in a tangle, bleary and haggard.

"Oh, it's you. I thought it might be you." Then, before he could apologize or offer to leave: "Well, you might as well come in. Leave your overshoes in the hall."

She had the downstairs half of the building, behind the boarded-up windows, which were sealed, on this side, with strips of carpet padding. A coal stove on a brick platform gave off a parsimonious warmth. With a creaking of springs Lady Astor returned to bed. "You can sit there," she said, gesturing to a chair covered with clothes. When he did, its prolapsed bottom sank under him like the seat of a rowboat. At once a scrawny tabby darted from one of the shadowy corners of the room (the only light came from a small unboarded window at the back) and sprang into his lap. It nuzzled his hand, demanding a caress.

While he stumbled through the necessary explanations (how he happened to be passing, why he hadn't visited before) she sipped vodka from a coffee cup. He assumed it was vodka, since a vodka bottle, half-empty and uncapped, stood on the cash register that served as a bedside table. Most of the shop-fittings had been left *in situ*: a glass counter, full of dishes and cookware; shelves bearing a jumble of shoes, books, ceramic pots, and antique, probably defunct, electric appliances. A bas-relief Santa of molded plastic was affixed to the wall behind the bed, its relevance belied by layers of greasy dust. The room's cluttered oddity combatted its aura of poverty and demoralization, but not enough: he felt stricken. This was another first in the category of emotions, and he didn't know what to call it. Not simply dismay; not guilt; not pity; not indignation (though how could anyone be drunk at ten o'clock on a Saturday morning!); not even awe for the spirit that could endure such dismalness and still appear at Naropa every Wednesday evening, looking more or less normative, to lecture on the theory and practice of (of all things) Consumership. All these elements, and maybe others, were fuddled together in what he felt.

"Do you want a drink?" she asked, and before he could answer: "Don't think it's polite to say yes. There's not much left. I started at six o'clock, but you have to understand I don't *usually* do this. But today seemed special. I thought, why not? Anyhow, why am I making excuses? I didn't invite you, you appeared at the door. I knew you would, eventually." She smiled, not pleasantly, and poured half the remaining vodka into her coffee cup. "You like this place?"

"It's big," he said lamely.

"And dark. And gloomy. And a mess. I was going to get the windows put back in, when I took the lease last summer. But that costs. And for winter this is warmer. Anyhow, if I did try to make it a shop I don't know what I'd sell. Junk. I *used* to throw pots. What *didn't* I used to do. I did a book of poetry based on the Tarot (which is how I latched onto the job at Naropa). I framed pictures. And now I lecture, which is to say I read books and talk about them to people like you, too lazy to read books on their own. And once, long ago, I was even a housewife, would you believe that." This time her smile was positively lethal. There seemed to be some secret message behind what she was saying that he couldn't uncode.

He sneezed.

"Are you allergic to cats?"

He shook his head. "Not that I know of."

"I'll bet you are."

He looked at her with puzzlement, then at the cat curled in his lap. The cat's warmth had penetrated through the denim, and warmed his crotch pleasantly.

"God damn it," she said, wiping a purely hypothetical tear from the corner of her bleary eye. "Why'd you have to pick this morning? Why couldn't you have phoned? You were always like that. You schmuck."

"What?"

"Schmuck," she repeated. And then, when he just went on staring: "Well, it makes no difference. I would have had to tell you eventually. I just wanted you to get to know me a little better first."

"Told me what?"

"I was never erased. I just lied about that. It's all there on the shelf, everything that happened, the betrayals, the dirt, the failures. And there were lots of those. I just never had the guts to go through with it. Same with the dentist. That's why I've got such lousy teeth. I *meant* to. I had the money—at least for a while, after the divorce, but I thought . . ." She shrugged, took a swallow from the cup, grimaced, and smiled, this time almost friendlily.

"What did your husband do?"

"Why do you ask that?"

"Well, you seem to want to tell the whole story. I guess I wanted to sound interested."

She shook her head. "You still don't have a glimmering, do you?"

"Of what?" He did have a glimmering, but he refused to believe it.

"Well then, since you just insist, I'll have to tell you, won't I? *You* were the husband you're asking about. And you haven't changed one damned bit. You're the same stupid schmuck you were then."

"I don't believe you."

"That's natural. After spending so much money to become *innocent*, who would want to see their investment wiped out like . . ." She tried to snap her fingers. ". . . that."

"There's no way you could have found me here. The Institute never releases that information. Not even to their employees."

"Oh, computers are clever these days (*you* know that), and for a couple thousand dollars it's not hard to persuade a salaried employee to tickle some data out of a locked file. When I found out where you'd gone, I packed my bags and followed you. I *told* you before you were erased that I'd track you down, and what you said was, 'Try, just try.' So that's what I did."

"You can be sent to prison for what you've done. Do you know that?"

"You'd like that, wouldn't you? If you could have had me locked up before, you wouldn't have had to get erased. You wouldn't have damned near killed me."

She said it with such conviction, with such a weariness modifying the anger, that it was hard to hold on to his reasonable doubt. He remembered how he'd identified with Judd Gray, the murderer of Albert Snyder.

"Don't you want to know *why* you tried to kill me?" she insisted.

"Whatever you used to be, Ms. Astor, you're not my wife now. You're a washed-up, forty-year-old drunk teaching an adult education course in the middle of nowhere."

"Yeah. Well, I could tell you how I got that way. Schmuck."

He stood up. "I'm leaving."

"Yes, you've said that before."

Two blocks from her house he remembered his over-shoes. To hell with his overshoes! To hell with people who don't shovel their sidewalks! Most of all, to hell with her!

That woman, his wife! What sort of life could they have lived together? All the questions about his past that he'd subdued so successfully up till now came bubbling to the surface: who he'd been, what he'd done, how it had all gone wrong. And she had the answers. The temptation to go back was strong, but before he could yield to it the bus came in the homeward direction, and he got on, his mind unchanged, his anger burning brightly.

V

Even so it was a week before he'd mustered the righteous indignation to call the Delphi Institute and register a formal complaint. They took down the information and said they'd investigate, which he assumed was a euphemism for their ignoring it. But in fact, a week later he got a registered letter from them stating that Ms. Lady Astor of 1972 Follet Avenue in Boulder, Colorado, had never been his wife, nor had there ever been any other connection between them. Further, three other clients of the Institute had registered similar complaints about the same Ms. Astor. Unfortunately, there was no law against providing erasees with misinformation about their past lives, and it was to be regretted that there were individuals who took pleasure in disturbing the equanimity of the Institute's clients. The letter pointed out that he'd been warned of such possibilities while he was at the halfway house.

Now, in addition to feeling angry and off-balance, he felt like an asshole as well. To have been so easily diddled! To have believed the whole unlikely tale without even the evidence of a snapshot!

Three days before Christmas she called him at work. "I didn't want to bother you," she said in a meek little whisper that seemed, even now, knowing everything, utterly sincere, "but I had to apologize. You did pick a hell of a time to come calling. If I hadn't been drunk I would never have spilled the beans."

"Uh-huh," was all he could think to say.

"I know it was wrong of me to track you down and all, but I couldn't help myself." A pause, and then her most .amazing lie of all: "I just love you too much to let you go."

"Uh-huh."

"I don't suppose there's any chance we could get together? For coffee, after work?"

When they got together for coffee, after work, he led her on from lie to lie until she'd fabricated a complete life for him, a romance as preposterous as any soap on TV, beginning with a tyrannical father, a doting mother, a twin brother killed in a car crash, and progressing through his years of struggle to become a painter. (Here she produced a brittle Polaroid of one of his putative canvases, a muddy jumble of ochers and umbers. She assured him that the Polaroid didn't do it justice.) The tale went on to tell how they'd met, and fallen in love, how he'd sacrificed his career as an artist to become an animation programmer. They'd been happy, and then—due to his monstrous jealousy—unhappy. There was more, but she didn't want to go into it, it was too painful. Their son . . .

Through it all he sat there nodding his head, seeming to believe each further fraud, asking appropriate questions, and (another First) enjoying it hugely—enjoying *his* fraudulence and her greater gullibility. Enjoying, too, the story she told him about his imaginary life. He'd never imagined a past for himself, but if he had he doubted if he'd have come up with anything so large, so resonant.

"So tell me," he asked, when her invention finally failed her, "why did I decide to be erased?"

"John," she said, shaking flakes of dandruff from her long black hair, "I wish I could answer that question. Partly it must have been the pain of little Jimmy's death. Beyond that I don't know."

"And now . . . ?"

She looked up, glittery. "Yes?"

"What is it you want?"

She gave a sigh as real as life. "I hoped . . . oh, you know."

"You want to get married again?"

"Well, no. Not till you've got to know me better, anyhow. I mean, I realize that from *your* point of view I'm still pretty much a stranger. And you've changed too, in some ways. You're like you were when I first met you. You're—" Her voice choked up, and tears came to her eyes.

He touched the clasp of his briefcase, but he didn't have the heart to take out the Xerox of the letter from the Delphi Institute that he'd been intending to spring on her. Instead he took the bill from under the saucer and excused himself.

"You'll call me, won't you?" she asked woefully.

"Sure, sure. Let me think about it a while first. Okay?"

She mustered a brave, quavering smile. "Okay."

*   *   *

In April, to mark the conclusion of the first year of his new life and just to glory in the weather that made such undertakings possible again, he took the lift up Mount Lifton, then hiked through Corporation Canyon past New Focus and the site of the pyramid—only eight feet at its highest edge so far, scarcely a tourist attraction—and on up the Five Waterfall Trail. Except for a few boot-challenging stretches of vernal bogginess, the path was stony and steep. The sun shone, winds blew, and the last sheltered ribs of snow turned to water and sought, trickle by trickle, the paths of least resistance. By one o'clock he'd reached his goal, Lake Silence, a perfect little mortuary chapel of a tarn, colonnaded all round with spruces. He found an unshadowed, accommodating rock to bask on, took off his wet boots and damp socks, and listened as the wind did imitations of cars on a highway. Then, chagrined, he realized it wasn't the wind but the shuddering roar of an approaching helicopter.

The helicopter emerged like a demiurge from behind the writhing tops of the spruces, hovered a moment above the tarn, then veered in the direction of his chosen rock. As it passed directly overhead, a stream of water spiralled out of the briefly opened hatch, dissolving almost at once in the machine's rotary winds into a mist of rainbow speckles. His first thought was that he was being bombed, his next that the helicopter was using Lake Silence as a toilet. Only when the first tiny trout landed, splat, on the rock beside him did he realize that the helicopter must have been from the Forest Service and was seeding the lake with fish. Alas, it had missed its mark, and the baby trout had fallen on the rocks of the shore and into the branches of the surrounding trees. The waters of Lake Silence remained unrippled and inviolate.

He searched among those fallen along the shore—there were dozens—for survivors, but all that he could find proved inert and lifeless when he put them in the water. Barefoot, panicky, totally devoted to the trout of Lake Silence, he continued the search. At last, among the matted damp needles beneath the spruces, he found three fish still alive and wiggling. As he lowered them, lovingly, into the lake he realized in a single lucid flash what it was he had to do with his life.

He would marry Lady Astor.

He would join New Focus and help them build a pyramid.

And he would buy a car.

(Also, in the event that she became orphaned, he would adopt little Rochelle Rockefeller. But that was counting chickens.)

He went to the other side of Lake Silence, to the head of the trail, where the Forest Service had provided an emergency telephone link disguised as a commemorative plaque to Governor Dent. He inserted his credit card into the slot, the plaque opened, and he punched Lady Astor's number. She answered at the third ring.

"Hi," he said. "This is Richard Roe. Would you like to marry me?"

"Well, yes, I guess so. But I ought to tell you—I was never really your wife. That was a story I made up."

"I knew that. But it was a nice story. And I didn't have one that I could tell you. One more thing, though. We'll have to join New Focus and help them build their pyramid."

"Why?"

"You can't ask why. That's one of their rules. Didn't you know that?"

"Would we have to live up there?"

"Not year-round. It'd be more like having a summer place, or going to church on Sunday. Plus some work on the pyramid."

"Well, I suppose I could use the exercise. Why do you want to get married? Or is that another question I shouldn't ask?"

"Oh, probably. One more thing: what's your favorite color?"

"For what?"

"A car."

"A car! Oh, I'd *love* a car! Be a show-off—get a red one. When do you want to do it?"

"I'll have to get a loan from the bank first. Maybe next week?"

"No, I meant getting married."

"We could do that over the phone if you like. Or up here, if you want to take the lift to New Focus. Do you want to meet me there in a couple hours?"

"Make it three hours. I have to have a shampoo, and the bus isn't really reliable."

And so they were married, at sunset, on the stump of the unfinished pyramid, and the next week he bought a brand new alizarin crimson Ford Fundamental. As they drove out of the dealer's lot he felt, for the first time in his life, that this was what it must be like to be completely human.

ABOUT THE AUTHOR

THOMAS MICHAEL DISCH became a freelance writer in 1964 after working in advertising. He was born in Iowa in 1940, and educated at New York University. His first published science fiction story, "The Double-Timer," appeared in *Fantastic* in 1962. His novels include *The Genocides, Echo Round His Bones, 334, Camp Concentration* and, most recently, *On Wings of Song*. He has also published several short story collections, such as *Getting into Death* and *Fundamental Disch*. Thomas Disch was involved with the popular television series, *The Prisoner*, and has edited several anthologies of short fiction.